Long Odds

Long Odds

Stories by Gordon Weaver

University of Missouri Press

COLUMBIA AND LONDON

University of Missouri Press, Columbia, Missouri 65201
Printed and bound in the United States of America

5 4 3 2 1 04 03 02 01 00

Library of Congress Cataloging-in-Publication Data

Weaver, Gordon.
Long odds : stories / by Gordon Weaver.
p. cm.
ISBN 0-8262-1291-3 (alk. paper)
I. Title.

PS3573.E17 L66 2000
813'.54—dc21 00-024574

∞ This paper meets the requirements of the
American National Standard for Permanence of Paper
for Printed Library Materials, Z39.48, 1984.

TEXT DESIGN: LIZ YOUNG
COVER DESIGN: VICKIE KERSEY DUBOIS
TYPESETTER: CRANE COMPOSITION, INC.
PRINTER AND BINDER: EDWARDS BROTHERS, INC.
TYPEFACES: CAROLINA, PALATINO

For Kristina and Matthew,
Anna Lynne, and Jessica and Greg
and for Barbara Frances
and not least:
for Aisia Katherine Neubert

Also by Gordon Weaver

Novels

Count a Lonely Cadence

Give Him a Stone

Circling Byzantium

The Eight Corners of the World

Story Collections

The Entombed Man of Thule

Such Waltzing Was Not Easy

Getting Serious

Morality Play

A World Quite Round

Men Who Would Be Good

The Way We Know in Dreams

Four Decades: New and Selected Stories

Poetry

Small Defeats

Contents

Long Odds

Depend upon it, Sir, when a man knows
he is to be hanged in a fortnight, it concentrates his
mind wonderfully.

—*Samuel Johnson*

Mannequin

"... to hold, as 'twere, the mirror up to nature."
—*Hamlet*

I consider myself an archetype of the artist. My origins are both remote and obscure, yet there is a seed of the distinctive in my lineage, and I bear a royal name. I have had a patron and a muse, and wrought a revolution in my art. And, not surprisingly, I am both alienated from and wholly ignored by the public.

Do not confuse my art with mime. Mime is elementary, easy. What is a mime except an ordinary actor without props, costume, voice? Stop a mime, freeze him in place—would that we could!—at any point in performance, and what do you have? A man (rarely a woman) in black leotards, chalked face, body in some arbitrary posture all but impossible to decipher.

Agile, yes, supple, but exaggerated, and yielding nothing without his (or her) narrative. And so trite! The invisible wall, the absent mantel, the host of unseen commonplaces. Take any premise you like.

A morning's ablutions for example. Your mime peers into the medicine cabinet mirror, hams it up with extended tongue, sleep-bleared eyes, bared teeth, turns on the taps, squeezes dentifrice on a brush, spits, rinses, splashes, combs, preens—this is art?

All this I do, and more, complex and subtle, in but a single instant stopped in time, held for as long as you like, suggesting an otherwise incalculable past, an undreamed, unlimited future, as precise as my audience's imagination, as universal in implication as all humanity's sad, comic history.

I define *mannequin* as: living statuary, fleshly symbol, breathing (though you will *not* detect this!) embodiment, feeling manifestation, sentient icon, tangible commentary on the quotidian, palpable form of the unguessed, concrete evocation of ephemera . . . rendering in a single pose an unalterable (once chosen) depiction giving shape, substance, meaning to the innumerable possibilities of our vulgar experience.

Mine is a solitary art, seldom rewarded. Little wonder there are so few of us.

My patron—yes, the term is inflated!—Mr. Stan(ley Zucker), sole proprietor of Fashions by Mr. Stan, believes he can make me rich and famous.

Says he, "Zog, listen what I'm telling you! With the television, what's impossible? You know from Mr. Whipple who said don't smush the toilet paper? You know from Mrs. Whatshername brewed instant coffee? Madge who did your fingernails with dish soap you heard of? It could happen. A video we'll make, local at first, but this could catch on. You'll get rich, I'll get richer, pretty soon millions know from both Mr. Stan and Zog Hocha!"

"Television," I tell him, "lacks intimacy." I tell him, "TV likes quick cuts, dissolves, music, computer-generated special effects. Your average Joe Blow surfing the remote won't stop to watch me pose. And how long," I say to Mr. Stan(ley Zucker), "a spot can you buy? They'll think I'm a department store window dummy."

"It could happen," he says. It can't.

My muse, Miss Jasmine Jankowski, who professes to love me, says, "I don't need to understand what you *do*. It's enough for me that it's *you* doing it."

I tell her, "You can't know *me* unless you understand what I *do*."

She says, "Isn't love enough?"

I tell Miss Jasmine Jankowski, "Are you kidding or what?"

I was destined for a life in art. I am named for Zog I, last king of Albania; my great-uncle Enver was the last Supreme Chairman of the Central Committee of the People's Republic. His last official act (one of the few benevolent) was to grant a permit to my mother to leave Tirana for the West. But it is the nature of my seminal memories that marks the source of who and what I became. What I am.

King Zog's official portrait betrays the weakness and pretense that ripened him for bloodless overthrow. His military kepi would be suitable on a toy soldier, for comic opera, the *Nutcracker.* His large eyes bulge, glassy with the effort to show character, soft with irresolution, dissipation. His mustache, waxed into horns, looks theatrical, something pasted on with spirit gum. His mouth is a slit, lips pale pink, an effort to project resolve, as flagrantly artificial as the rows of gewgaw medals on his narrow chest.

Great-uncle Enver Hocha's huge wall posters blare his ideological simplicity and rigidity, his hand raised in a clenched-fist salute, the sure sign of his long, tyrannical reign. When he died, only Mao paid public tribute.

My memories are static, like the poses mannequins strike.

My father, the Chairman's nephew, sits at our kitchen table, a small apartment in Tirana. His head in his hands, shoulders slumped, he despairs because there is no way out of his despair.

My mother, travel papers pinned to her underclothes for safekeeping—*impossible* to obtain without political connections—stands at the steamer's rail, gazing across the Adriatic as her homeland melts into the sunset. Her body is weary, but her spine stiff, chin up, determined to find a new life in the West. For me.

Suffice to say she died soon, that I spent my tender years in an orphanage in Wisconsin, that I learned to cope with privation and brutality by simply standing aside, mute and immobile until danger passed or circumstances improved. It is ironic that my survival to manhood came of the very tricks of the trade I transmuted into art, is it not?

Like this metropolis's handful of rude, crude mimes, I began in the streets, performing for pennies. Unlike them, I did not stake out busy intersections or crowded malls.

It was at an unremarkable suburban bus-stop, an unremarkable day, Mr. Stan(ley Zucker) discovered me. I struck a pose: distracted commuter, a clerk, a semi-soulless drudge, his pointless day's labor over, waiting for a bus to take him home to his shoddy tract house, his homely wife, a single child absolutely without promise.

So I stood, cheap briefcase in hand, box on the curb baited with some nickels, dimes, quarters, looking straight ahead at nothing, soon surrounded by half a dozen in my image gathered for their bus. So perfectly had I struck this pose, none among them noticed me.

Until the bus pulled up with a whine of brakes, doors whooshed open, the half-dozen entered like cattle going up a chute to slaughter. The driver looked at me, frowned, whooshed shut his doors, left with a diesel roar and stink of exhaust, and I was alone, immobile. I sensed, of course, the approach of Mr. Stan(ley Zucker), did not break my pose until he spoke.

"Mind telling me once what you're doing here?" said he.

"Practicing my art," said I.

"First off," he said, "I thought you was one of them waiting on that bus. Then I see you don't move, not a blink, they get on and you're still here. For a sec I thought you was a damn statue."

"That," said I, "is the art," and looked down at my box of bait coins, nudged it with the toe of my worn shoe.

"You do this for *money?*" said he.

Said I, "Everybody's got to eat."

"Oh," said he, and took a bill from his vest wallet, placed it in the box, anchored it with a quarter against the light breeze. And said to me, "I got a idea you can make regular salary if you're interested." He handed me his business card: *Fashions by Mr. Stan.*

Thus it was I acquired a patron.

Like ordinary actors and ordinary mimes, laymen believe art is all technique. Muscle control, slowed breathing, strength, endurance, the mental capacity to blind consciousness to any distraction, the ability, through practice, to avoid blinking, to erase any slightest hint of expression from the eyes.

Of course technique is essential! But only as means to end, like the actor's props, script, stage direction, the mime's leotard and face paint. What comes first is *imagination!* A kind of knowing, from which stems *feeling.* I imagine, I feel, only then turn to technique, my mannequin's bag of tricks. Anyone can learn technique. An artist imagines, feels, *creates* from this an entire cosmos!

I was an instant success at Fashions by Mr. Stan.

Said he, "Traffic is up! Sales is up! Profits is up!"

Said I, "I'm glad for the money, but, Stanley, there's really no challenge in this."

Said he, "Keep doing what it is you're doing, I'll make you a salary raise, I'll make you a bonus comes Christmas!"

Said I, "I need to find ways to explore the potential in this. I require horizons."

Said he, "Horizons, schmorizons!"

I noticed Miss Jasmine Jankowski at once. She stood well back from the display window, apart from the ever-present crowd jammed cheek by jowl, intent, puzzled, amused, astounded. Employed at the mall's Hallmark franchise, she was on her afternoon break.

How long I hold a pose is strictly up to me. So, attired in, say, a crimson blazer, white slacks, open-neck shirt, two-tone shoes (Fashions by Mr. Stan), I step through the curtain, step up on the low platform, strike a pose, any pose.

I am, I decide, a very eligible young bachelor attending a poolside party—I have just walked into the cabana, left hand inserted in the blazer's patch pocket, right raised in greeting to my friends gathered at the bar, face lit with a casual, effortless smile, lips parting to speak.

Shoppers pass on the mall tier. Then someone stops in place, does a rough double-take—am I *real?* He or she steps closer, still unsure. Another shopper wanders over. Another. Now a couple. Now a mother pushing twins in a stroller. Then three teenagers, their total egocentricity breached. Another. More. A crowd. My audience.

And still I stand, very eligible bachelor in blazer, open-neck shirt, white slacks, two-tone shoes, hand in pocket, hand raised in greeting, easy smile, parted lips. So exact is my stance, my expression, so totally do I interact with the nearby (imagined!) pool, the shady cabana, the bar, my waiting friends . . . I—*we*—are more real than the audience on the other side of the glass, lone shoppers, couples, families, teenagers. They lose themselves in me, in what I have become, where.

Teenagers will attempt to resist, pull faces, wave their arms, jiggle in place, as if frantic to protect, preserve their tenuous existence. To no avail. The very eligible bachelor, so impeccably attired, is forever—*forever*—poolside, greeting, smiling, a world as complete as the portraits of King Zog and Chairman Hocha, my static, unalterable memories of father, mother, Tirana, the blue-gold Adriatic at sunset seen from a ship's rail. The callow teenagers subside, stare dumbly as the rest, wander off devastated.

Miss Jasmine Jankowski stands apart. She is, I see at once, drawn most fully in, suffused with wonder and delight by this eligible bachelor at his poolside party, as lost to her Hallmark world as I am to distant Albania.

When I have seen enough, the crowd beginning to seethe with impatience, frustration, beginning to fidget, I break the pose. Bachelor, poolside, cabana, friends, party disappear as if they never were.

There are grins of relief, breaths exhaled, often spontaneous, sincere applause—Miss Jasmine Jankowski is saddened, bereft. I duck back through the curtain, hurry to my changing room. My patron is exalted.

"You see how traffic's up, Zog? You hearing my cash registers clicking?"

Says I, "I need a dramatic change. I think the walking shorts, aloha shirt, sandals," I say. "I think I'll take a walk on the beach in California."

"Wear what you want, pick from my whole stock," says my patron. "It don't matter what you wear, everything sells!"

Miss Jasmine Jankowski waited outside Fashions by Mr. Stan as I left for the day. "You probably don't know I've been here to see you every day on my breaks for two weeks," she said.

"I know."

"You see people from up there?"

"I see everything."

"Your eyes never move. You don't look at anyone."

"That's how it's supposed to seem. In fact, I see everyone. I see you standing back, away from other people."

"That's wonderful," said Miss Jasmine Jankowski, and, "I just wanted to tell you how wonderful I think you are. And now you're more wonderful even than I thought."

"You are," I said to her, "very kind." Praise makes me, I confess, uncomfortable. But now I had my muse.

I was inspired by Miss Jasmine Jankowski. Was there something I could do, I asked myself, to give her something to replace the cruel sense of loss she felt when I broke a pose? What good was there in the art of Zog Hocha if he only gave to, in turn, take away? Was any art truly *art* if it only confronted its audience with the vision of what they were not, could never be? How, I wondered, inspired by Miss Jasmine

Jankowski, might the mannequin's art of Zog Hocha be something more than a brief illusion, a refined amusement, a passing show?

My aesthetic breakthrough, the onset of my ascent to a higher plateau of artistic achievement, had an origin as humble as my own. It was a moment of pique, a flare of irritation, perhaps underlain by boredom, that catapulted me into a new and brilliant realm of my art. Great oaks from little acorns grow.

I was dressed formally, a white tuxedo jacket, stiff shirt with frilly cuffs and jeweled studs, cummerbund, a swatch of pleated fabric shot with gold (more ascot than bowtie), a sateen stripe down each trouser leg, patent leather shoes (Fashions by Mr. Stan). I had just passed through the curtain into the display window, my patron's "You look a million bucks!" echoing in my indifferent ear. I had not settled on a vision of who I was to be, where, doing what.

I saw him in the instant I stepped up on the platform—there was a collective *ah!* from the small crowd assembled for my entrance, a smatter of applause. I saw him.

This obnoxious man stood at the rear of the gathering, only a few paces in front of Miss Jasmine Jankowski. Was it his proximity to her that set me off, or only the sheer arrogance of this man, the almost palpable aura of self-satisfaction and social superiority he oozed like a foul miasma?

This man was tall, slender, his posture an evocation of health, confidence, muted aggression, social pretense—a kind of soft, disingenuous power pulsed in a halo about him. His coiffure a silver-white meringue, each hair choreographed in perfect place, so solid with mildly scented spray no wind could ruffle it. His eyes were small, narrow, a bit too close together, an icy greenish hue, a flickering in them indicating both intelligence and amorality. Beneath his fine straight nose lay a trim white mustache, like a slug's trail. His complexion faintly ruddy, glowing, his mouth curled at one end in the suggestion of a contemptuous sneer. He wore a gray suit clearly tailored to his model's build, clearly more expensive than anything on Mr. Stan's racks. He stood with folded arms, leaning a degree or two back on the heels of his buffed Italian shoes, like some dignitary come to review a parade, a critic perusing a second-rate gallery. He was a man obviously petted by fortune, an unself-conscious worshiper of Mammon, a scion of old wealth sprung from pedigreed loins.

Naturally, I hated him. It would have been too easy to simply replicate him for my audience, mock him, strike *his* pose, show them—and him—his pompous absurdity, his facile elegance, the bombast of his presumptions.

As an artist, I do regret having stooped to the personal.

What I had to accomplish was no less than a telling dramatization of his *humanity,* the core of that essence beneath all the gloss of his facade he shared with my hoi-polloi audience, that he shared with Miss Jasmine Jankowski and Mr. Stan(ley Zucker). It came to me at once, pure epiphany.

I stood on my platform, fixed my eyes, seemingly sightless as any Greek statue's, on him, struck my pose. I became, in seconds, that obnoxious man.

I became that man seated (a mere flex of the knees sufficed) on the padded seat of his commode in his large tile and chrome master bath (forearms resting on my thighs, hands clenched, fingers interlaced). I became that obnoxious, meringue-haired man in the precise moment of attempting to expel a painfully large stool—a rock-hard turd long and round as a policeman's flashlight. On my—*his*—face I formed a tooth-grinding, eye-squinching, near-shuddering expression of powerfully focused effort to pass this excruciating plug of shit! This I did, in seconds, and held it, veins bulging in my forehead, face flushed, filmed with sweat.

It was, without question, an episode of genius!

The effect on this obnoxious would-be elitist was immediate, all I hoped for. My audience saw, not what they were not, but what they *were*—they saw, as tangible as their own blood and bowels, their basic animal natures. And he saw it. And I saw it, the abolition of all his arrogance, his pseudo-superiority, the unexamined (until then!) sham of his being. Gone was any distinction between him and the hoi-polloi he had, until that moment, so harshly disdained.

There was a beat during which my audience was as immobile as I—did I hear an infant cry? Then a kind of contagious shiver coursed through them, a seismic shock of recognition. Then a tremor of movement as they stepped back, as if their nostrils were assaulted by toilet odors. Then a drifting apart and away, each of them self-absorbed in the contemplation of what they now understood of what, in truth, they were.

And the object of my art, his fabricated persona in shards, turned and ambled down the mall tier, perceptibly unsteady on his feet, his attire a little rumpled.

As I broke my pose, I saw tears pool in Miss Jasmine Jankowski's eyes, brim, overflow onto her pale cheeks. Had I given her a reward worthy of a muse? I was not, am not, sure.

I felt weak, my breathing shallow and fast as I ducked out through the curtain. "What's?" Stanley said to me, one eye on his sales staff, customers, one ear tuned to the click and clatter of his cash registers, the zip of his credit card machines. "You okay, Zog?" he asked.

"Stanley," I told him, sighed, "you are a footnote to a seminal juncture in the tradition of the mannequin's art."

"Can I ask you what your name is?" says Miss Jasmine Jankowski.

"Zog Hocha."

"That's a funny name."

"It's Albanian. I am named for a king and a great-uncle who was an absolute monarch in all but name."

"Oh. Well. Well, I was wondering if you'd, like, like to, you know, like to do something?"

"Do?"

"Go get something to eat, see a movie? There's twelve theaters in the mall."

"Motion pictures are for children, a rudimentary craft at best."

"Oh. Get some supper then? There's Chinese, Mexican, pizza, all kinds." I was hungry. Miss Jasmine Jankowski is, in an unremarkable way, modestly attractive.

"What you doing with this funny stuff all of the sudden?" asked my patron.

"Taking," I said, "my art into a new dimension."

"It looks funny. Funny strange, not funny yuck it up."

"Is traffic up?"

"It's okay the traffic."

"Are sales up?"

"Sales is maintaining."

"Are profits up?"

"Profits is good for now."

"Then please allow me," I told him, "to pursue my art, Stanley."

"Art schmart, don't mess what works if it ain't broke," he said.

"I am making," I said, "my art interactive with its audience in new and exciting ways. I am allowing my audience to participate in ways heretofore undreamed of."

"Me," said my patron, "I'm selling the *schmatta* to affluent gentlemens who want stylish at a price not so high they can't afford."

I told him, "You simply wouldn't understand."

"And what is your name?" I said.

"Jasmine. Jasmine Jankowski."

"Unusual. Jasmine, I mean."

"I think my mom named me after her favorite perfume at the time."

"A complaint, Zog."

"From whom?"

"That guy just walked out. He said you made fun from him because of a condition he has, his spine's crooked, scoliosis he said, from childhood."

"I remember him. I held that pose no more than fifteen seconds, I assure you. It was a warmup. He must be very perceptive."

"He's complaining me you mocked him his medical condition from birth ain't his fault his back's humped."

"Did he make a purchase?"

"Socks and a belt is all he bought, but also complained."

"Traffic," I tell Mr. Stan(ley Zucker). "Sales," I say. "Profits."

How many artists, I ask myself, can boast they advanced their art? I have, it is clear to me, redefined the meaning of *mannequin.*

Where once the problem was *duration,* holding the given pose beyond the probable capacity for total immobility (a series of purely mechanical efforts—my bag of tricks!), I have progressed to *virtuosity!* How many poses can I strike in, say, ten minutes? Fifteen? Twenty?

I am, in turn (I *am!*): the morbidly obese man slurping a super-sweet soft drink, the pregnant woman who leads a toddler on a leash like a dog, the sickly mall-rat with dirty hair and droopy shorts, the bookish boy goggled with thick spectacles, the grubby laborer in his stiff coveralls, the haughty dowager crowned with blue-rinsed hair, the pouty sex pot displaying her bared belly, one button too many unbuttoned at her cleavage, the dour ascetic who pauses before my window, reeking with disinterest, the tattooed freak whose pet boa winds up his forearm, the frail oldster leaning on his metal walker, the prim couple wearing identical smirks of sheer vacuity . . . *ad nauseam.*

Am I too proud? So be it.

"I seen!" says my patron. "I went out the back delivery door all the way around the tier so's I could see. I seen what you did in there today!"

"Of course you did, Stanley," I say. "And I saw you as well. And did you not see the pose I struck just for you? The greedy eyes? The feral mouth? The grasping hands? The sagging abdomen? Shoulders hunched by years of counting receipts?"

"I seen!" says he, spittle flecking the space between us. "I seen it was *me* you was doing!"

"Bravo," says I.

"How could you, Zog?" he says. And his face softens from outrage to remembered pain. "How could you make fun from me who did you so much, took you off the street, pay you good! Zog, I feel like a father his only son betrayed."

"You overdramatize," I tell him, and, "Consider it a distinction. I have turned you, if only for a few seconds, into a work of art."

"I'm so hurt!" he says, clutching his chest as if smitten with angina.

"I'm not staring," says Miss Jasmine Jankowski, "it's just I can't take my eyes off you. I don't think you're handsome, not *handsome* handsome, but, I mean, I felt something special the first time I saw you in Mr. Stan's window. Oh," she says, "I'm embarrassing myself."

"Not at all," I say, but within I feel such . . . *discord.* This is easily masked. I strike a pose, seated across a table from Miss Jasmine

Jankowski at the Orange Julius: on my lips sits a faint smile of amusement, my eyes project a genuine sympathy, my head tipped just a degree down to indicate sincere modesty.

Says she, "I'm making such a fool of myself! Oh, you must think I'm *so* stupid! Why should you care what I think, I'm just a foolish person who sells the greeting cards and scented soap and assorted notions at Hallmark, you couldn't possibly care what I think or feel!"

I strike a pose: I lift my head, fold my hands under my chin, fill my eyes with warmth, the smile gone from my lips, say, "On the contrary." I am rigid, my warm eyes locked on hers, which flush suddenly with joyous half-tears.

I prepared to enter the display window, checking myself in the full-length mirror provided me for the purpose, my costume a golfer's togs, flaming pink slacks, spiked saddle shoes, canary yellow pullover, white sunshade, left hand gloved, putter gripped in my right (Fashions by Mr. Stan) when he confronted me. I could see how agitated he was, eyes wide behind his hornrims, collar open, tie askew, beads of sweat on his brow, spittle flying off his tongue.

He said, "A official complaint! You got to quit this, Zog! A official complaint from mall management, signed by all the tenants on this tier, a petition it is! Karmel Korn, Shoe City, Fireplace Stuff, Health Haven, all complaining from this foolishness you do in my window!"

"And how flows traffic?" I asked.

"Chocolate Factory, Radio Shack, also both complaining."

"Are sales still vibrant?"

"They sent watchers to watch you, Zog, even the fancy jeweler's my friend, Diamond Trust, they saw you do *schmutz* in my window. Stop!"

"Profits?" I asked.

"Will you hold my hand?" I take Miss Jasmine Jankowski's small, damp hand in mine, swing our arms as we stroll the mall's third tier, on our way to one of the dozen movie screens she is so drawn to. I strike a pose—yet continue to walk beside her!—I am a swain, sodden with infatuation for her, lyric with ardor, tingling with the delight that comes only of the submersion of one's self in the self of the beloved.

As we pass through the ceaseless stream of shoppers, their eyes, their entire beings mesmerized by the piped music, the recycled air, the profuse and garish displays of merchandise heaped in cornucopia windows, I am confident in this incarnation: love-struck swain.

This is remarkable—I do not need to *hold* a pose, have transcended stasis (*sine qua non* of my art!). This is alarming!

"Will you please kiss me?" asks Miss Jasmine Jankowski. I strike a pose: my lips open (tongue at the ready!), eyelids flutter, press my face to hers, release a thin moan of ecstasy—so wholly am I the substance of mounting passion that I scarce feel her in my arms at all!

My muse's little apartment is hopelessly predictable, the miniature kitchenette, a cramped, cell-like bedroom, tacky plush sofa, obligatory television monitor (sound muted by remote control) casting the only light, strobe-like, in this perfunctory darkness she has arranged for the purpose of my seduction.

"Will you please touch me?"

"Where?"

"There. Here. Yes. More."

I strike a pose: mouth clamped wetly on here, I caress her calf, thigh, her yielding breasts.

"Let's do it," says Miss Jasmine Jankowski.

"Do *it?*"

"Yes. Now."

"Do *what?*"

"It. Please." My brain swirls, surveys galleries of what I presume must be appropriate poses—I am giddy, gut full of butterflies, all agog. I feel her grope for my buttons, claw at my zipper. Her eyes pop open like a mama doll's when I spring to my feet.

"No," I say. "That is," I say, "I am not at all certain." I say, "I am unprepared." I say, "I did not anticipate." I say, "I really must go." And I do.

Outside her door—I tried not to slam it—I hear the awful sound of her weeping, sobbing, near-screeching, and I grieve. But of course, I have done her a mercy, though I suppose she will never see it that way.

Says Mr. Stan(ley Zucker): "Zog, my heart it's breaking, but I got to let you go."

"I am dismissed from my engagement?"

"Sort of like," says he, "but only because if I don't they'll take my lease, bum's rush me from out of the mall, in violation of my lease, a morals clause they say, a nuisance I'm doing with you in my display window, Zog."

"I rather expected this. Or something like it."

"I personally like you lots," says my former patron, "like a son almost to me. But business is business, Zog."

"Traffic?" I ask. "Sales? Profits?"

"Don't make no matter," says he. "A severance pay I could give you, a little, so's to tide you a little. I'm sorry, Zog."

"Grant me," I say, "one last request?"

"Name it. If it ain't too much."

"A final performance."

"Okay," says my ex-patron, "but then I don't pay you a severance, okay?"

It is a classic, my classic performance. I don no costume, dressed simply as who I am—Zog Hocha, Mannequin—step through the curtain, onto the platform. I know she will be there, and she is. I ignore the crowd awaiting me, meet her eyes for just an instant, so she will know this is exclusively for her, dedicated to my ex-muse. I strike my pose.

I become Miss Jasmine Jankowski. To perfection, my hair is lank, damaged by frequent bleaching; my skin is sallow, dull; my eyes go empty, no least spark of quick intelligence or delicate feeling; my lips are bloodless, expression one of stunned disappointment and baffled pain; my shoulders are narrow, my bosom near-flat, my hips too wide, legs thin and stringy with muscle, long feet splayed; I clasp my bony fingers together at my waist, shudder with the shock of recognition she replicates there at the edge of the bewildered audience.

And I can smile—inwardly—for I have done her a generous mercy, freed her forever from her absurd obsession, this parody of a passion I should never have encouraged in her.

Oh, Jasmine Jankowski, I can only pray you will be grateful somehow, sometime! And I break my pose, liberated from my muse, step back through the curtain, take my leave of my former patron.

Says he, by way of parting, "Zog, we could of made millions except you had to do *schmutzig* foolishness art!"

It is fitting, I think, to end where I began, on the inhospitable streets, posing for pennies. I seldom despair.

I have memories: my father, Tirana, my mother, Zog I, Great-uncle Enver, the Adriatic Sea, Mr. Stan(ley Zucker), Miss Jasmine Jankowski . . . and marked with the names of a monarch and a despot, I have my little-known, wholly unappreciated art!

Perhaps I will be recognized someday, even revered, celebrated, perhaps only after my demise. Perhaps never?

But here, down the sidewalk toward me and my box of small coins, comes a family trio. The father is large, hirsute, lumbers like a circus bear uncomfortable on its hind legs; the mother is squat, dumpy, face plain as mud; clutching at her skirt stumbles a boy (girl?) with smeared face, snarled hair, barefoot. I conjure the sound of a coin rattling in my box.

I strike poses.

Ed Stein, Ed Stein, Speak to Me!

So here I am, waiting for Ed Stein to get back to me. On my uppers, the psychic scam kaput, no new game in sight—I'm of course assuming and still somewhat hopeful Ed will point me in whatever direction's in the cards—a few days, a week tops, from the streets. For a guy liked to think he knew what's what, it's strictly on the stupid side, dumb as the dumbest mark I ever conned.

Ed, where are you, man?

Ed Stein. In life so crooked he had to screw his pants on, supposedly the worse for being a Jewish person, since the religion is especially unforgiving, or so he told me. Deceased a decade. And out of the blue speaks to me from what he calls The Other Side. Which can translate as The Beyond, the term I used for the marks I had on line with the psychic scam, which I'll admit was about played out before he spoke to me anyhow.

The first time, I thought I was losing it, having a mini-stroke or some such, beginning Alzheimer's, though I think I'm too young for that yet.

I'm in my month-to-month-no-lease rented apartment—one big room with a bed pulls down out of the wall, kitchenette the size of a submarine galley shared with various vermin in residence before me, bathroom featuring semi-hot water and a toilet runs nonstop no matter how I shake the handle. Admitting at least subconsciously to myself my cons are all behind me, the recent psychic scam proving a loser, admitting I'm verging on semi-panic at my plight. But I'd like to think I could still get in there and swing again.

So there I was standing at the bathroom sink, semi-hot water splashing in the bowl, watching myself in the cracked medicine cabinet mirror as I'm shaving, cleaning up from a moderate hangover for my late-morning appointed session with this Norweda Brown woman, one of only the four marks I have on-line with the psychic scam. I'm going over some things in my head, what I can say to Norweda Brown this time to keep her on the hook, watching myself shave my face, and Ed Stein speaks to me from The Other Side.

What, Luthi, more from the hokum still? Get off it, Luthi!

When I say he speaks to me, I don't mean out loud, but a voice in the bathroom there with me, like he's invisible. I mean a voice I hear sort of from inside my own head. But clear, fairly loud, and I know it's not me thinking something in words. He has the Jewish accent, it's an old man's voice, deep, gravely. *Come off from this hokum, Luthi, it ain't working no more!* he says. I of course don't know it's any Ed Stein, his name, or The Other Side from where he's addressing me yet.

What I did was I sort of froze. There I was looking in the mirror, but it could have been another person, not me, I'm seeing there, holding a safety razor against his cheek, stopped still in its track through the lather. It was a little like the Out-Of-Body thing some operators use in the psychic scam, which of course I was familiar with from my basic researches before I set up this con. It was like this voice speaking pulled me out of my body, left me standing—not hovering, which is usual in that con—there looking at this absolutely motionless body in my bathroom mirror. Like I was suddenly dead or in a trance, looking at my physical body in that mirror.

But I wasn't, of course. Dead or in some trance—another feature of some psychic scams, The Trance, like Edgar Cayce spoke from. And to prove it I spoke. Out loud in my bathroom, over the gurgling sound of my commode running. I said, "What?" and "What the hell?"

You heard me the first time. You got wax in your ears, Luthi? The voice I didn't yet know was Ed Stein on The Other Side.

I said, "What the fuck's going on here?"

The voice said *Such a potty mouth! You eat with such a mouth? So, do I got your attention, do I? You listen good to me, Luthi!*

See, the psychic scam was about played out.

To begin, I didn't have a sufficient stake from my previous venture to set it up right. I'm working from a storefront, bad racially mixed neighborhood where the Koreans and Pakistanis and some few Jews have metal screens they pull across their windows and lock when they close shop. Winos sit on the curbs with bottles in brown paper bags until the cops roust them off to the alleys. Nights the gangbangers take over to do their drugs and shoot each other from cars, but it's all I can afford, hoping to build up this con to where it pays fat and fast at least for a while, at which time the agenda was, as usual, pull out, move on to something of higher quality, less risk and bigger returns. I'll admit to being on something of a severe downcurve with the cons to this point.

So my scam's a storefront, pretty shabby, but cheap, so I clean it up some, sign in the window—*Luther: Wisdom From Beyond.* Notice I alter my name as a precaution. Adopting the alias is basic to any con, all right? But I lack the stake to dress up in costume, robe, turban, Gypsy hokum. Nor can I afford drapery or incense or candles or music or crystals, so it's just a small table with two chairs, but I keep the room very dim, hoping the mark's imagination will fill in the blanks. But it's a tough go.

Competition's fierce. In our contemporary times the TV gets a lot of the play, the phone pitch, talk to certified sensitives and what not. Much of the game goes to the national organizations with local chapters, A.R.E. and such. Plus this depressed neighborhood's already spoken for regarding what street trade there still is. A Madam Ashanta, a tall and very fat African lady, three blocks over, her storefront's all decked out with gold stars, the zodiac signs, a large pretty bad painting of herself looking down at a crystal ball giving off light turning her black face kind of gold. I steer clear of her—make no enemies you don't need to! That leaves me with the spillover, which is not much.

Four. I've got just the four marks on this scam, so only barely making my nut. I foresaw, frankly, this game was doomed. Even if Ed Stein never spoke, I was due to cut and run sooner rather than later. But I'm still in there swinging at this time.

My pitch was simplicity, the straightforward approach. I said to my mark, "Don't look for hocus-pocus with me. I don't read lines in your palm, I don't deal out Tarot, I don't make noises come out of the walls, I don't pretend to conjure up ghosts or that phlegm-goo, I don't divine lottery picks or policy numbers, I don't brew love potions or cast spells on your enemies, okay? The dear deceased don't speak from my mouth." Straightforward, the sincerity approach. Disarming if done right.

So what *do* I do?

I have a Control. The Control con. We face each other across my table, I take your hands in mine, I ask you to keep quiet, don't even breathe loud. Close your eyes. Closed tight? Okay. I close my eyes. I make contact with my Control in The Beyond. Right, the same thing as the Channel Guide thing, minus frills. No name, no gender, no speaking gibberish, no ancient lost Atlantis civilization. I tell the marks I don't know where my Control comes from, it's a gift since early childhood, etc. We hold hands, we sit quiet. When I figure it's gone on long enough, we're both getting bored, fidgety, I open my eyes. Open your eyes, I tell the mark. We let go hands. Then I tell them what my Control told me to tell them. Simplicity.

A slim con, but every game is less than meets the eye.

Cash and carry. I'm too wise to certain legalities to suggest investments or sell cures, no emptying bank accounts or borrowing from friends and relatives. It's pay per session, whatever I think the traffic will bear. As many sessions as I can hook them into. Looked at objectively, it's a kind of counseling. Therapy. I just don't have appropriate credentials, so a scam, a con, but nobody gets hurt beyond the price per session, all right?

Given I actually do try to use common sense in my utterance from Beyond, it's theoretically possible I might on occasion accomplish some good. I mean, how can I possibly further damage somebody who'd sit still for this con to begin with? I had only the four marks at the time, but still in there swinging, hoping for word of mouth maybe, the rare chance of sudden fast and fat returns. And certainly not in any way troubled with guilt for anything. I never, to that point, my whole life on one con or another, was troubled by any guilt.

Ed Stein said *Luthi, such a mess you made from your life! But not so late we can't fix. Listen what I'm saying, Luthi! You was once a good little boy, we all was, a nice-ish young man for a while you were, or could have been. Now look. Still we can fix if you listen. You hearing me, Luthi?*

My first impulse was, seeing how loud and clear his voice was, was to just talk right back out loud, like he was an ordinary living person talking to me, right? Except I'm walking down the street with other persons of all sorts passing close by enough to overhear, and then I'm sitting at the counter at Slick's, the local soul diner, about to tie into my one main big meal of the day to start off hearty on the con, and Slick himself is turning chicken and barbecue over the coals, other patrons alongside me, at the few tables, and then I'm riding the bus—notice I do not work the con in the immediate vicinity of my residence, which is an old rule worth obeying. So I have to sort of think my words to answer Ed Stein back. Sort of hear my own voice in my head, where I hear him.

I say *What's so wrong with my life?* I say *What do you know about me as a little boy?* I say *Save your fixing for someone asks for it and welcomes same, all right?*

Ed Stein says *From The Other Side I know all I got to know for dealing with guys like you, Luthi.*

It's odd for me how quick it was I got used to hearing him, listening, answering back. It's very odd to me still how our conversational exchanges got feeling natural so quick, as real as whatever I said out loud to real living persons, my marks on the psychic scam, casual exchanges I had with whoever in the course of my everyday day.

The only difficult part was when I'm working my con on the marks, of which I had only the four in this almost played-out game, at which times I'm having to talk to two persons all at once, the mark and Ed Stein.

Norweda Brown. That first day.

Norweda Brown was—is—this very large, frankly hog-fat African girl. Woman, aged thirty or so. So fat she only wears these big sack dresses, though very colorful in what I suppose are African native colors. Fat to the extent her behind spreads out over the edges of my chair she sits across me on, fat even in her feet swelling out the tops of her shoes, big dimples where her elbows are, her neck's all fat rolls, ever her facial fat pinches her eyes. And big fat hands on my table. Her fatness is exaggerated by her hairdo, which is perhaps some African native style, cut short like a man's or as if she had ringworm recently. Add to this she sort of perpetually perspires so her skin looks on the slippery side, plus the air's close and still in my storefront, weather's warm, so she smells on the ripe side, plus she wheezes when breathing and talking, I suppose from overweight also.

Norweda Brown says she wants love.

So I am naturally telling her, in roundabout fashion in order to keep her on the hook as long as possible, how my Control says she can have it. Provided she renders herself worthy of receiving same.

Norweda Brown says, "I don't be caring if it be a man or a girlfriend or some child come into my life, I just wants me someone to love me. Ain't nobody loves me. Nor never did."

"Give me your hands, Norweda," I tell her. "Let's see what my Control has to say today. Close your eyes. Closed? Now we'll be silent, I'll listen to Beyond." All I'm actually thinking is how long do we have to sit in such proximity this way, given her odors, her wheezy breathing. If I think anything specific it's how long can I keep her on the hook—and where's she getting the hundred fish, all crisp twenties, I charge her per session? And rehearsing some baloney lines about rendering herself worthy of love in order to receive same.

I shouldn't have been surprised Ed Stein chimes in at that moment.

Ed Stein says *Luthi, try telling her some truth for a change. Worthy for love? Ain't we all? You know from what she needs, tell her!*

To which I say—I've got my hands all folded inside Norweda Brown's fat sticky ones, frankly smelling her odors, pretending I'm listening to my Control from Beyond—*Can you see I'm working here? How should I know what she needs? Don't blow my game here, all right?*

To which Ed Stein says *If Ed Stein knows*—this is when I first learned his name's Ed Stein—*Luthi knows. We ain't that different, you from me. Look at her, Luthi. Go on, look, she won't see, she's got her eyes shut like you told her to.* So I take a peek. Norweda Brown's got her already scrunched up from fat eyes closed to where it looks like she was born without, all of her fatness kind of heaving with her wheezy breathing, perspiring hard, her sweat rolling down her face, making her skin glisten like it's greased. I can even see sweat beads on her scalp in that short African-style hairdo. *Sad, ain't it. Poor thing* Ed Stein says.

I say *I'll grant that* and *Like it's any of my fault* and *You're so smart, tell me and I'll tell her. Ed Stein, is it?*

He says *Love's a fancy word. What she wants is a man will give her a poking, which she's never had one in her life because she's fat and also pretty ugly. Tell her go find a man'll slip it to her if she asks nice, she'll have what she needs, Luthi.*

I'm about to tell him I don't suggest immoralities could get me cross-wise with legalities, when Norweda Brown kind of sighs long and loud, speaks, says, "I don't feel good! Ain't your Control done said nothing yet?"

I open my eyes again, see she's opened hers, so I yank my hands free, hot and moist from hers. I say, "You broke the celestial contact. I was just getting in touch. That's all this time. Come back in three days, same time, we'll try again."

To which Norweda Brown says, "A hundred dollars for just that?"

To which, thinking fast—a necessity of any con—I say, "Okay. I'll discount twenty percent for incomplete contact, but you caused it. Next time I feel sure we'll get what you need, all right?" And I'm relieved she gives me four crisp twenties she takes from between her enormous bazooms, and they're oddly not hot or damp. And she leaves, amazingly graceful on those fat feet of hers.

Ed Stein says *She's stealing them dollars from her poor ma who cleans ritzy houses for rich white ladies, her life savings she stashes in new twenties she's stealing from to pay you, Luthi, and you ain't decent enough to tell her get laid?*

I say *Not my concern, Ed Stein.*

If not, then who? Says Ed Stein. *Come off from it, Luthi. Do some good for somebody, it could maybe fix what's basic wrong with yourself, maybe.*

I say *I don't need fixing, and further don't welcome it if I actually did.*

He says *Oh, Luthi, you do!*

Ed Stein wasn't blowing smoke. He did know all about me, things I'd forgotten myself. On The Other Side, they seem to know everything. Wouldn't that be nice if we all did!

He said *When you was a little boy you was probably decent enough, but already you stole things from kids in your neighborhood and also at school.*

I said *I never!*

Ed Stein said *The Schwinn bike you stole from out a garage the door was left open, you took it and rode all day in a park and then left it there when it got dark, you had to go home for your supper.*

It was more borrowing than stealing I said. *It was a pretty nifty bike. The kid could have found it easy if he searched in the park. For all I know he did.*

Money Ed Stein said. *Change from your ma's coin purse. Change from your pa's pants he left on a chair when he took a nap. A dollar once from out a little girl's wallet she put down with her books and lunch bag on the playground to go swing on the swings, you slipped it under your sweater so's you could go off and take the money, you put her wallet down a sewer grate.*

I said *I forgot that, but I recall it now you say it, her name was Sally Gronski, she was in my class in third grade. I don't recall what I spent the buck on, but I remember she cried about losing her wallet with her favorite pictures in it. I don't think she missed the buck. I did feel bad she cried.*

You were mostly a decent kid, Luthi he said.

I said *I consider myself a basically moral person at heart. I just happen to lead an unconventional lifestyle.*

Luthi Ed Stein said—he said it loud, like he was angry—*you are a thief! A cheater! Strictly no good! The worst sort of person! Since you was a boy you been this, Luthi!*

Which he backed up by telling me much of my past history on the con, how I solicited donations door to door—this was when I was in junior high as I recall—for charities didn't exist, crippled children, burn victims and such. How I was expelled from high school for breaking in lockers to grab lunch money and other valuables. How I was an absolutely ace shoplifter for a time, complete with deep pockets sewed into my winter coat lining, I could conceal any amount of goods therein. How when I was drafted into the military service I was the barracks thief they never identified, and at which time I became adept through much practice with crimped playing cards and dice I could roll in my favor at key moments. How, after a less than honorable discharge deriving from the theft and sale of some assorted military hardware I did very well for a considerable period working the pigeon drop and the Philadelphia bankroll you flash, two fifties like bookends on a wad of singles can be manipulated to look like all fifties in the eyes of the given mark on the line—this attracts greedy small-time investors, but led to an embarrassment causing me to relocate at great distance from my original stomping grounds, and thereby distancing me for good from my mom and dad.

Ed Stein said *What hurt you gave your poor ma and pa, Luthi.* Which, as I think on it, I suppose I did. However, they were very simple people who could not appreciate the bent I had taken, and legalities required my keeping out of touch, to the point I dared not try to get what little inheritance they left. Doubtless they'd be ashamed to this day if they knew all Ed Stein did. I try not to think of them, as it tends to make me gloomy. Candidly, my folks were a pair of basic marks, all right?

You were cruel to several women, Luthi he said.

I never raised a hand in anger to a one of them, Ed! I said. Which is mostly true. With whores I paid the going rates, and paid with my time and attention to the nonwhore ones, which were not numerous in my case.

I'm saying cruel to their romantic feelings he said. *The two who truly loved you, Luthi.*

Which ones? I wanted to know, couldn't imagine. Which question he never responded to, saying that was spilled milk, water under the bridge, ancient history. He seemed pretty upset.

You embezzled in positions of trust he said. Which I have. *You made false representations regarding joint ventures.* I did. *You peddled fake Rolex watches from a suitcase on the street.* Which I would have preferred he not remind me of, that debacle. *You dealed from the bottom of the deck. You forged payroll checks on a machine you stole from a warehouse office. You defrauded numerous innkeepers. You made people to believe you was rich and educated, once you told you owned houses and estates on three continents!* Candidly, I was very ambitious in my younger years.

I said *Ed, a guy's got to make his nut, all right? The bulldog's got to be fed, Ed!*

So he said. And said *And now the worst, you swipe from people's dreams, what most they need and want and hurt for, you take advantage with this psychic medium hokum. The Beyond! It's the worst yet, Luthi.*

I was looking to tell him, hey, it's not all that different, this con, from, say for example, psychological counseling, all right? But I had a sudden brilliant inspiration I hoped would get him off my case, which was making me uncomfortable in the extreme. I said to Ed Stein *So I suppose you never did anything wrong or immoral or unethical in all your life, right, Ed?*

He said *I did worse than you, Luthi.* He didn't sound angry any more.

Such as? I asked.

The very worst Ed Stein said. *I stole from people their graves. Cemetery plots. All on paper and phony. I sold them graves weren't there when they passed, final resting places they bought from me but didn't have when they died thinking they had a place for eternal peace everlasting. This I did.*

I heard of that con, but I never played it I told him.

Ed Stein said *Almost as bad, what you do now, Luthi, taking money for giving them just hokum.*

Ed I said *I only got four marks, it's playing out, slim returns, how much harm can I be doing?*

Luthi he said *you could do them some good if you try, smart guy like you think you are.*

What, for example? I said to Ed Stein.

Wait and see.

Then I said *Would it be too personal if I were to inquire how you happened to, like, die?*

Hanged myself. From shame he said.

Oh. I know that's a sin for Catholics, but also for the Jewish persuasion?

The worst Ed Stein said.

So you of a religious bent?

Strictly not. It never took. The biggest tragedy from my life he said.

Angelo Vitucci is maybe sixty, but looks younger, dresses very dapper, loud sport coats, bright ties, crispy shirts, knife-blade creased slacks, buffed shoes. For a guy whose line is poor-mouthing, he looks pretty natty, and never so much as blinks when he forks over the hundred after a session. "I think of it as investing in the hope of manifold returns," he says.

"Exactly, Angelo," I tell him. And, "Shall we commence?" I take his hands in mine. He's got big hands, hard, like he did manual labor, though he told me he was a chef until recently, had his own Italian place, Angelo's, which just went—he says—bankrupt, not from this neighborhood. He also sports a couple of rings look to me like the real thing on his knobby fingers. "Close our eyes," I tell him, wait to be sure he does, then close mine. His hands feel strong, like some thick wooden sticks in mine. So we sit while I'm supposedly locating my Control out there in The Beyond. For Angelo Vitucci I sway a little on my chair, hum a very soft humming sound to make for a little theater, all right?

Ed Stein says *You're right, Luthi, it ain't money he's seeking.*

So what is it then?

See for yourself. So I do, open my eyes, look him over close. I don't see anything so special, just this natty-dressed older Italian man in his later prime. He gives off a sweetish scent, aftershave and hair tonic I think.

So what am I supposed to be seeing?

Ed says *Money he's got. Plenty. That's a big fib he told you, from his restaurant he lost. Them finger rings alone cost a bundle. He didn't bankrupt, he sold out to a chain bought him out for a stiff price.*

What a lying old prick! I say, and *So?*

Notice, Luthi, how neat and clean he gets himself up? Like he's got a hot date waiting.

So he's hygienic. Big deal, the lying old prick!

He's lonesome is what he is Ed says. *His wife from forty years, a very happy union, she died sudden, his daughter she's married and lives far away on the coast. He had a son but the son died from a disease he was born with, this is the one big tragedy from his life. He's got nobody. He comes to see you for what he don't know ails him.*

Lonesome? I say.

So bad it hurts him. He's a shy man don't know how to meet people. He's a good man, Luthi, he goes regular to church and contributes to United Way pretty hefty, but he's almost dying from lonesome.

So what am I, some dating bureau?

Use your imagination, you're the sharp operator Ed says. Like he's disgusted with me, as if I'm obtuse, slow on the uptake.

I open my eyes, release Angelo Vitucci's gnarly hands, say, "Open your eyes, Angelo. This was a super one! My Control's giving me hot stuff today!" He claps his hands, rocks in his chair, leans close to get the latest news from Beyond. I say, "There's money coming, big money, Angelo! I'm not certain as to the source, it could be a bequest, you might have a valuable art object in your attic you forgot about, possibly the government owes you big-time for taxes you overpaid on your business, but I distinctly heard money's in the offing."

I've teased him some with such talk before, but never this emphatic. So I'm surprised he doesn't break out with a smile, some show. Ed Stein says *Not money, Luthi!* Angry again. *Something for his lonesome!*

Angelo Vitucci says, "That's heartening," but is no way convincing.

So it occurs to me to say, "Also, Control indicates this money will be attached in some manner to a person. I think female. Somehow this female personage will be the bearer of money, but you'll get very attracted to this female, which will be mutual, possibly developing into a lasting relationship the exact tenor of which I'm still fuzzy on."

Now he gives with the smile, all big white teeth, nice gold inlays between them. I mean, a wide smile with gusto, and his big black eyes dancing. *Ed* I say *you hit him where he lives I think.*

You hit him, Luthi, I'm just provoking here.

Angelo Vitucci says, "Now that's very intriguing. I'll tell you, I had a premonition coming today this might be the day we'd learn something substantial."

"Maybe you have a little gift of your own there, Angelo," I tell him. And, "So, be on the alert for any female contact, no matter how casual, all right? Come back in three days, could be Control'll give me a name and address for all I know."

"Oh, I will!" says he. And forks over my hundred like it's small change. Ed's right, it's not the money. "I consider this well expended today!" Angelo Vitucci says.

On the one hand I tell Ed as I squire my mark out the door *this will keep him on the hook until he gets tired of waiting for some gal to brace him. On the other, he's in for slow death by disappointment, Ed.*

Ed Stein says *So don't disappoint the man, Luthi.*

And just how do I manage that, Ed?

Use your imagination, you're such a sharpie in the brain department from working the con all your life, okay?

Leander Foley, Jr., an African man I see sometimes on the street because he's employed at this big full-service valet carwash just down the block, and also takes some meals at Slick's diner, spouts the line he's ambitious with respect to advancing his career. He says, "I wants me a decent clean job pays me some real money. I done worked all my lifelong, got nothing to show, live paycheck to paycheck washing and waxing, cleaning up other folks' automobiles, don't pay for shit and shitty tips too. You dig, man?" With a life on the con, on this severe downward curve, I can certainly dig.

This Leander Foley, Jr., is the color of ox-blood shoe polish, a tall thin man, so lean it's like there's fire burning him up from inside. He reminds me of a long stick of beef jerky, tough as cured leather, spicy-bitter. He's a nervous man, jumpy, twitches, tics, snaps his fingers a lot. I'm frankly a tad wary he could be dangerous if crossed, so never speak when we happen to meet on the street. This is a good rule of the con, do not mix the business with sociability. I don't tease Leander Foley, Jr.

I say, "Mr. Foley, I can only tell you what my Control tells me from Beyond. Like I said, I'm told your case is not hopeless, but I'm not getting concrete possibilities here so far."

Says he, "I be getting something soon or you don't be getting my money no more soon, man."

"Let's close our eyes," I say, make sure he does, take his hands, all long fingers and knuckle bones and ropy tendons, in mine, get a grip to where I feel I can hopefully restrain him if need be, shut my eyes once I feel somewhat secure. I don't employ any hokum for Leander Foley, Jr., just hold tight and hope to wing it one more time.

Ed Stein says *So, Luthi, make up some whopper for this poor guy, why don't you?*

I'm trying to think of something, Ed. This man's not all that stable, I don't think. I tell him he's going to get hired by some big corporation, he's the type'd come back and slit my scrotum when it doesn't happen, all right?

So tell him go to night classes, learn a skill, get a diploma, study computers, get a license for selling real estate maybe, huh?

Get real, Ed! This guy washes cars for a living. He probably can't write his name the same way twice.

Get real yourself Ed says. *It ain't no career opportunity he wants. So give me a clue.*

What he wants says Ed Stein *is getting laid.*

Come off it, Ed!

See for yourself, Luthi.

I sneak a peek at Leander Foley Jr. I see this rock-hard man, maybe forty, long, lean and mean, a little tremor going in his head and shoulders, eyes and lips shut so tight he looks about to burst.

Do I hear a sort of moan coming from inside him somewhere? I feel him pulling against me, half-rocking in his chair. His ox-blood skin glows, stretched drum-tight over his sharp-edged facial bones. I feel his hands sort of pulse in mine.

I think maybe you're on to something, Ed.

Ed Stein says *He's a walking boner, Luthi! Help this poor man washes off cars all day, ain't got any regular nookie since when he was a youth.*

Ed, this ain't a whorehouse I'm running, and I'm no pimp, all right?

Did I say you was? Be creative, Luthi, you're so smart, conning people your whole entire life.

I yank my hands away. Leander Foley, Jr., pops his eyes open, looks at me like I woke him up from a good dream. Says, "Say what?"

"Control broke off all of a sudden, Mr. Foley," I say.

"So I don't gots to pay?"

"Half-price today," I say, and, "Come back in two days, I think we're close to getting something good here soon."

"We best had, man," he says as I show him the door, pocket his fifty—I'm not going to make my nut this way! I lock the door after him as a precaution.

I say *Ed, I think I'm in over my head.*

Ed Stein says *I got faith in you you'll figure solutions, Luthi.*

Phoebe Davison is this old gal could be anywhere from fifty to seventy. Hard to tell because of the heavy cosmetics she lays on her face, caked foundation, blue eyeshadow, brows drawn in dark, lips very glossy bright red and matching her long fingernails I presume are real, not glued on. Her hair's dyed about canary yellow, sort of sculpted like a helmet. Big dangly earrings, bracelets that slide up and down her skinny arms, rattle, cocktail rings which are likely junk jewelry. But dresses nice, though in styles very younger than she is, and too much perfume, a kind of cloud follows her around, blankets me as we join hands. A classic hypochondriac.

I naturally tease her with vague nostrums, say, "Are you taking the vitamins, Phoebe? The ginseng? The herbal tea? A mild laxative like I suggested last time?"

"I do everything Control says," says she, "but nothing helps. I ache all over, I'm constipated, I still get shooting pains up my legs, I feel a migraine coming on." She's very near tears, which I do not wish to deal with, nor do I enjoy dwelling on her bowel conditions either.

"Relax, Phoebe," I say, take her hands—she's shaking a little, whimpering. "Close your eyes, Phoebe. Maybe we'll get that elixer we need today, all right?"

Doctor Luthi Ed Stein says *what's your hokum expert medical opinion today? How about you tell this sad lady she should get healing massages, or could be acupuncture's the ticket, needles, that's a good one!*

Give me a damn break, Ed! This is tricky. I don't dare even looking like practicing medicine without a license, all right? She's a chronic, nothing better to do than bitch she's ill, right? I'll get her to exercise, take long walks, it can't hurt her, and I guarantee she'll come back for more. Phoebe here is your classic mark, Ed.

She ain't sickly, Luthi. Except in her head, which is to say in her heart.

Another lonesome you're saying? You got a one-track mind, Ed.

Ed Stein says *It's a prevalent human condition, Luthi. Universal in fact.*

So I should tell her find a pen pal or maybe do some volunteer work?

You can do better if you try, Luthi he says. And *This lady's a spinster lady, no family left in the world. What does she look like to you, Luthi?*

I peek. *An old retired hooker.*

Shame! Ed says. *Ain't you got a speck from decency left for an old lady so alone she has to pretend sick so she can come to a cheater-pants like you for something to do in her life?*

I got I respond to this, watching whimpering Phoebe Davison, hands shaking like baby birds in mine *probably as much basic decency as the next average person.*

Then show it! Ed shouts at me so loud for a second I think Phoebe can hear it.

So I tell him *All right, damnit, maybe I just will!*

I say to them, "I appreciate your all being able to come in today. Sorry for any inconvenience, but Control said all of you jointly, this is a breakthrough we're onto here today, all right?" They don't look like they much like the idea.

Norweda Brown's in a heavy sweat, heaving and blowing to get her breath—she looks even heavier, put on a few more pounds maybe. Angelo Vitucci's decked out as per usual, but I can tell he feels disconcerted. Leander Foley, Jr., looks plain mad at the world, which I suppose is personified in me. Phoebe Davison's shaking like she's got a fever or else bad scared. I look at them, my marks, think, this was supposed to be my nut, the psychic scam, this was supposed to perhaps build into something fast and fat, a potential ace con.

Ed Stein says *Ain't you the smart guy! I knew you was capable from creative innovations, Luthi!*

Don't count your pigeons before they hatch, Ed.

Don't you be a pessimistic!

You forget I've seen too many cons dry up and blow away before the payoff.

He says *I got confidence in you.*

I say, "Okay here. Let's all get seated," thinking how I dug into my nut for three additional folding chairs on discount, like you'd get with a card table. "Norweda," I say, "next to Mr. Foley here. Angelo. Phoebe, next to Angelo. All right?"

Norweda Brown says, "It too hot and stuffy in here!"

Phoebe says, "My head is splitting."

Angelo says, "I'm not sure I see what we can profitably accomplish," giving the two African persons a semi-fisheye.

Leander Foley, Jr., says "We gots to pay the same with all at the once?"

I say, "Take hands, please." They do, Norweda and Leander, Angelo and Phoebe—with my right I'm clutching Phoebe's fingers, fluttering like something wants to fly away, with my left I've got Norweda's fat, hot, moist hand, like a handful of rising hot dough. We're a circle. The classic medium scam ploy, of course, but it can work. "Close our eyes," I say.

I watch a beat or two to be sure they do. Ed Stein says *They wouldn't cheat on you, Luthi, they need too bad.*

Will you leave me do this my way, Ed?

Pardon me for mixing in.

I need to concentrate, get some lines ready to spiel. Eyes shut, I listen to us, Norweda's huffing, sharp little snorts from Foley, smell Phoebe's scent-cloud, Angelo's talc and brisk aftershave. I can't think of a thing. *Ed, maybe you could possibly assist me a tad here?*

You're doing good on your own by yourself so far. I said I won't mix in.

I can feel them getting fidgety, like a mild electrical something passing through all the clasped hands to me, hear somebody shuffle feet under the table. *Ed? Please?*

Do what you know's right, Luthi!

I hold off as long as I can stand, then take one huge deep breath, hold it until it hurts, blow it out like a whale breaching. Okay. I'm back from Beyond, right? Now what? *Do!* Ed Stein says.

"Open eyes," I say. So we're sitting, still holding hands, a classic medium scam circle, all looking at each other. I say, "Control was very specific today, folks."

"What he be saying?" Norweda asks.

"If he don't be he better look some like being," Leander grumbles.

Phoebe says, "My head hurts me so!"

Angelo says, "Do you intend betraying confidences? I prefer to hear anything pertinent in private."

"No, Angelo," I say, and, "Control insists we share. Please don't let go each other's hands, all right?" *Ed?* Ed Stein is silent. So I wing it. Like always on the con.

I say, "Control was very precise. Listen to me, all right? I'm translating sort of from the language of The Beyond, right? It is desired that you, sort of, like . . . pair off." I stop for a reaction, questions, protest, but they sit, waiting for me, perfect marks. "Mr. Foley," I proceed, "you and Miss Brown are to become . . . acquainted." They look at each other, but I can't read them. "The two of you in conjunction will combine to enable each the other to realize that which is most needful for the given individual. Both spirit and flesh, as it were." I'm not at all sure they fathom this gobbledygook, not sure I do. Where am I getting this spiel? "Angelo," I resume, "you and Phoebe here are likewise enjoined to conjoin in order to complement one another to the purpose of mutually supporting the other toward the ends innermost sought for personal fulfillment." Hokum. No reaction, excepting they look at each other. I say, "You can let go hands, we're done here. Control's spoken, this is all straight from The Beyond, all right?" I pull my left loose from Norweda's clammy mitt, my right releases Phoebe's jittery digits. I slide my chair back from the table, stand. I'm all of a sudden very tired.

I for certain didn't have expectations. But it seems to work, a perfect con. Was the jargon all that good? Norweda and Leander kind of rise in unison, still holding hands—they'll burn each other up to cinders!—head for the door. Angelo stands, a gentleman, holds Phoebe's chair as she stands, walks her to the door supporting her bony elbow with his free hand. From the look of her I don't think her head hurts her any.

I call after them, as if I had planned to, "In case anyone's concerned, this is a freebie! On the house courtesy of The Beyond!" And they're gone. And there's the end of my scam. My nut. Another con down the dumper.

Ed Stein says *You done good, Luthi!*

To which I reply *Yeah. And so now what, Ed?*

That's your business, he says. The last thing I ever heard him say so far.

Which leaves me at what I have to term sort of an impasse, right?

Ed, will you please just say something, anything?

I'm owing rent on both the storefront, from which I took down my sign, and this fleabag apartment also, money I do not have, rationing my nut to cover one good meal per day at Slick's, all right?

Ed, did I do or say something inadvertent to piss you off?

I've considered numerous options, but, candidly, lack the heart to come up with a new con, much less the energy to get it going, all right?

Okay, Ed, the marks live happily ever after, what about yours truly?

What I'd like if I had my druthers is some sound advice. Where do I go from here? No nut, no con, and I'm too old a dog to learn new tricks, all right? I'd panhandle, fake a limp or a twisted torso and work the streets if it weren't I still possess at least a little pride. That—pride—as with basic decency—and a buck will purchase a cup of coffee, the way I see it.

Ed, is this your not so coy way of telling me I should do your number with a rope, turn on the gas, locate a sharp instrument?

I know I'm hurting when it occurs to me to shell out what little's left of my nut, drop in on Madam Ashanta not so many blocks away. And I note TV psychics offer free introductory minutes on the phone. And there's bound to be one of those A.R.E. Edgar Cayce study groups I could run down if I wanted. As if I was just another mark waiting for the hook!

Ed? Ed? Hey, Ed, the universal human condition you called it, right?

Candidly, I'm getting pretty tired of listening to myself.

Ed?

Viewed from Lanta & Wally's

" . . . the center cannot hold . . . "

—Yeats

I'm in the ideal position to see what's happening. My table—everyone knows it's my table—has the only window. I not only see everyone passing by outside, a regular gallery, I also have a view of the five-way intersection, maybe the busiest in town. So it's possible to say I pretty much have the whole town up close and personal there in the window from my table.

And then there's inside. Wally cooking at the grill, his wife Lanta waitressing the counter and handling the register. Their daughter Gina waitressing the five booths. And my table.

In addition to which there's the black-and-white TV up on the shelf on the back wall, just above the doorway to the toilets and Wally's storeroom. It's far enough away from my table I have to squint if I want to see the screen clearly, but I *can* see it. So I don't miss anything on TV. Add to that my newspaper, which I buy out of the machine just outside the door, every morning on my way in to my table. So I get everything in the daily paper.

Plus of course the customers on stools at the counter, and in the booths, coming in, sitting, ordering, eating, paying Lanta at the register—not to mention how I eavesdrop all I care to while they're here.

I figure my position is about ideal.

However, something's happening. And I'm in a position to maybe be the first to know.

Lanta and Wally's may be just possibly one of the best diners in all of America.

Wally can cook anything, on the menu or not—just ask for it. It's mostly standard stuff, naturally, eggs and omelets, sausage and bacon and steaks and pork chops, sandwiches, potatoes any way you prefer, juice and milk and soda and coffee. My favorite is the French toast. Wally doesn't use those little pats wrapped in foil, he slaps a lump three times that size right on the edge of the plate, and always more than enough syrup in a small pitcher. I also like a specialty called *Eggs a la Walter* on the menu. It's excellent with a couple drops of Tabasco, which is always on the table along with sugar, salt and pepper, ketchup. Also, no chemical nondairy powder in packets. The coffee's marvelous, strong, and you lighten it with fresh actual cream from a shiny metal creamer Gina brings with my coffee every time because she knows I use it. I don't have to ask, she automatically brings it.

Sure it smells of cooking, but it's a good cooking smell. When I come in each morning, I catch a big whiff of the smell when I open the door, my paper under my arm, and it makes me hungry. It makes me feel good, starting another day. It's like it signals it *is* another new day, everything starting over again. I couldn't hardly start another day without my window table view at Lanta and Wally's.

I don't say this is the *perfect* diner. By no means. Wally smokes while he's cooking. I've never seen it, but it figures some ash has to fall on the grill. Lanta could use a fresh apron to start the day, but I've seen her use the same one for two, sometimes three days. I can tell by specific spots and stains. Their daughter Gina doesn't wear a hairnet, which is probably against health law. I don't complain because I've never found ashes or hairs in my food. And because this is where I start every day, where I spend the biggest part of what I'd call my day. Because I so value the position I occupy at my table, where I can take everything in.

I go back to Wally at his grill, say, "My compliments to the chef."

He says, "Yeah, and I can take that to the bank, right?"

Something very funny is going on. Funny-strange, not funny-ha ha. It took me a while to catch on at first.

I'm *not* talking eccentric. Oddness is normal enough. On the TV above the door to the toilets and storeroom, I see some television woman on one of the morning shows interview a rock-and-roll singer just got elected a congressman. In the paper I read about a woman, her husband told her he was dumping her for another woman, he leaves, she goes to kill herself, jumps out the window of their fourth-floor apartment, she lands on him, she's unhurt, he's killed instantly. Out my table window I watch a woman walking her dog. The dog does his business on the sidewalk, she nicely scoops it up with a scooper into a plastic bag. But then she takes a Kleenex and *wipes* the dog while it stands there like this is routine, then puts the kleenex in the bag too, and they walk off like this is routine for them. Right here in the diner, there's a regular whose name is Melvin, he wears Bermuda shorts no matter what the weather. Below zero with wind chill factor, he's in Bermudas like it's summer.

I'm talking absolutely *strange,* not normal oddity.

In small ways at first. I look up from my newspaper, notice Wally at the grill is wearing an earring. A little gold hoop right through the lobe. Wally is a good fifty years old. Shortly thereafter, I notice his wife Lanta, who I never saw smoke before, is smoking. She sets orders on the counter with a cigarette stuck in the corner of her mouth, always has one burning in a glass ashtray beside the register. When it gets slow and she takes breaks, she stands leaning against the doorway to the toilets and storeroom, smoking, dropping ashes on the floor, drops the butt right on the floor, grinds it out with her shoe, lights another one right up.

The topper was Gina's hair. I'm aware she doesn't wear a sanitary net, but then suddenly one morning she's dyed a big white stripe front to back on one side, like a skunk. Then she's suddenly cut it very short, like a boy's. Two days later, she's had her head half-shaved, one side is hair with a white stripe like a skunk's, the other's slick baldness like she's getting x-rays for cancer.

This is only the beginning.

Paying Lanta at the register, I say, "I never mind paying out for quality food and service."

She says without looking at me, "Like as if you got a choice, right?" I notice she drops my change in my hand, never touches me with her fingers.

* * *

I watch part of a talk show on the black-and-white TV, the guest's a famous actor in the process of surgery and drug injections to change from a man to a woman. The host asks him if he's going to date men once he's completely a woman. The famous actor says, "No, I've always thought of myself as a lesbian."

I read in the paper where the county's turning almost all the mental diseased out into the streets because warehousing is wrong, and also it'll save on the budget. I start watching out my table window to see if I can spot any on the street.

I eavesdrop. Lanta says to Wally, "Your damn snoring is driving me bats!"

He says to her, "It's my fault I sleep with my mouth open?"

To which she says, "I hope a cockroach crawls in your mouth while you're asleep and chokes you!"

To which back to her he says, "Say that again, I'll brain you with this here skillet!"

They talk loud enough the whole diner can hear. When Gina comes to refill my coffee, I say, "All is not domestic bliss I'm guessing."

Gina says to me, under her breath so only I can hear, "I'd like to murdalize the both of them."

Wally's quit smoking. When she's not working the counter or the register, Lanta stands and glares at him. He doesn't look at her, at least when I'm watching. Gina's got a gold earring just like her father's now, except she wears hers in her nose.

I eavesdrop customers:

"I couldn't fucking believe he fucking asks me to fucking sit in the fucking back seat!"

"Everything I eat or drink gives me the gas."

"So he goes, 'Cut me a little slack, I'm short this month.' So I go, 'You're short, grow! I'm not in the slack business, right?' So he goes, 'Can you not give me a damn break?' So I go, 'You want it in the neck or your legs?'"

"I say *two* strikes and you're out. First offense, minimum ten years in the pen. Second offense, castration! No exceptions."

"My motto is, all good things and all bad things come to an end sometime."

I'm never certain which are the nut cases let loose by the county, which are normal people passing my window. Some are obvious. Nut cases tend to overweight, and they shuffle when they walk, they carry bags usually because I suppose they're homeless or afraid to leave their belongings anywhere for fear of theft, and they tend to have small eyes and mouths in large faces. Their haircuts are bad. But not all of them by a long shot.

Just such a person, shuffling, carrying two big shopping bags, small eyes and little mouth, puffy face—he had a hat on so I couldn't tell the haircut—comes in, shuffles up to the counter, asks Lanta, "May I please use your lavatory?" She explodes at him.

"Out!" she says. "Out! Go back and use your loony bin john instead of you people coming in and stinking up mine! Outside, I said!" Even Wally turned away from the grill to look at her. Gina thought it was a hoot, giggling behind her hand.

"Forgive me. Pardon me, I meant no inconvenience," this guy who was clearly *not* one of the cases turned loose by the county says, and he shuffles out the door. I watch him cross the five-way intersection. Lanta stomps over to the toilet entranceway to smoke. Gina's laughing so hard her eyes are wet.

Wally says, like he's talking to his grill, "He's not the only one could maybe benefit from some professional help."

The TV does a story on a famous politician's wife visiting a famine country in Africa. This woman hugs a nearly naked man who's so starved he looks like a skeleton with brown paper wrapped tight over his bones. She hugs him to her so hard I'm afraid he'll snap in pieces, feeds him from a baby bottle, not milk, some soybean mixture. The TV reporter says there are rumors this politician's wife could be a candidate for one of the Nobel prizes.

My newspaper's front page features an upcoming auction of things owned by a serial killer who also cannibalized his victims: a saw and knives he cut them up with, a vat and chemicals he used to destroy body parts, a motel-size refrigerator he kept certain parts in to eat later, a log he wrote of victims' names and descriptions, his clothes and various other personal effects. All bids will be sealed so buyers' names can be secret.

Regular Lanta and Wally's customers are a mixed bag. Melvin with his Bermuda shorts could pass for one of the county's nut cases. On the other hand, there's a young guy—I don't know his name—is always in a suit and tie, sometimes even a vest, takes his coffee black, reads the *Wall Street Journal* he brings in with him, smokes menthol cigarettes, never stays long. About as normal as you can get, I'd say. A pair of blue-collars, could be brothers? They both have long ponytails, dirty hands, dirtier work clothes, take the same booth every morning like I take my personal table at the window. They think they're funny, flirting with Gina. "Are you married?" one asks her. When she says no she's not, he says, "Too bad, I am, but she could die, right?" Not funny after the first time. A woman with a little kid, I can't tell if it's a boy or girl, she leads in on a leash with a harness, like her kid's a dog she's walking. This mother eats a full breakfast, feeds pieces of it to her kid even though there's kids' portions on the menu. The kid spills a lot and would run riot in the diner if it wasn't for the leash—I have trouble concentrating when she's here with her kid. The beat cop, his nickname is Tubby, which is perfect, he's so gut-sprung. He sits at the counter, eats two crullers with coffee he never pays for because he's a cop.

I keep wondering why Lanta and Wally are so cheerful with him, given he's freeloading. "Have a good day, Tub," Lanta says when this cop finally hauls his bloated self off the stool to leave.

"Take care, Tubby," Wally calls out from the grill. And this cop Tubby never so much as says boo, much less thanks for the free crullers and coffee.

It's no big stretch for me to imagine sometimes this is the dining room at the nuthouse, these regulars are inmates waiting for the county to toss them on the street.

I say to Gina, "I hope you notice I always leave you the larger than average tip."

She says, loud enough for others to hear, "Don't do me no big favors, huh?"

* * *

The quality of food served at Lanta and Wally's is declining. I order my eggs over easy, but they're almost runny when Gina brings them. There's less butter on the plate with my French toast. My bacon could be crispier, since I always specify extra-crispy. I could almost read my paper through it, it's so half-cooked. My first cup of coffee's only three-quarters full. "Is Wally distracted?" I ask Lanta when I pay up at the register.

"Like as if I'd know," she says, jams the register drawer harder than necessary to close it.

Both the TV and the newspaper feature the unusual weather this past year: record snowfall, spring tornadoes, first summer drought, then flooding.

Out my window I see: a woman pushing twins in a double-wide stroller. She stops right in front of my window, walks around in front of the stroller, leans down and slaps both twins, one after the other, hard, goes back behind the stroller, pushes them, screaming, out of sight.

A woman I thought at first was one of the county's nuts because of her semi-mongoloid face, but probably isn't because she stops in place, opens her big purse, takes out a wad of bills, fans them out like a canasta hand—I see all hundreds—counts it, could be a couple thousand dollars in all, folds the wad up and puts it back in her purse, walks on.

A teenager in baggy shorts, baggy T-shirt, stops, faces my window, turns his ball cap backwards, admires his reflection, sees me staring at him, flips me off with both hands, pivots, dashes away.

A regular, the guy who wears suits and ties and vests, smokes menthols—he strolls past with the fly of his trousers wide open, business fully exposed.

A sort of dwarf in an electric wheelchair does a wheelie, a three-sixty, another wheelie, zips away.

I make myself turn to the black-and-white TV to focus on the coverage of various wars going on around the world.

The quality of service is declining. My table is not wiped properly. Gina took a careless swipe at it after I sat down, tucked the damp rag under her arm and stood tapping her foot while I tried to concentrate on the menu this morning.

I saw my order sit several minutes on the counter where Wally set it for her, distinctly not hot by the time Gina picked it up and brought it to me. Lanta only half-filled my first coffee, and I had to catch Gina's eye with a gesture before she brought me my free refill. I left her a smaller than usual tip to let her know I take note. Paying Lanta at the register, I said, "I see your daughter shaved the rest of her head there."

Her mother spoke with her teeth closed, said, "No shit, Dick Tracy!"

From my table, I watch two men outside, just standing and talking—they're young men, ordinary—they look really ordinary, no possibility they're county cases. They talk a long time, then come inside. Inside the diner, they both pull little stacks of cards out of their pockets. One goes all the way to the back, to the farthest booth across from Wally's grill. The other one comes to my table, hands me one of his cards.

The card says: *I am deaf and dumb from birth, but want very much to live a normal and productive life. I would greatly appreciate any donation you might wish to make to assist me in my desire to contribute to the life of our community. Thank you for your generosity!*

I look up at him. He smiles at me, points to the card I'm holding, makes a kind of gurgling noise in his throat. I'm trying to think of something to say when Wally starts shouting.

"Move it or lose it, sonofabitch!" Wally yells. He has the other fake deaf and dumb guy by his collar and the seat of his pants, marches him toward the door—everyone's looking. "You too, deadbeat!" Wally yells at the guy standing at my table. Wally lets go the one guy's pants, grabs the guy at my table by *his* collar, jerks the two of them to the door, outside.

"Hands off the threads, man!" the first guy says on his way out.

"Mister, I'm just trying to make a living for myself!" my guy says. I watch from my window as they run off, talking.

"Talk about your brass!" Wally says on his way back to the grill.

"If you'd held them I could of called the cops," Lanta says.

"Yeah," says Wally, "what I need is Tubby around here even some more. I want advice, I'll request it," Wally says, and tells Gina to pick up the printed cards they dropped on their way out.

"Anybody for a souvenir?" Gina announces to the customers when she has them picked up. I shake my head no to her, I still have the one my guy gave me.

The newspaper has a little filler item about seventeen people who lived through the atom bomb on Hiroshima. These seventeen fled to Nagasaki right after Hiroshima, so they got atom bombed again, and lived through that one also.

The morning show on TV does a humorous piece about a farmer in Mississippi who was sitting in his outhouse when it was hit by lightning, which killed him.

What are the odds on these, either of them, being pure chance?

I eavesdrop:

"Frank Snotrag and Hungry Blowfart."

"Pardon my boardinghouse reach."

"Keep your glommy meathooks to yourself. That's my toast."

"I wish I may, I wish I might, I wish I would get laid tonight."

"He's so tight he'd fart on a rock to save the grease."

"My ass and your face."

"So out of the blue, she says to me, 'I'm not sexually available.' I come right back at her, I says to her, 'That's perfect! I'm not sexually competent!'"

"Your Republicans are historically always for big business. Check the record out."

"My farts and your breath."

"Communism in its pure form would be ideal. Unfortunately it's been perverted."

"Sometimes I wish I had the magic power to kill people, or maybe just paralyze them, just by giving them a magic look."

"My balls and your tonsils."

"I wouldn't mind screwing me one of them space women you see in the movies."

"You hear about Decker?"

"I heard double pneumonia."

"Like hell. AIDS."

"Can I get a refill here if it's not too much trouble, Miss?"

"Who cut the cheese?"

"The scientific reason your niggers excel is, one their skull bone is thicker, two, they have longer Achilles tendons."

"Opinions are like assholes, everyone has one."

"There's a hair on my eggs."

Wally is getting a hair transplant. What's odder is the little hair plugs he's got from the back of his neck, which is graying, are dyed reddish.

Gina is having her face tattooed with zebra stripes. It makes her look like a cat's face, sort of. Also she paints her fingernails black and glues sparkles on top of that.

I see Lanta close up when I pay at the register. There's a bruise not covered very well by makeup on one cheekbone, and her lip's swollen, and she's lost an upper tooth in front. She keeps sticking the tip of her tongue in the gap.

What set me off was coming in at the usual time to find this large guy with a brush haircut at my table. I was polite.

"I think you're sitting at my table." He looked at me, looked at the counter, where there were several free stools, looked at the booths, of which one was empty.

He said to me, "I don't see your name on it, or am I missing something?"

"It's just my table. Every morning. You can ask the management, they'll verify me." He looked at Lanta behind the counter, looked at Gina serving a booth, craned his thick neck to look down at Wally at the grill.

"Are you some whacko or something?" he said.

"It's my table is all," I said.

He said, "What I want is for you to get the hell out of my face, you old fuck." He was quite a large man, even sitting down, so I wanted the management to settle it.

What it is, is the world's coming unglued. When everything changes from day to day, you can't predict. Am I the only person aware of this? I don't have a name to call it, but it's happening. I'm in a unique position allowing me to observe.

I turned away from the large man sitting at my table, my place, almost bumped into Gina, carrying an order to the nearest booth. "That person's sitting in my seat," I said to her. She looked at me like I was speaking gibberish.

She said, "Mind getting out of my damn way?"

I said, "Make him move to the counter or a booth that's free." I said, "Everyone knows that's my place by the window."

Gina said to me, "I ain't got time for this hassle," and stepped around me to serve her order. I looked back at the large man in my seat, but he was looking out my window, as if nothing had happened.

I stepped up to the counter, leaned between two people on stools to speak directly to Lanta. She looked at me like she'd never seen me before. I said, "Make that man move from my place, Lanta."

She said, "You," and, "That does it!" and untied her apron, balled it up, threw it on the floor behind the counter. Now everyone in the diner was looking at me, except the large man, who stared out my window.

I said to Lanta, "Don't blame me, he's the one stealing my seat there!"

Lanta said, "You little creep, I had you up to here," and drew her finger across her throat like it was one of Wally's big knives.

I said, "Are you going to get me my place back?"

She said, "What I'm gonna do is come across this counter and bum's rush you out on your keester!" She actually started to climb up on the counter. So I scooted back to Wally at the grill. I could hear his wife and daughter behind me.

Gina said, "Nail him, Ma!"

Lanta said, "I'll call the cops and get you tossed in the clink is what I'll do!"

Wally faced me, his back to the grill, holding a big fork he uses to turn bacon. I said, "Wally, a person's got my personal seat by the window, make him give it back."

He said, "Come a step closer, I'll stick this here fork in your eye."

Up front, Lanta was almost screaming. "Loonies and creeps, what the hell's next?"

Gina was laughing hard. She said, "Ain't we got the fun?"

"I can't sit someplace else," I said to Wally. "Couldn't you please make him move so I can sit down and eat my breakfast?" Wally laid his fork on the grill, came out to the aisle. I said, "I *always* have that spot by the window, Wally!"

He said, "So you say," and, "What I don't need is cranky old farts complaining the eggs is runny and the toast's burnt and the coffee cup not filled full and the service sucks!"

Lanta shouted from up front, "Kick his bony butt, Walter!"

Gina said, "This is way better than on TV!"

When Wally, who is a largish man, started toward me, I said, "Okay, I'm going, but this better not happen again." I was partially running for the door because he was coming fast toward me. When I got to the door, I stopped, and what I said I was saying to the whole diner.

I said, "When I come in tomorrow I expect to see my window place waiting for me. I overlook it this once."

A lot of customers said a lot of things loud enough it was not eavesdropping on my part:

"Does this happen a lot, or is this a rare event here?"

"What is the old coot, high on something?"

"Can a man not eat his breakfast in peace?"

"Hey, don't look at me," the large man in my seat said, "I come in, sit down, he jumps me, see?"

"They should put persons like that away somewheres."

I said, "I'll forgive it this once, but don't let it happen twice ever."

That's when Wally said, loud, like it was a public announcement, "There won't be no other times. Because you are as of now officially barred. Permanent. You come through that door there ever again, I'll not only personally put the blocks to you, I'll have Tubby get you jailed."

All I could think to say was, "I'm banned from ever coming in forever?"

"You heard him the first time," Lanta said.

"I swear this is better than the effing circus," Gina said through her laughing. And then I went out the door, because Wally was about to put his hands on me, throw me out.

* * *

I don't risk going in. Lanta's just crazy enough to sic Tubby on me, and Wally's mean enough to get physical, and I don't relish putting on a show to amuse their daughter.

In any case, it's not so very different.

I buy my newspaper out of the same machine right outside the door, I just read it later. I miss the good cooking the way it was before it all blew up, but there's other places to eat if I'm hungry, fast food or whatever.

They can ban me from entering, but no law says I can't look in my same window. I have to cup my hands beside my face to see in. I can't make out the black-and-white TV in the back except to see it's always on, like always. But everything else is the same. Gina's zebra-stripe face and shiny shaved head are the same, the ring in her nose. Wally's hair transplant is filling in, dyed reddish. Lanta chain-smokes. The regulars are still the regulars.

Melvin still wears his short pants no matter how cold or if it's raining. The young guy in the suit and vest hasn't so far had his fly open again. The woman keeps her kid on the leash, like a dog. The two blue collars still wear dirty clothes and don't wash their hands, and probably think they're funny when they're not.

We don't talk when they come and go, though some of them give me looks, which I ignore. I don't doubt jokes are made about me inside.

Every once in a while, Tubby speaks to me, says, "Okay, that's long enough, move it on," or, "You desirous of a loitering citation?" so I have to walk away. Which does not prevent me from coming back to my window once he's out of sight. And of course I see all I care to of the county cases and odd persons and plain ordinary normal people on the sidewalk outside the diner, and just over my shoulder is the five-way intersection full of traffic I can check on.

I don't know if it's the same or getting worse, or if possibly there's some improvement, but I take it all in, keep watch. I can't yet put a name on it, but I'm aware. I confess I do miss eavesdropping, but that's almost all.

I'm in the perfect position to be the first to know whatever it is.

Solidarity Forever!

"Once you put it in writing . . .
everything looks normal."
—Günter Grass, *The Flounder*

I am the best one to tell this story. Disregard what you have heard until now; the truth about a schism will not come from schismatics. Forget all the fragmented, narrow accounts: television interviews, the panel discussions on National Public Radio, magazine articles, three—the last time I counted—books. All polemics and pontification, cold analysis and spiteful anecdotes. Only I can tell the truth about NUALA's destruction.

Documents can support lies. Facts can be twisted. The Department of Labor held weeks of hearings, and what was the result of that? Our government washed its hands, cursed all our houses with equal fervor. History is always revised. It is like a novel the author still gropes to shape, an imagined mass whose center has yet to emerge, a vision without focus.

I will not fictionalize. I was there, at the beginning of the end, with Weinberg in Las Vegas, Caesar's Palace, and I promise to tell exactly what I saw and did, no more, nothing less. It is an important story—and so sad!—and I am the one to best tell it.

NUALA. The National Union of American Literati, Amalgamated. NUALA. We were NUALA, all of us, me, Weinberg, D. W. Weathergood, Academics, the Poets Claque, Roaring Boys, Minimalists and Symbolists and Meta-Fictionists, Gays, Blacks, Hispanics, Native Americans, Smallpressmen and Smallpresswomen, Regionalists and Local Colorists, the Electronics and the Mixed Medias, Feminists and Feminist-Lesbians and Feminist-Lesbian Radicals, the Iowa Gang, Commercials and Slickies and Hacks—all of us, factions, caucuses, single-issue advocates, but all pledged to the Broad Consensus Declaration of Boston, all together in NUALA.

It bound us in a unity as profound as the cement of our common language, welded us like the very discipline of our crafts, made us all something as tangible and glorious as the tradition of our shared art, made us all greater than ourselves, transcended the rich chaos of our individual sensibilities!

The National Union of American Literati, Amalgamated! NUALA. And it is gone, a wreck of sterile splinters and effete rumps and self-appointed ad hoc voices clamoring in the unceasing cacophony of their quarrels over turf and funding and influence and franchise, charge and counter-charge! I was there.

I was there when we forged our magnificent charter, at the founding in Boston, took my union card at the birth. And I was there, in Las Vegas, at Caesar's Palace with Weinberg, when he launched his takeover, shattered us into a hundred powerless pieces, broke our solidarity the way you break a pencil by bearing down too hard on the page.

Why tell it? Because it is true! And because there are generations to come, just learning the alphabet, or how to write cursive, or sitting down for the first time at a word processor. Maybe, just maybe they—the generations of literati to come—can rebuild what we lost, resurrect NUALA from its cooling ashes the way a writer can sometimes find a new and better story in the scraps of a draft gone so bad the author is ready to chuck it for good.

Las Vegas was going to be the biggest and best ever. I flew in, took the shuttle to my motel just off The Strip, found Weinberg's message waiting for me at the check-in desk: *come instanter my suite Caesar's Palace utmost urgent future of NUALA also American letters strictest confidential! Weinberg.*

I did not hurry to meet with Weinberg. I unpacked, showered away the taint of the long flight, walked to Caesar's Palace instead of grabbing a cab; it was still late morning, the heat only beginning to accumulate like a heavy blanket in the dry desert air. Even in daylight, I thought The Strip was beautiful.

I stood outside Caesar's Palace, stood for a moment in the middle of the passing stream of tourists, gamblers, and celebrity gawkers, looked at the marquee billboard. There was the headliner's name, and the times of the floor show, but it also said *Welcome NUALA* and *Scribble, Scribble!* I cannot swear to the memory, but like to think I stood there and sang the opening verse of *Scribble, Scribble!* to myself, because I could hear a band playing NUALA's anthem just inside the big glass, brass-trimmed doors.

I took my time getting to Weinberg's upstairs suite.

I dallied in the foyer, listened to the Random House Band play *Scribble, Scribble!* almost too loud, drowning out the Simon & Schuster Chorale singing the words, mixed with the buzz of noise from the casino; the roulette wheel's rattle, clack of the chuck-a-luck cages, shouts of encouragement and despair from the crap tables, the grind of slot machine levers. I registered for the convention at the reception booth sponsored by Farrar, Straus, picked up my badge and delegate's credentials.

I was about to find the elevators when I ran into Suzi Dodsworth, wearing her neon-pink bikini and heavy plastic clogs, on her way in from catching the morning rays at poolside. We hugged, and I congratulated her on the publication of *The Fey Heart,* told her I loved it, thought it the best thing she had ever done; though I lied, I did promise myself to get a review copy and read it first thing when I got back home. "I'm on my way up to see Weinberg," I told her, "he's got himself a suite upstairs here."

Suzi Dodsworth said, "He's cooking something up. He left me a note to get together for the Vegetarian Fruit Brunch Scribner's is laying on tomorrow."

"You know Weinberg," I said.

"Do I ever," Suzi Dodsworth said. Before I could ask her what she thought Weinberg had up his sleeve this time, a bunch of the Iowa Gang came in, Suzi's friends, and there were the hugs and mock-kisses, congratulations for *The Fey Heart,* and for one of the Iowa Gang whose name I missed; he has just published a chapbook. So I drifted away.

I took my time. I looked in on the convention floor, scatterings of delegates straggling in to take their seats for the opening ceremonies, admired the bunting and balloons and the forest of poles carrying caucus placards. I stopped on my way to the elevators to check out the New and Recent Display, pleased to find my *The Big Irony,* surprised and delighted because it had been out six months already, scheduled for remand soon because of weak sales. I scanned the rows and rows of designer book jackets, felt that meld of bittersweet envy and chill disdain a writer feels confronting his peers' successes.

I suppose I experienced a moment of depression, the deadness at the center of me, a little like the effect of a monumental block stopping a narrative dead in place. But I reminded myself of where I was, who, *what* I was—NUALA! I listened to the Random House Band and Simon & Schuster's chorus, and I patted the credentials in my pocket, pinned on the badge with my name on it in gold, went to the elevators.

When I reached Weinberg's door, I thought: even though he was on the Executive Council, NUALA would not spring for a private suite; either Weinberg was flush with another of his grants or fellowships, or else he had something in mind worth dipping so deep in his own pocket. Then I knocked on the door, waited while Weinberg checked me out through the peephole, unhooked the security chain, threw back the bolt, and let me into his Caesar's Palace suite.

Inside, Weinberg leaned forward from his seat on the sofa cushion he plopped on the floor of the conversation pit, spoke low, almost a whisper, as if we were closeted alone. "I'm going for it," he said, "I'm going for the presidency of NUALA. It's all set up to nominate me from the convention floor, and I've about got the seconding speeches lined up."

"You haven't got a chance," I told him. "The Commercials and Slickies will all be behind the Nomination Committee slate. It's pro forma, it always is."

"We crunched the numbers. It can be done," Weinberg said, "even with all their automatic proxies."

"Weinberg can count for starters on the Poets Claque as a core vote," David Gordon said. I did not much like David Gordon; he was—still is—America's best known Smallpressman, editor of *Tabula Rasa,* where I had long since stopped submitting my manuscripts. When I sent him *The Big Irony,* which I was calling *Life's Ironics* then, he rejected it with a little note that said, *nice, but doesn't quite bestow the literary "hit" I always seek.* He had published reams of Weinberg's New England poem-cycles, had a stack of the new issue of *Tabula Rasa* with him in Weinberg's suite, the one featuring the in-depth interview. "I can deliver the small presses for him," David Gordon said, handed me a copy of his new issue.

I glanced through it. It was the one featuring Weinberg, his white paper, Weinberg's comprehensive platform, bracketed and punctuated with a generous sampling of his new poems, the ones collected recently in *A Regional Suicide's Manual.*

"I'm forging a coalition," Weinberg said.

"And with you helping me we'll deliver the Academics," Professor Meyer Jackson said; he had grown a beard since the last convention to hide his small chin; it made him look like a reincarnation of Lenin. His sonnets, *Professor Jackson's Tenure Jeremiad,* had just gone into a fifth printing as a result of its adoption as a workshop text by his friends in the Iowa Gang.

I said, "I'm out of touch. My book's scheduled for remand any minute, I couldn't deliver my blood relatives."

"See those?" Weinberg said, lifted a leg, pointed with his bare foot at the half-dozen telephones sitting on the period escritoire. "WATS lines," he said. "We'll put you in touch. I've got phone numbers, home and office, for every Academic with a NUALA card, you can take their proxies orally."

"So who do you deliver?" I asked D. W. Weathergood. The author of the prize-winning *Troutstream America* lay flat on his back in the bottom of the conversation pit, like a turtle sleeping through winter in the mud, eyes closed, as if the gloom of Weinberg's Caesar's Palace suite—the drapes were closed against the desert sun—hurt him. He lay with his hands behind his head, logger's boots crossed at the ankles.

"Me, myself, and I," D. W. Weathergood said without opening his eyes, as if he spoke in his sleep. "I hate politics. I really wonder sometimes why I pay my NUALA dues, it doesn't help me with my prose that I ever noticed."

"He's prestige, a figurehead," Weinberg said. "There's more Guerrilla Independents out there writing away in total isolation than you think. They'll come in with Dwayne Willie, and there's hundreds of novices with union cards out there who wish they had it in them to go off in the woods or the mountains or the desert or some shack somewhere and just write the way people like Dwayne Willie or Marengo up in the wilds of Wyoming do it."

"I prefer D. W. if you don't mind," Weathergood said. "And I promised you my vote and you can use my name because I'm sick of the damn Commercials and Slickies with their bad *New Yorker* stories. I never promised you I'd do you any good, Weinberg," he said without opening his eyes or uncrossing his logger's boots.

"Which," I asked Weinberg, "is also the rationale for our Roaring Boy here?" I looked at Sean Ignatius Kennedy, who got up, walked—a sway already in his gait—to the fully stocked hospitality bar for a refill.

"You got it," Weinberg said. "Think," he said, "how many novices holding NUALA cards out there see themselves as Roaring Boys. Most of them don't have the digestion to play the role, but they'll go for the image."

"Scotch?" Sean Ignatius Kennedy said to me from the bar. "Irish? Vodka? Gin perhaps? Bourbon? Potato Schnapps? A cordial? Red and white wine or a shade betwixt the two? Ale? Stout? Beer, imported and domestic, of course—my Christ!" Sean Ignatius Kennedy said, "I've died and gone to heaven!" He tossed back his drink, poured another.

"Paddy Casey can't be here, he's trying to dry out before he starts another novel, but he's on board, too, and so's Dizzy Denny Bormann down in Florida," Weinberg said.

"You've got Paddy and Dizzy Denny?" I said. "Okay, you've got the Roaring Boys, real and would-be," I said.

"Here's to dear Patrick!" Kennedy toasted from the bar. "A good man with a glass in his hand, but I daresay he's never passed out at a lectern whilst reading to an audience the way I have countless times!"

"Nadjia's already spoken for me to all the feminist caucus leaders," Weinberg said. I had never met Nadjia Bogosian before, but recognized her at once from her book jacket pictures, the mop of dirty hair twisted into one braid long enough to sit on, steel-rimmed granny glasses, bag lady's dress, a canvas shoulder bag adorned with sleigh bells, jammed with the paperbacks she hawked at her readings, along with what looked like granola bars. She talked and chewed at the same time.

"I think I can bring in a lot of the Ethnics, too," she said. America's only publishing Palestinian, her ties with the State Department's Cultural Bureau, which sponsored her frequent Third World reading tours, were solid.

"I can believe it," I said.

"Rod here's going to solicit the Minorities for me. Have you ever tallied," Weinberg asked me, "the combined Black, Hispanic, Native

Americans, not to mention Chinese and Japanese on the West Coast, plus clots of Vietnamese here and there starting to get into print these days?"

"Red, Black, Brown, Yellow, we're all in the same pickle, we need a voice on our side running NUALA," Rod Echohawk said. He was not wearing the full eaglefeather bonnet, but he did have a beaded headband, fringed vest, moccasin leggings.

"You've been active," I said to Weinberg, and laughed, pointed to his mastiff, Juggernaut—he took him everywhere; the dog stank horribly, but people always indulged Weinberg's love for the fat beast. "Juggernaut's going to catch the sympathies of NUALA's animal lovers, I suppose?" Nobody laughed with me.

"Are you for us or against us?" Weinberg asked.

"You and me, we can wrap up the Academics," Professor Meyer Jackson said, setting his jaw, looking like Lenin addressing a mob of workers and peasants. Sean Ignatius Kennedy drank deep, looked up at the ceiling of Weinberg's Caesar's Palace suite, began mumbling one of the Roaring Boys' infamous obscene ditties.

"Female Commercials and Slickies don't appreciate feminist concerns," Nadjia Bogosian said, spewing flakes of granola from her mouth.

"Red, Black, Yellow, Brown, we're fed up with being down!" Rod Echohawk intoned; I recognized the meter, the line from one of the poems in his *Who Killed Our Buffalo?*

"Would you mind taking a few copies of *TR* and seeing if you can sell them down on the convention floor?" David Gordon asked me.

"You've got my name and my vote, don't ask me to politic," D. W. Weathergood said from the bottom of the conversation pit. "I go politicking," he said, "what happens to my credibility with Guerrilla Independents?" Weinberg's mastiff, Juggernaut, looked up at me, brow furrowed, from between his paws, whined.

It was a Caesar's Palace suite, but Weinberg had already put his mark on it. There was the hospitality bar and the conversation pit, two bedrooms, a bath and sauna, a kitchen, a balcony overlooking Vegas and the desert horizon, the patio doors behind heavy draperies. But, as always, Weinberg had unpacked wherever he happened to drop his luggage, suitcases split open, shirts and socks and underwear, toilet articles, books and magazines and poetry manuscripts—typed and holograph—strewn about the sitting room.

Weinberg was a notorious health nut, carried sacks of fresh fruit with him on his reading tours, a sworn foe of tobacco and spirits except for the occasional recreational toke, but the bar was fully stocked, the air conditioned suite's atmosphere rank with the smoke of Sean Ignatius Kennedy's cheroots—concessions to the exigencies of union politics.

Weinberg, shirtless, barefoot, wearing only shorts printed with hearts and dancing monkeys and the words *Let's monkey around!*, dressed for the opening ceremonies while we talked, rummaged in his bags, tossing things behind him, over his shoulder, like Juggernaut digging for a favorite bone, finding his trademark denims, cape, and red beret.

I told them, "It comes down to clout. Sympathies and affinities don't matter. The New York publishing houses won't back away from their own people. What have you got to offer them?"

"Wise the man up, Professor," Weinberg said, trying on his floppy beret in front of a mirror with a gilded frame, fine-tuning the angle.

Meyer Jackson scratched at his beard, said, "If we put a lock on Academics, we can control textbook adoption for curricula. We'll make the kind of sales figures the Iowa Gang brags about look like peanuts. I'm talking a centralized book ordering bureau run through NUALA's Executive Council," he said.

"How many copies of *Big Irony* did you flog?" Weinberg asked me, buttoning his bleached denim jacket with the *Poets Are, They Don't Mean!* logo on the back. He said, "How many of those bricks would you move if it was on a required reading list for every Master of Fine Arts writing program in America?"

"Thousands," I said.

"We're going," Nadjia Bogosian said, swallowing loudly, "to go through some of my friends at State and the Department of Labor to put the squeeze on the National Endowment to process grants and fellowships directly through NUALA."

"What's the last grant you snaked?" Weinberg said, smoothing his patched jeans over his narrow behind, turning to check the effect in the mirror.

"And readings!" Sean Ignatius Kennedy said, drained his glass, smacked his lips. "We'll by the love of Jesus call it the NUALA Visiting Writers Consortium or such, you'll not get a reading or a lecture or a workshop at so much as a community college without the say-so of the Roaring Boys! Oh," Sean Kennedy said, "the reading-workshop-writers conference circuit will thrive in my benevolently despotic clutches, me and Paddy Casey and a few select others. Mad Mike Murphy and Dizzy Denny from down Florida way if he asks nice, old son!" he said to me.

"How many reading invitations do you get in a year?" Weinberg asked me, donning his cape, stepping back to the edge of the conversation pit to consider the whole man in the mirror; he struck the pose I knew from his readings, the one where he raises one hand, looks up as if seeking the Muse's presence and blessing before declaiming the first line of the first poem, Juggernaut squatting at his side.

"We're envisioning a Smallpresspersons Editorial Board to regulate all the crap being published by amateurs and novices now," David Gordon said.

"Guerrilla Independents will find their books kept in print long enough to find an audience for a change," D. W. Weathergood opened his eyes to say, rose from the floor of the conversation pit, unbuttoned the top two buttons of his L. L. Bean flannel shirt, the way he wore it in the jacket photo for *Troutstream America.*

"Are you in?" Weinberg asked, twirling to make his cape flare, observing himself in the mirror. I looked at him; I looked at David Gordon, Professor Meyer Jackson, Nadjia Bogosian, at Rod Echohawk, who took Sean Kennedy's arm to prevent his falling as he stepped out of the conversation pit. Juggernaut barked and began to cavort in anticipation of our leaving.

"I'm in," I said, and we left Weinberg's Caesar's Palace suite, went down in the elevators to NUALA's opening ceremonies.

We were just in time. As we walked on the floor, made our way to our respective caucuses, the delegates were already singing *Scribble, Scribble!* along with the Simon & Schuster Chorale, the Random House Band accompaniment drowning out the adjacent casino's gambling noise. I found my chair among the Academics, put the bundle of *Tabula Rasa* David Gordon stuck me with under it, stood to sing the final verse of NUALA's anthem with my brother and sister literati.

I remember, in everything that followed, the nomination from the floor, the flap over the seconding speeches, I left the magazines there, forgot them; David Gordon billed me for them, but I've never paid, not even when he threatened, just recently, a civil suit.

NUALA's entrenched leadership knew what Weinberg was up to; his pre-convention maneuvers warned them, and the solid block of Commercials and Slickies were ready for him, for us. They drew their wagons in a circle, pulled up the drawbridge, dug in their heels—they were shoulder to shoulder, armed with proxies, the ear of sympathetic media, financed by magazine syndicates and New York publishers. Their stooges presided at the podium, sat on all the standing committees governing parliamentary procedure, circulated on the floor to erode our ranks, spreading rumors, casting aspersions, invited uncommitted delegates to their suites upstairs in Caesar's Palace where they plied them with hospitality and brokered to retain their power.

We never really had a chance; I must have been blind not to have seen the writing on the wall!

D. W. Weathergood was our first defector. After Meyer Jackson nominated Weinberg for the presidency from the floor, the author of *Troutstream America* went to the podium to give a seconding speech, found his path blocked by a half-dozen Sergeants-at-Arms, big men who wrote commissioned articles for trade publications and house organs, men with few scruples.

Weinberg's Poets Claque rose in protest; Meyer Jackson and I stood on our chairs, led the Academics in a chorus of outrage, waved our signboard. *Free speech! Free speech!* we cried. *Poetic license! Poetic license!* chanted Weinberg's claque. We marched down the aisles, hoarse with shouting to be heard above the Random House Band, which, cued by the leadership, struck up *Scribble, Scribble!* again to drown us out.

The Convention Chair, Max Godwin, author of a sleazy novel about divorce and wife-swapping and esoteric perversions that had been on the best-seller list for fifty-six consecutive weeks, pounded his gavel. D. W. Weathergood struggled with the house organ goons, cursed them as journalistic prostitutes, invited the largest of them to step outside with him.

When order was restored—our demonstration gradually ran out of energy, like a narrative with insufficient conflict to animate it—Chairman Godwin recognized the chair of the Membership Committee, Loretta DeJong, author of two dozen Romance paperback originals on sale in every supermarket in America; she reported Delegate Weathergood was ineligible to address the convention, having failed to pay his NUALA dues, though repeatedly dunned. D. W. was summarily jostled out the door by a trio of the trade publication sluggers, shouting he was not to blame, it was a point of integrity with him not to open unsolicited mail.

Because Sean Ignatius Kennedy was already past the point of slurring his words, I made Weinberg's seconding speech.

After we adjourned that first session, I tried to talk Weathergood into staying in Las Vegas, to at least give us moral support, set an example for all the real and would-be Guerrilla Independents out there in the sticks who looked up to him. "No way," D. W. said. "They can have my NUALA card. I never joined anything before, not even the Izaak Walton League, and I never will again!"

"What will you do if you leave NUALA?" I asked him.

"Write!" he said. "And go fishing." And he strapped on his knapsack, picked up his poles and tackle-box, and left Las Vegas, hitch-hiking back east to his Vermont hills.

I often wonder, now, whatever became of D. W. Weathergood. I once tried to call Marengo, up in Wyoming's wilds, to see if he had heard from him, but his phone was disconnected. I like to think he—Dwayne Willie, Marengo, all the genuine Guerrilla Independents—that all of them are still out there writing, even though nobody publishes their work.

"That hurt," I told Weinberg when we gathered in his suite to assess strategy just before the first evening session.

"Who needs him?" Weinberg said. "I thought *Troutstream America* sucked anyhow. I couldn't get through it."

"His stuff," Rod Echohawk said, "shows no real spirit of reverence for our sacred environment."

"Is it really that bad?" Nadjia Bogosian asked. "I never got around to it. I was giving readings in Bangladesh for the U.N. when it came out, I think."

"Bottoms up, muck in your eyes!" Sean Ignatius Kennedy said, waking up. "Say, where's my boy-o Dwayne Willie got to?"

"Gone fishing," I told the Roaring Boy, who shrugged and tipped back his glass. Something started Juggernaut barking, and Weinberg had to lock the mastiff in the sauna before we could get on with our discussion of tactics.

"We can do without the Guerrilla Independents," Professor Meyer Jackson said, stroking his beard, "if we just pull together."

After Weathergood's ejection, the convention, on its surface, was routine, business as usual. We opened and closed each session with the singing of *Scribble, Scribble!*, we heard the presentations of ad hoc and standing committee resolutions, made and seconded motions, debated the questions, voted by voice and by secret ballot if the issue was at all sensitive.

NUALA closed ranks to accept the Membership Committee's recommendation that the petition to join our union filed by the WASP Heterosexual Monogamists, purged as reactionary troublemakers at the first convention held after the Boston Consensus, be denied; at least, I think now, we stood together in NUALA against those neo-fascists!

And we stood together behind the ac hoc Committee on the Closed Shop recommendation to censure the states of Mississippi and Oklahoma for their continued enforcement of the antiquated Literary Right-to-Work statutes. A large majority voted to establish the NUALA Hall of Fame, recommended by the Awards & Honors Committee, empowering the Executive Council to seek government funds to build a suitable edifice in which to display effigies, manuscripts, publications, and other memorabilia of deceased members distinguished for their literary achievements; site selection from among competing bids from Fayetteville, Arkansas, Montpelier, Vermont, and, of course, Iowa City, was tabled for further study.

The last day, at the morning session, when Weinberg moved from the floor that NUALA budget funds for the purchase of a fleet of motor-homes, said vehicles to be provided gratis to poets engaged in cross-country reading tours, we watched the voting for an indication of how the membership might lean when we got to the crunch of the presidential election. But when the chair of the Finance Committee, a Slickie who published a nationally syndicated book review column under the nom de plume of De Gustibus, reported NUALA's treasury, while sound, could not absorb the impact of the initial expenditures in addition to maintenance and liability insurance complications, the convention voted to table; we naturally suspected he lied, cooked the accounts.

But I suspected it was all moot by then, the last day, anyhow. I do not claim to have foreseen exactly what happened, but I knew a disaster lay in wait for us, for all of us, for NUALA, the way you feel a story's conclusion coming before you reach it—you fear the author will not be able to pull off his intentions, his purpose too blatant.

It was early in the morning of the second day, in Weinberg's suite, that Nadjia Bogosian and Rod Echohawk left us.

I was there alone when they came to break the news. Weinberg was out, giving Juggernaut a run somewhere on the edge of the Nevada desert, where the mastiff could roam free of his leash and choke-chain. I didn't know where Meyer Jackson and David Gordon were—we all found *that* out later! Sean Ignatius Kennedy was there with me, but, still sleeping it off, didn't get up to seek his hangover remedy until it was over.

"We need to talk to Weinberg," Nadjia said when I let them in; I sensed something because Echohawk—dressed in full regalia, eagle-feather bonnet, spear and shield with tassels and dangling artificial scalps, face painted for war—stood silent, bare arms folded across his chest, as if guarding a tobacco shop, while the Palestinian poetess told me what they had done.

"He's out taking Juggernaut to crap somewhere besides in the conversation pit for a change," I said.

"Then give him a message for us," she said. "Rod and I are leaving Las Vegas."

"You can't do that," I said. "Why?" I said. "What did they offer you?" I asked. She told me, Rod Echohawk standing by her side, as unmoving as if he were made of wood.

They had conferenced until the wee hours with a group of publishers' reps flown in from New York by the union leadership, a cultural affairs specialist from the Foreign Service Officers Corps, and a middle-level bureaucrat from the B.I.A. Nadjia Bogosian told me they resisted as long as they could, held out, but the ante kept rising, and they sold out, us, NUALA, just as dawn broke over the desert; she said Rod found the moment prophetic, a favorable sign from the Spirit World.

"It's not just Weinberg," she said, "who by the way I happen to feel isn't really, truly sensitive to minority racial and ethnicity concerns. We're resigning from NUALA, and we think a lot of the Blacks, Browns, and Yellows feel the same way. It's time we asserted our respective identities in dramatic fashion." Rod Echohawk grunted agreement; Sean Ignatius Kennedy stirred and groaned in his sleep on the chaise lounge where he lay in fetal position.

I asked her, "How many pieces of silver did you settle on?"

What they got, of course, turned out to be the Racial-Ethnic Artistic Congress; they got Heritage Imprints, the book series funded by the New York cabal; they got Global Village Reading Safaris; they got a large majority of the Minorities to abandon NUALA in the middle of the convention. They got what we, those of us still here, now like to call the Minorities Rump Parliament, which is what Weinberg first called them when I passed on the news.

And he called them scabs. "Literary scabs!" he said to me, to Meyer Jackson, and David Gordon when we finally all got together before the morning session opened downstairs with *Scribble, Scribble!* "Where were you when we needed you?" Weinberg said to Jackson and Gordon. "If you'd been here you could at least have tried to talk her out of it!"

"I was having breakfast with some Academics I'm doing my best to line up behind you," Professor Jackson said.

"I had to stop by a Smallpresswomen's caucus," Gordon said.

Of course, as we all learned soon enough, they lied.

Sean Ignatius Kennedy woke up, moaned, sat up, clutched his throbbing head with both hands. "I need," he said, "a hair off that hound that fanged me. I think I need his whole damn hide!" Juggernaut, frisky from his desert exercise, barked.

It wasn't all convention floor business and back-room politics. My memory of it is distorted by the hours I sat in Weinberg's suite, using his WATS lines to call English department writing programs, flattering and pleading for proxies, but there was also socializing, entertainment, play. Suzie Dodsworth and the Iowa Gang camped by the swimming pool, oiled themselves, donned sunglasses, stretched out to darken their tans. There were the nonstop poetry and fiction readings, marathon book-signings, literary agents roaming the halls of Caesar's Palace, on the prowl to contract new clients. The New York publishers rented suites, laid on catered buffets and open bars. NUALA delegates took time out to watch the floor shows, tried their luck at blackjack and poker and roulette, fed coins to the slots. Sean Ignatius Kennedy won ten thousand dollars for guessing the exact number of jellybeans in a huge jar, using the number of words in his last memoir, *Dipso's Diary,* then lost it in less than an hour shooting craps. I had a long, ultimately unproductive talk with an editor about a possible paperback edition of *The Big Irony.*

It did not matter; we might as well have given ourselves over to enjoying Las Vegas. We were doomed. NUALA was doomed.

Late in the evening of the day the Minorities walked out, David Gordon went, taking almost all of the small presses with him; he made his deal early that same morning, while Nadjia and Echohawk were with me in Weinberg's suite—he was with the American Booksellers Association, in a private party room at Circus Circus, selling us out.

"Distribution!" Weinberg screamed. "The fat little Judas threw us over for distribution!"

"It's hard to blame him," Meyer Jackson said.

It was difficult to blame Gordon only if you put aside the damage to NUALA. David Gordon got his own network, United Smallpresspersons, Inc., a contract linking his U.S. to the booksellers; you see their chapbooks and broadsides and prose-poem postcards now in every Waldenbooks and B. F. Dalton's in every shopping mall in America.

"I blame him," I said, and asked, "Can we still swing it without him and the Minorities?"

Professor Jackson said, "It'll be as tight as the prosody of a closed heroic couplet."

"We can do it!" Weinberg shouted. "What are there more of than anything else in NUALA? What are there more of than anything else in the whole damn country?"

"Poets," Meyer Jackson said.

"Academic writers," I said.

"And don't forget," Sean Ignatius Kennedy said, popping the cap on a bottle of warm Guiness, "you've got the Roaring Boys of America with you still, faithful to the bitter end, pals o' mine! Let's drink on it!"

"Gordon's going to move a lot of inventory," Meyer Jackson said.

NUALA was doomed. As I think of it now, it was like a very bad story, one in which suspense is important, but the reader sees the end before the narrator or any of the characters. *Presque vu.*

We doubled our efforts, did not concede. Weinberg had his vegetarian fruit brunch with Suzie Dodsworth, made a good pitch to the Iowa Gang, worked at holding his demoralized Poets Claque together—I can still see Weinberg as he looked then, running from hotel to hotel to caucus, his trademark floppy beret and flowing cape, Juggernaut on a short leash at his side. Meyer Jackson—or so we thought—was also constantly on the go, running down stray Academic delegates, negotiating with the university presses. I stuck with Weinberg's WATS lines, hustling proxies, trying to quash the rumors that we were on the verge of collapse after the loss of David Gordon, the Minorities, the Guerrilla Independents. Sean Ignatius Kennedy scoured the convention floor, the casinos, the cocktail lounges, our roving ambassador of inebriated goodwill and confidence, flourishing his portfolio, telegrams of unqualified support from Paddy Casey, Mad Mike Murphy, Dizzy Denny Bormann.

"Where's Jackson?" Weinberg asked when we met to evaluate the situation during the third day's recess.

"Ain't seen him in an age," Sean Ignatius said, drank, wiped his mouth on his sleeve, said, "Perhaps the Muse jumped him unawares and he's gone off in the desert to compose one of those long rhyming things of his I'm forever seeing in the stuffier quarterlies? Ah!" Sean Ignatius Kennedy said, "he's no true poet, you know! Tastes a toddy at bedtime, nurses the odd pint now and again, likes sweet cordials, for the love of me! Professor Jackson," he said, "is no tippler, more what I'd call a sipper, a pure puddle-jumper, but a good man for all that!"

We all knew Professor Meyer Jackson was not a good man. Professor Meyer Jackson was an opportunist, a rat who jumped off NUALA's ship when he discerned her listing, taking on water. And he lacked even the decency to tell us to our faces what he had done for himself in the bargain.

The university presses were Meyer Jackson's undoing. I still think the consultancy they combined to give him has no real responsibilities—I don't think he functions as the czar of scholarly and critical publishing, the popular misconception—but the stipend is rumored to be substantial, and the promise of it was enough to erode the ranks of the Academics I had labored to bring to Weinberg's cause. Professor Meyer Jackson disappeared from Las Vegas, did not surface until the press conference in Cambridge announcing his new position. It is no coincidence the news of his contract to edit the multivolume *Poet's Complete Encyclopedia* broke a month later. Professor Jackson was our Trotsky.

"Is it over then?" Sean Ignatius asked when we understood what Meyer Jackson had done to us.

"They're gutting NUALA to spite me," Weinberg said. He did not take Jackson's treachery well, huddled with Juggernaut in the conversation pit, did not bother to shave or dress—he stared for long minutes into his mastiff's large, fluid eyes, stroked and patted the big dog's flank, all the fight gone out of him.

"We can't give up," I said. "We've got the Poets Claque, the Iowa Gang might still throw in with us, I've got a lot of Academic proxies, there's more than a few didn't go out with that traitor!"

"And the Roaring Boys!" Sean Ignatius cried, "The Roaring Boys will be true blue all the way so long as there's a drop left in the bottom of the jug," and he waved his telegrams from Paddy Casey, taking the cure in California, Mad Mike Murphy out in Boston, too broke to make the trip, Dizzy Denny Bormann paralyzed with classic writer's block down in a Florida swamp.

"If we hold," I told Weinberg, "NUALA will fall into our laps tomorrow night!"

How could I have known, as the convention went down to the wire, the presidential balloting, how it was going to end? Now, in retrospect, it was self-evident; all it would have required was a simple tabulation of the numbers, a check of the Convention Rules appended to the Boston Consensus. But I was too busy calling long-distance for every last possible Academic proxy vote, dashing downstairs to the convention floor to rally the faithful who refused to walk out with the betrayers of NUALA. I might have set Sean Ignatius Kennedy the task of assessing total numbers, put him to reading the Rules for fine print, but he was hardly in condition for work that needed a clear head. Or Weinberg . . . but I thought every available minute of Weinberg's time was devoted to his dwindling Poets Claque, to prolonged negotiations with the Iowa Gang.

My memory of that last day is a kind of exile I felt, alone in Weinberg's Caesar's Palace suite—Weinberg gone to politic, Sean Ignatius downstairs on a barstool, introducing himself to showgirls and cocktail waitresses—he still does that, walks right up to women, tells them his name, presents them with an autographed copy of one of his books, asks them if they have ever seen a real writer with all his clothes off.

I was alone in Weinberg's suite, calling on the WATS, Juggernaut asleep in the conversation pit.

The final evening session began, the delegates on the floor standing to sing *Scribble, Scribble!* when I rode up the elevator to get Weinberg, bring him down for the election. "Come on," I said to him, "they're about to call for the balloting. Where have you been? Sean Ignatius said he looked all over Vegas for you, your dog's been going stir crazy in here all day!"

"I won't be going," Weinberg said. Then I saw he was packing, throwing the mess of his dirty clothes, books, loose manuscripts into his bags, forcing the lids shut, snapping latches, buckling straps. He buttoned his cape at his throat, put his beret on, stood at the mirror to adjust its flop rakishly over one eye as he spoke. "I'm not humiliating myself," Weinberg said.

"Don't do this!" I said. And I said, "We're close! Your Poets Claque will stick with you, I've got a bag of proxies, there's a lot of literati on the floor down there mad as hell at the leadership for the way they've tried to buy this election, don't fold on me!" I urged Weinberg.

He assembled his luggage, looked around the suite for anything forgotten, whistled Juggernaut to his side, clipped the short leash to his choke-chain collar, faced me in his trademark denims, cape, beret. "Give it up," Weinberg said. Weinberg said, "NUALA's dead meat. The leadership's splitting off, there's going to be a new organization for the Commercials and Slickies, you'll have to qualify for membership by proving your income from writing with your tax returns every year."

"Then it's ours!" I said. "Poets and Academics and Roaring Boys, whoever else wants to hang with us, *we'll* be NUALA!" I cried, and for just a moment I really believed it could happen that way.

"No," Weinberg said, "the Poets Claque's going with me." Then I understood what he had done.

"What did you get for yourself?" I asked Weinberg there in his suite.

"I don't have time for this," he said, "they're coming up for my bags, I've got a cab coming."

That was how Weinberg got Poets Union, Inc.—P.U. Stink, Sean Ignatius christened it. From the start, the leadership determined to ruin rather than risk losing their rule. They nibbled us to death: bullied Dwayne Willie Weathergood and his Guerrilla Independents out of Las Vegas, cut up the pie, pieces for the Minorities and Smallpresspersons, Professor Meyer Jackson's Academic followers and the university presses . . . Weinberg's Poets Union, Inc. was just the last and biggest slice. That was how Weinberg got P. U. Stink and the enormous motor-home he calls Poemobile Calliope he lives in on the road, his cross-country reading tours.

"It makes more sense this way," Weinberg told me before I left him there with his mastiff, went down and did what I did. "Our respective interests are too divergent," he said. "NUALA was a flawed idea from the start back in Boston," he said. "Poets," Weinberg said, "just naturally by virtue of their special and peculiar sensibilities feel more affinity with their fellow poets. If you're smart you'll find someplace for yourself before it's too late. *Sauve qui peut,*" Weinberg said.

It was already too late for me; I had no place to go except back downstairs, to what was left of NUALA.

I was not responsible for what happened, did not orchestrate or manipulate events there on the floor that night, what was supposed to have been the final session of the Las Vegas convention. Rumor to the contrary, it happened quickly, spontaneously.

When the call for the vote was made, the vice-chairman of the Membership Committee, an Academic named Learst, author of impressionistic sketches profiling disaffected Vietnam veterans, reported the resignation of all standing candidates from NUALA's rolls. There was momentary chaos until Sean Ignatius Kennedy rose, stood on his chair, inspired by whatever he had been drinking, shouted until he was recognized, and entered my name in nomination for the presidency. The nomination was seconded by one of the Iowa Gang, perhaps confused as to who I was, and I was elected by acclamation. When I reached the rostrum to make my acceptance speech, Learst took me aside, whispered in my ear that NUALA, membership decimated by mass resignations, lacked the quorum necessary to adjourn.

"Then," I told him, "we won't adjourn."

"What'll we do, extend the convention until Caesar's Palace throws us out the door?" he asked.

"If need be," I said, and went up the steps to the podium microphone, gaveled the floor back to order. "If need be," I told Delegate

Learst, "we'll stay in session forever, as long as it takes to make NUALA what it should be!"

The floor returned to order, I made my acceptance speech, and then I led them—the remnants of NUALA gathered below and before me, in the Resolution of Censure; I *did* orchestrate and manipulate the condemnation of all who had abandoned us: Commercials, Slickies, Minorities, Guerrilla Independents, Smallpresspersons, the Poets Claque.

That was what drove the Iowa Gang away, out of Las Vegas, back to the Midwest, where they charted their own organization, membership restricted to graduates of the Writers Workshop.

And so the convention at Caesar's Palace continues. I suppose it is inevitable; when we exhaust NUALA's treasury, we will be evicted, tossed out by the management to wander in the Nevada desert. But NUALA will never die. Weinberg was wrong—it is too grand an idea, too wondrous a creation of our collective imagination to just disappear!

Meanwhile, we continue at Caesar's Palace. We open each day with our a cappella singing of *Scribble, Scribble!*, we hear ad hoc committee reports on the status of efforts to reconcile with splinter elements, on the new membership recruiting drive, on the treasury funds that sustain us. We try to remain hopeful. We hear of renegades considering rejoining NUALA, disgruntled Minorities, Poets, Academics, a few of the less successful Commercials and Slickies, and we welcome their return to NUALA's bosom—we have hope of attaining a quorum to adjourn sometime soon. We seek constantly to find those literati, spread all across our mighty nation, who might see the value of petitioning for readmission to membership. We are hopeful.

We have not forgotten, will not forget those who destroyed us. Each night, before we close the evening session with *Scribble, Scribble!*, we renew the Resolution of Censure, and we name them: D. W. Weathergood, Nadjia Bogosian, Rod Echohawk, David Gordon, Meyer Jackson, Weinberg . . . Weinberg most of all! Anathema, all of them, to the card-carrying brothers and sisters of NUALA. We do not forget, cannot forgive!

There are so few of us left here in Las Vegas: a scattering of the faithful, myself and the Roaring Boys—Sean Ignatius persuaded Paddy and Mad Mike and Dizzy Denny to join us. We gather in the casino bar each night, pay for our drinks with funds from NUALA's rapidly diminishing treasury, and, I confess, we all get quite drunk, sentimental about the old days, Boston. It is very sad.

What is most sad of all is that none of us, not me, not the Roaring Boys, none of NUALA's faithful, has written a thing since it happened. That, that we are America's only true literati, and we write nothing, have written nothing, that is the saddest thing of all in the story I have to tell.

But we do not talk of this here in the casino bar at Caesar's Palace. We get drunk and talk of the old days, Boston, and we sing *Scribble, Scribble!* to the amusement of the gamblers and revelers. We link arms and sing, trying to forget we are not writing anything these days.

Without Spot or Wrinkle

What I said to myself as I got out of the rental car was: *What do we come to?* And: *Jesus.* And: *God's mercy!* It was like stepping out of the world, into some dingy, shabby, skewed approximation of any world I knew, walking into one I might only half-remember from a bad dream dreamed a long time ago. *Roddy boy, Roddy Mullins, how in the name of anything holy did you end up like this?*

I stepped out of the air-conditioned bubble of my rental Oldsmobile, the door shut behind me with a clean, sharp, metallic smack, and there I was, breathing the thick humidity hazing the evening's dimming air, walking through a close heat I felt clamp my skin like a hot, moist hand, hearing the crunch and crackle of the cinders paving the parking lot under my shoes, a little giddy from the flight from Boston, the slow drive from the Jackson airport, nothing substantial eaten since Roddy's wife called.

Then I stood for a moment on the buckled sidewalk, looked about—sagging clapboard houses, some up on blocks, two trailers, a get-and-go gas station, shallow ditches instead of curbs lining the pocked, washboard street—and realized I was the only soul there. No people, a few old cars and pickups parked in driveways, front yards, under scraggly trees and tilting carports, nothing but me and the humid heat, sky darkening, and for just an instant I was somehow terrified, as if a great danger were about to break loose upon me.

And then I turned to the funeral home, the name *Coleman* painted above the double doors, and then I saw the sign on the sparse lawn, the kind churches use to post sermon titles in white letters on black felt, and read it in the last possible light allowing this. *Mullins* it said, and *Visitation 8 PM.* I said my brother's name to myself, as if it could repel that irrational danger lurking nearby, then started up the short walk, clenching my fingers into fists, preparing myself to look upon his remains inside this rattletrap of a funeral home in this parody of a residential neighborhood in this weary and ancient small town in the benighted state of Mississippi—this place, this Negro funeral home in this Negro side of town. *Oh Roddy!* I said to myself.

Then suddenly I wasn't alone there, and I wasn't afraid of anything except whatever might be usual in the falling evening dark of this improbable place.

The double doors popped open, a light in the small porch's ceiling blinked on, and there were half a dozen Negro people there with me, and I thought to myself I must say *black* and *African-American,* not *Negro.* I tried a smile that was friendly but also solemn for the occasion. This little crowd parted as if at a command, and an old woman, elegant in her way—white hair perfectly arranged, big gold rings, a splashy gold brooch set on her large bosom, her dress a flaming pink—came slowly toward me, walking with a shiny black cane, free hand out to me. I took it in mine, felt her papery skin, the surprising grip of her bony fingers, smelled the strong lilac scent of her perfume flood the air around us.

"Kenneth Mullins. Kenny," I said, and, "Roddy's brother. From Boston," I said. She cracked her too-red lips, flashing gold inlays between her big teeth, an almost-grin, as if I had stated the too-obvious.

"I am Mrs. Faylennete Coleman," she said. "Mr. Coleman begun this business. I am the proprietor." She released my hand. "We are quite proud," she said, "to service Mr. Mullins. He is the first white man to be buried from out one of us's establishment in all this county ever."

"Thank you," is all I could think to say. And then she hobbled past me, off the porch, down the walk, cane tapping, a younger woman with her, supporting Mrs. Coleman the proprietor of Coleman's Funeral Parlor, fading into the growing dark as I turned back to meet the half-dozen or more black/African-Americans who had come to mourn my brother's death with me in this impossible place that had proved his last.

It was very strange, but I felt relaxed now, easy, well able to shake hands and utter the purely formulaic and perfunctory things one says at funerals, weddings, and other ceremonies we sleepwalk through because we cannot or do not wish to truly participate.

There was an obese man, skin so black it looked tinged with a purple afterglow. The only person I saw dressed in ritual black, a suit far too heavy for the season, sweat coursed down his balloon cheeks into his stiff, snowy shirt collar. I took his swollen hand, said, "Thank you" when he gave his name as Livingston Jones, told me Mr. Roddy Mullins had been his client. Was he a lawyer, insurance agent, bartender? There was no time for actual conversation, to me no seeming need for it. It was men's and women's faces in shades from pale tan to Livingston Jones's ebony, their proffered hands in mine, the shibboleths.

"I am Miss Minnie McWilliams. I am China Mae's aunt." She pronounced it to rhyme with *taunt,* a woman surely younger than Roddy's wife had to be, yet her aunt, hair bleached a bizarre reddish blond, her crisp pant-suit coral blue, gold necklace and bracelets, a large diamond ring flashing like an ice shard.

"I am Hector Robinson. Very sorry Mr. Mullins is passed so sudden."

"I am T. C. Green," said T. C. Green, muscular, coffee-colored, shaved skull, gold chains splayed on the glossy expanse of his chest revealed by his polyester smock's open neck. He squeezed my hand as if we were competing, said, "Roddy be my man, we get together afore you leaves, Mr. Kenneth. Oh yeah, Roddy be speakin' about you to me!" I nodded yes, we would get together before I left, spread my fingers to ease the hurt of his aggressive clasp.

"I be China Mae's cousin by marriage? We be having our dinner with her and Mr. Roddy jus' las' week 'fore he die."

"Mr. Roddy a *nice* man, I always say. He help me when my old car stop on me sudden."

"I am Mrs. Celestine Flood, and I am ninety-one year old. It a shame one so young go from us!" Mrs. Flood had no teeth, but walked as sprightly as a girl, dressed as if she were twenty, all in white, gloves, handbag, earrings like sugar cookies.

"Muchly sad for your loss," said a man.

"We say we be doin' this and that tomorrow or directly, we don't *know* what or *if* we gon' *do* nothing if our time come!" said a woman.

"Luther Givens. You Roddy's brother, was you?"

"I am Alberta Coggs. You don't know me, 'course, but I knowed your brother and his Mrs. good."

"I believe you favor your brother some, but he lots larger than you until he losed so much pounds just recent here. I guess did he die from losing all them pounds so quick, did he?"

I shook their hands, said *Thank you* and *Thank you for being here* and *It's good of you to come* and *Yes it was sudden, unexpected* and *I'm glad you were his friend,* all the things one says without having to think—it is well we have such things so easily, effortlessly said; it allows us to absorb ourselves in immediate things, the varied hues of skin, the redolence of perfume and pomades and perspiration, the dazzle of bright, multicolored attire chosen for this moment by these people in this place.

I felt very much at ease with these Negroes, confident I would never use the word, felt I would come through this well, behave well, be free after just another day to drive away in my air-conditioned rental Olds, fly away back to Boston, resume my life without difficulty in the world I knew and understood.

Roddy's widow—had she waited aside until everyone else met me, come forward as a kind of finale? She said, "I know you from Roddy's picture album. He never sent you a picture of me? I'm China Mae. Do you recognize my voice from the telephone. Should I call you Kenneth or Kenny? Roddy always said *Kenny.*"

China Mae Mullins—my brother's widow—was the only other one there dressed in somber colors, a dark brown business suit, besides the obese Livingston Jones. And the only other besides myself with something like an expression of mourning on her face. She dabbed at the corner of one eye with a frilly hankie as I took her free hand in mine. I did not expect her to embrace me, but she did; her perfume had a coconut flavor to it, and for a thin woman she felt very solid, very strong as she hugged me, once, hard, then stepped back. Standards of female attractiveness are absolutely arbitrary, I know, but I thought her a plain woman, not at all the type Roddy fancied in life—his former wives, four of them, for example.

"Kenny's fine," I said, and, "Whatever you feel comfortable with." She smiled a small smile, as if to say she forgave me for something awkward or boorish I had said.

"I'm very glad you came all this way," she said. "There was no warning except he didn't feel chipper lately, and he wasn't one to see doctors, you probably know." And she said, "Your wife, Mrs. Mullins, she wasn't able to come so quickly, I understand," she said.

"She's a very busy person. And we have children," I said.

"It's a shame," my brother's widow said.

"Yes," I said, not sure what she meant, what I meant. Roddy's death? My family's inability to come with me? That I had a wife and children?

"I want you to meet our pastors," China Mae Mullins said, and took my arm as if I were blind, led me up the carpeted aisle—it was badly worn in spots—toward the casket banked by flowers I was close enough to smell now. Behind me, the mourners who greeted me gathered at a card table filled with stacked cans of soda, a coffee urn, a tower of Styrofoam cups, paper napkins, plastic stir sticks. They talked, chattered, as though they were parents gathered to watch a school play or concert. *Here, Roddy?* I thought, and, *This?*

The Coleman Funeral Parlor was vaguely church-like. There were pews, stained-glass windows, something like an altar or stage behind the casket we neared, a large, crude picture of Martin Luther King on one back wall. But the ceiling was low, giving it a barracks-like feel, something prefabricated, jerry-built, and now I heard some faint recorded organ tones.

The pastors sprang up from the front pew, stood side by side in the aisle, each holding a Bible to his chest, blank expressions, as if braced to block my path to my brother's remains. "This is Kenny, Roddy's baby brother," his widow said. Roddy was only sixteen months my senior; we were sometimes taken for twins when we were toddlers.

"Your sorrow is ours, our faith to withstand is yours," said the younger pastor. He wore a dog collar, could have passed for a priest. He said his name was Pastor Hightower.

"Consolations in the Word, always," said the much older man. China Mae told me later he was emeritus, very reluctant to give his duties up to a successor. She called him Dr. Watts. He wore a gray suit, his hair like white wool, pale brown face freckled.

Did I say *Thank you?* Did I say anything?

Then China Mae Mullins said, "Would you like to view Roddy now?" and took my arm again. The pastors stood aside, bowed their heads, eyes closed, presumably praying—for my brother? For me? And then I stood at the open casket all but smothered in floral displays, looked down at my only brother Roddy, dead in this unlikely place.

I had not expected to weep. I wept, copiously, dug for my handkerchief, mopped my eyes, but the blubbering noise I made was bursts of laughter—cynical, callous guffaws—I clenched my teeth against, threatening to erupt into this absurd place of ostentatious flowers, canned organ music, cloying scents, the backdrop of chatting mourners over coffee and soda, the pair of silent praying pastors, Mrs. China Mae Mullins beside me, clutching the crook of my arm as I shook with weeping and suppressed, ugly laughter.

"He looks nice," she said.

He did. Roddy looked only a little older than the last time we met, years before, his hair grayed some, a haircut I had never seen him wear in life. And he was leaner, the weight that grew on him through the years trimmed away, his skin sallow, folded hands almost emaciated, his burial suit a dark blue flannel I could not believe he would have picked. And I did not know his sullen expression, the petulant set of his mouth.

"It's Roddy," I said, "but it's not Roddy," wiped at my face, handkerchief soaked. I tried to make myself think of him in life, our childhood, the good and crazy times, and this made me want to weep, but my eyes cleared and I could see all the excessive floral tributes with ribbons, gilt script sentiments, mundane snapshots of Roddy and his last wife set in the casket with him, the folded flag waiting to be draped over it when the lid was closed and sealed, and all I heard was recorded organ, the pop of soda cans opening behind us, mumbling pastors flanking me like sentries, felt the firm hand of my sister-in-law on my elbow. I sighed for breath, tipped back my head, looked into the portrait of Martin Luther King, looked back at what had been my beloved only brother, looked down at my shoes, balled my drenched handkerchief and shoved it in a pocket. I said, "It's sort of like a statue of Roddy."

His widow said, "I think he looks nice, but I mean to keep him in mind as he was living." And she said, "We can sit," and turned me, led me to a front pew, pastors parting to give us way, seated me like an unruly child condemned to a corner.

I said, "Everybody in our family's buried in Boston," did not know why I said that. My sister-in-law looked at me, frowned, but said nothing in return.

And there we sat through the hours of visitation.

The mourners, their numbers greatly increased now, left their coffee and sodas, marched up the aisle in pairs, threes, sometimes four in a rank, stopped at the casket, looked at my brother as if he were a sign they could not decipher, turned to me and China Mae, leaned down, shook hands, said the things they said before. Some stayed a while, sitting in the pews behind us while the recorded organ droned, the insufficient air-conditioning struggled to cool us, got up and left. The double doors made a clapping sound when they opened and closed behind them.

"How are you holding out?" I whispered to China Mae.

"I am maintaining," she said. "Are you?"

"I think so. I'm frazzled from the trip, I think. Jet lag."

"You need a sleep," she said, and, "Did you get your reservation?"

"I confirmed in Boston," I said. "The Ramada?"

She said, "That's brand new. It'll be nice."

"I hope," I said, and, "I passed it coming in off the highway."

"It's brand new," she said, the way its owner might have bragged of it.

We sat, the organ never ceased, and I shook hands again with Livingston Jones and Hector Robinson and the aged Mrs. Celestine Flood, and a host of cousins and in-laws and near neighbors whose names are lost now forever. T. C. Green said, "Roddy were my man. We get us a little taste and talk some after the burying and all, huh?" I agreed we would.

"Is he a relative too?" I asked China Mae.

She said, "T. C. tends to be wild. Roddy liked to go drinking with him once every so often."

"Roddy tried to go A.A. years ago. It didn't stick?"

"He abstained some and he drank some. I never faulted him for it," she said.

"Did he *know* all these people?" I asked her.

"Mostly," she said. And, "Roddy was a friendly person."

"He liked," I said, "a crowd."

"He also liked to just spend quiet time in our home," she said, which did not sound like my brother, but we had been so long apart, estranged, what did *I* know? This Roddy lying before me in his casket was as impossible as this place, these mourners, this widow. So we sat until there were no more mourners, and the pastors, Bibles in front of them like shields, said their good-byes, and we rose from our pew, and then I met the woman, Mrs. Faylennete Coleman's daughter, who managed the family business, was the mortician. Her name was also Faylennete, but she was or had been married, her last name Saucier—she pronounced it *So-shur.*

"Oh, lordy," she said, emerging suddenly from a doorway I had not noticed, her office—the mortuary? She said, "This *gots* to be Mr. Roddy's brother!" She embraced me before I could raise my hand to her, pulled me so close I felt her large breasts flatten on my chest, planted a moist kiss on my cheek that felt like it left the print of her silver lipstick, but when I checked in my Ramada bathroom mirror, there was no trace of it. She was a striking, vivacious, sexy woman, dressed as if for nightclubbing.

She said, "Now, China Mae, *ever-thang's* in ready a-plus condition! So you gots not to worry about *nothing!* And this big fella, he's all set up, is he?" Her hair was bleached gold-blond, coifed like a helmet. She reeked of a syrupy perfume I could not decide if I liked or hated, her skirt short enough to show off exquisite brown legs under translucent white stockings, her blouse open enough buttons to feature the high arcs of her bronze breasts, fingernails painted silver, rings and bracelets of silver, false eyelashes speckled with glitter she batted as though she meant to pick me up for the night. "You leave *ever-thang* to Coleman's, we gots it all *in* place, hear?" she said to me.

I thought . . . I thought so many things, so absurd . . . this blatantly sexy woman embalmed my brother? Did this voluptuous woman plant such lascivious kisses on the cheeks of those dour pastors? Why do I, here to mourn my brother, want to stare at this woman's cleavage? I think I was smiling as I swallowed repeatedly to prevent new weeping and laughter.

"Ten sharp!" she said. "Miss China Mae's house—you find that okay? The hearse and limo's gon' *be* there! And I be there to see it's all *right* all the while!" I nodded, I would find the Mullins home, I had a motel reservation—yes, I was sure the new Ramada would be nice. I would be punctual for the procession to the church.

I expected to embrace Roddy's widow good-bye, but this time she only gave me her thin, strong hand. Before I could offer my hand to her, this stunning mortician, Faylennete Saucier, grabbed me again, hugged, warm and fragrant, kissed my other cheek. And then I was able to leave; I did not look back at Roddy's remains, walked out the double doors into the stifling humid heat of full dark, ran my rental Olds's air-conditioning on high all the way to the town's outskirts, the new Ramada, was about comfortably cool by the time I reached my reserved room.

The brand-new Ramada was very nice. My room smelled that wonderful new smell that is more the absolute absence of any odor, everything absolutely clean, new. I might have been in any new Ramada anywhere. The beige walls sheltered me, the double bed made tight, sheets fresh, carpeting thick and springy, bathroom tiles glossy, faucets sparkling, plastic cups wrapped in plastic, the latest model telephone, clock radio, television set, scratch pad and ballpoint pen, room service menu, polished mirrors, efficient air-conditioning a soothing, incessant whisper, ashtrays and book matches, courtesy coffee-maker, drawers that slid without hitch or scrape, oversize pillows, a mattress solid as a padded slab of rock. It was like stepping back into the real world—I might have been miraculously transported back to Boston, anywhere.

I felt only pleasantly tired, as if at the end of a long but productive, rewarding day's work, felt sure a hot shower would send me to bed to sleep deeply, without dreams. I took a long shower in the frosted glass cage, lathered with the pristine packets of soap and shampoo, rinsed under the hot spray that stung like a vigorous massage. A long hot shower is a wonder, a respite during which everything troubling recedes, evaporates, washed away forever, or so it seems to me. It is like being wholly alive minus any of the complications of living. I closed my eyes, hummed, swayed under this marvelous, cleansing, restorative cascade.

But I did not sleep well. I slept hardly at all. When I did sleep, it was the semi-slumber in which half-dreams melt into immediate or remote memories, and so it is impossible to separate reality from the distortions flowing from the subconscious. So I did not want to sleep for fear I would dream about this place, these people, their accents, colors and sounds and smells so strange, bizarre, alien—that different, impossible, absurd world I had escaped at least until morning took me back into it.

I tried to make sense, coherence, logic and order of my brother's life, and this death, but failed. I found no pattern, no thread to lead me from beginning to this end; there were only juxtaposed moments, episodes, and too many blank spaces I could not traverse or link to what I knew and think I understood.

There was Roddy and myself, boys, close, happy, energetic, enthusiastic, loved—the world of South Boston, our good, decent parents, the most quotidian of lower-middle-class American lives, families. Then there was . . . *youth?* Roddy was an outstanding athlete, I was an excellent student, scholarships, B.U. and Northeastern. *Manhood* would be next? But things are already happening, changing—why don't I realize any of this as it is happening? Women. Roddy had far more than his share! My wife and I: love at first sight, just like the songs and soap operas. Work: Roddy sold intangibles, commodity futures and municipal bonds and growth stocks. I went into insurance, did well, not brilliantly, and today enjoy a very, *very* comfortable living on my client renewals alone. Roddy got rich, went bust, got rich again, broke, rich, broke.

I married my sweetheart, had a son and two daughters I am unreservedly, immodestly proud of to this moment. We will never leave Boston, do not wish to, but no longer live in the south end. Our grandparents were shanty Irish, our parents lace-curtain. We, I thought, are better than that. But my brother was gone, so there is only myself, my wife and children. I moved out of South Boston before I married.

Roddy drank, and he gambled, married and divorced and married, divorced, broke our parents' hearts over and over before they passed away. He *womanized* is, I suppose, the right term. Four marriages, all to beautiful women—I met only the first three—who were all wrong for him, he for them. Mercifully, he had no children. His divorces were bitter and expensive. He left Boston for Chicago to start over, joined A.A., but I criticized his life, he retorted by mocking mine, and we quarreled stupidly over our parents' estate, so we finally no longer communicated, lost each other. I wrote him off, the way I would an insurance loss; he considered me—one of the last things he said to me—so boring, so ordinary, so totally unremarkable a person he was ashamed to think we were related by blood.

I remember him saying: "Kenny, you always put me in mind of those geeks in zombie movies, living dead, you know?"

I said, "Roddy, you're not even the kind of man I'd care to have my children know for their only uncle on my side."

He said, "Ghost Who Walks. Holy shit, Kenny, how do you live with yourself? I mean, don't you worry ever you'll wake up someday and hang yourself or take the pipe?"

I said, "I think we've said enough. I think we should stop tormenting each other."

So we did. And there I lost him, for years, away in Chicago, I imagined, until his fifth wife, Mrs. China Mae Mullins, called me to come to the state of Mississippi to see my brother put to rest.

I think I did doze at least a little before morning, but woke weary and dreading the day, but determined to learn what I could of those blank spaces from his widow, from T. C. Green if there was time for that before I had to leave for Jackson's airport, my plane, Boston, the rest of my own life.

So it was morning, and I was back in that foreign place again, all hard, hot sunlight, smothering heat gathered like a fiery knot at the back of my neck, face filmed immediately with perspiration, lofty pines and the jawing of birds I did not recognize flitting among the greasy leaves of magnolias that blossomed with clumps of white, waxy flowers—my rental Oldsmobile's air-conditioning was only a brief reprieve as I searched my way through this grimy little Mississippi town to the countryside, my brother's last home. And then I was among all his mourning black neighbors and in-laws, the riot of their clothes: flowing dresses and floppy garden hats, sporty suits and hard-polished shoes, jewelry and slicked hairdos reflecting the merciless sun, pinks and reds and pale blues, yellows and oranges, all shades of pastel, the screeches and gutturals of their dialect in my ears.

"Could you use a breakfast before we go? There's time," his widow asked me.

"The Ramada had coffee in the room," I told her. Roddy's house was bigger, better than the worn frame houses around Coleman's Funeral Parlor, a squat brick ranch, broad Bermuda lawn, towering pines, shrubs and flower beds rivaling the mourners' attire for brilliant, clashing color. "You have a nice place," I said.

She said, "This land came to me from my people. We built when we came down from Chicago."

"I'd never guessed," I said, "Roddy would come way down here."

"We were very comfortable and content," she said. I told her that was good to hear.

I shook all the hands again, tried to smile back to all the smiles, thanked them, said everything I said before.

"As good a day as you gets for sad work," said Livingston Jones.

"My granddaughter say I too old to come out in all this heat," said the ancient Mrs. Celestine Flood, "but *I* says we owes it to peoples when they put to res'."

T. C. Green, flashy, grinning, said, "Don't forgets we gots a taste waitin'," and looked over his shoulder at a double-wide trailer across the road, a wide porch built onto its front.

And then it was time for the procession; Roddy's widow and I were escorted to the Coleman limo to lead. "Where's the hearse?" I asked the driver, a short brown man who wore something like a bus driver's cap and jacket.

"The departed," he said in a raspy voice, "already *in* church," opened the door for us. The limo needed a wash, upholstery tattered, dusty. China Mae Mullins beside me, her perfume thick in the stifling interior, we led the line of limping, noisy cars and pickup trucks down winding asphalt roads to The Church Without Spot or Wrinkle, her congregation.

"I don't suppose Roddy was very religious," I said.

She said, "He attended rarely."

"I'm surprised he attended at all. We were raised R.C., you know. Catholic. I guess we both fell away. My wife took our children when they were small, but we're not what you'd call religious people."

"He had a serious side," she said.

I said, "I don't think I saw that in him."

"You did not know him in recent years," she said, and I agreed. I tried to roll down the limo's window, but it would not budge, so his widow and I and the driver sweltered as we moved ever so slowly down the narrow county roads, long line behind us, lights on in the near-blinding light of late morning. The driver caught my eyes in his rearview mirror, told me these window cranks needed fixing bad. There was nothing to look at as we drove to the funeral except fields lush with whatever grew here, some few cattle drooping in patches of shade, and the high trees of the Piney Woods touching the white-hot sky everywhere.

I spoke because I did not want to think of anything, did not want to see this awful place. I said, "Forgive me if it's crude to ask, but what did you see in him?"

"Roddy? He was a nice man. He was jolly and cheerful and fun to be with. He had a difficult life of it. So did I. We were good to each other. We were good *for* each other."

"I suppose," I said, and, "Probably you can understand how surprised I am he married . . . I didn't know he married a colored person, much less got married again a fifth time. If he'd told me I wouldn't have believed it. I'm sorry if I'm awkward," I said. She turned to me, smiled a smile that seemed to reek of pity for me.

"He told me all that. You people," she said. "*Southies* he called you?"

"South Boston. We grew up there. I haven't lived there in ages."

"Yes," she said, and, "I know those attitudes. Some people like your brother can grow past *that!*" she said; it was like having my face slapped.

"Was it pretty difficult for the two of you? Here. Down here," I said.

"Some," she said. And she said, "My people are very accepting. It's not like it was twenty years ago," she said.

"I'm glad for that."

"We felt secure," my sister-in-law said.

"I guess that's what counts."

"Enjoying life no matter what is what counts," she said. My cheeks burned, so I stopped talking, tried not to think of anything, tried to ignore the oppressive heat, breathed long slow breaths, praying for her church to appear in the limo's windows, prayed her church would be air-conditioned.

The Church Without Spot or Wrinkle was a new building, set on the corner where two of the narrow asphalt roads met. Its name in large letters on a sign big enough to seem a billboard, it was too new for landscaping to decorate the rough Bermuda grounds; behind it, I got a glimpse of its small cemetery, stones, old floral tributes withering, the dark green canvas canopy over the grave dug for my brother. I tried to picture the cemetery in Boston where my grandparents and parents rested, all my relatives, where I would someday lie, but could not conjure it in this place.

Then we were out of the rattling limo, sun wicked above, the mourners stepping from their cars and pickups, lining up behind China Mae and me—we would lead them into the church, doors opened by our driver, the two pastors side by side to greet us. Faylennete Saucier, commanding and vivacious in her cerise pantsuit, kissed me again, her lips tacky-sweet white, hugged, said, "How is *this* big fella today?" and marshaled our file, nudged us forward into the church.

Pastor Hightower shook my hand, said, "Us *all* with you today, brother."

Dr. Watts took my hand, whispered, "Hear the Word!"

"I'm not sure I can actually do this," I said to my sister-in-law.

She took my arm, said, "I will support you if need be, Kenny," led me between the pastors who parted for us, up the aisle. The Church Without Spot or Wrinkle was, blessedly, chill with air-conditioning, so dark by contrast with the blazing sun I was blinded for an instant, would have stumbled on the aisle's runner were it not for China Mae Mullins holding me.

The funeral service is not complete, not wholly coherent in my memory. When I try to recall it, it comes confused with the vaguest memories of my Catholic Latin and beads. There was organ music again, but this time from a real organ, played by a young man in a short-sleeved white shirt and bow tie, horn-rim glasses giving him a scholarly look, distracted as he fingered the keys and pulled and punched the stops in some medley of hymns I did not recognize—this organ was a kind of filler, droning in the gaps between prayers and sermon and eulogy. Dr. Watts mumbled into the pulpit's microphone, head down, hands clasped, the usual prayers, mourners responding with perfect timing and rhythm behind the pew where I sat beside my sister-in-law. Pastor Hightower's sermon and eulogy came to me in bits and pieces as I stanched my flowing eyes on the handkerchiefs I had stored in pockets, in anticipation, at the Ramada.

The solemnity of the ceremony was shattered for me by his faulty grammar and pronunciation—we were reminded of mortality and morality by this man's passing; we were not to judge, God would do that, had doubtless already done that; we were to think on this man's joy in life, the joy he brought to those who knew him; we were enjoined not to forget God's mercy and the promise of Jesus; this life was a blessing if we would accept it, death a mystery revealing itself to us in God's good time. I tried to listen, tried not to hear, wept without let-up, wished to God I was not there in that place then.

Roddy in his casket lay before me, but I did not let myself look at him, the heaps of flowers transported from Coleman's Funeral Parlor. Beside me, China Mae Mullins did not weep, did not pray aloud, but I felt her shiver and shudder now and again. I tried to read the handout summarizing my brother's life, saw it was full of errors and misinterpretations—she was surely the author, did not really know my brother. *Who knows this man lying in all those flowers?* I asked myself. *Who knows anybody?*

I stood when she stood, heard the mourners rise and sit behind us, sighs and rustling, but I could not join the prayers led from the pulpit. When Hightower spoke Roddy's name in the eulogy, *Brother Roddy Mullins, Brother Roddy,* he called him, I tried to remember good times from so long ago, but nothing came to me. When he said, "Brother Mullins is sorely missed by his grieving beloved wife and also his brother with us here this day," it took me a moment to realize he meant me, the woman beside me.

Then it ended, we stood, Faylennete Saucier stood before the casket, called out, "Friends for flowers, friends for flowers," and mourners came forward to pick up Roddy's floral tributes, carried them back down the aisle, out of The Church Without Spot or Wrinkle. The pastors shook my hand again, walked toward the doors.

Faylennete Saucier took my arm, said, "Go on out to the entry, you two," and said, "Sweetie, you stand right in front the coffin, follow right on behind Pastor to the grave, sweetie." To me, she said, "Now you take your place beside the coffin when we brings it up to the entry after we close and drape the flag, hear?" That was how I learned I was to be a pallbearer.

The organ boomed us back up the aisle to the entry where I stood with five men—only T. C. Green and the limo driver familiar to me, but they were young, strong men. T. C. shot me a broad smile, winked; I look at my shoes, waited that way until Roddy's closed, sealed casket, covered now with the flag of his brief but honorable military service, was wheeled between our two ranks. The limo driver rasped, "Gentlemens, all take hold with one hand, lift on three," counted, and we lifted the casket free of its cart. It was the heaviest weight I have ever lifted.

I looked out the open doors, glaring sun bleeding into our shade, saw the walkway flanked by the mourners bearing flowers, a gauntlet we would pass through. *How far,* I asked myself, *must we carry this? I can't carry this all the way to his grave,* I thought, understood that was what we were to do.

Then the young organist struck up something almost martial, loud, Pastor Hightower opened his Bible, and, followed by Roddy's widow, followed by me and my fellow pallbearers, stepped out into the blistering heat and light. We shuffled, straining against the great weight of Roddy's blue enameled steel casket, through the floral gauntlet, turning left to proceed to the cemetery, Hightower singing out about the life and the resurrection, the quick and the dead, the valley of death and the everlasting glory hereafter—we shuffled, stumbled in the thick, dusty grass, sweated ourselves wet, carrying my brother to his grave in this place of heat and light and color.

I prayed then. I prayed I would not fall, would not release my grip on the casket's rail biting into my hand, prayed I would not faint, prayed I would not die from heat and exertion and bone-deep fatigue. *Jesus!* I said to myself, *you could die here!*

I did not let myself look at the green canopy nearing us in excruciating inches, would not hear the pastor's Scripture sung out to the pines, would not hear the involuntary grunting and wheezing we pallbearers emitted from our tight lips, did not look at my sister-in-law just ahead of us, only prayed my body would last long enough to do this last thing.

We reached the grave, the canopy's blessed block of dark shade, placed the casket, groaning, on the straps over the fresh hole, and there were folding chairs for China Mae and the pallbearers, and we sat, mourners crowding around us. A light breeze suddenly rose, stirred the canopy's fringe, blessed us. I sat, exhausted, near lifeless, my body's sweat suddenly a cooling bath on my skin, and my brother was buried there in that place.

Burial did not take long. We stood for Dr. Watts's mumble, Pastor Hightower's final prayer, Roddy's flag removed from his casket, folded by the limo driver, handed to his widow. I almost laughed when the limo driver closed the ceremony by standing at the head of the casket to deliver a short commercial for Coleman's Funeral Parlor. "We stands ready at Coleman to serve you needs at all times," he said. And then we all walked away from the grave, out into the burning heat and razor light.

Then it was as if we had gathered for some happy occasion, a picnic reunion of some extended family. The mourners broke into clusters of three and four, their voices loud with gossip, laughter, talk of the weather, of work and family. I felt dazed, like I had been yanked awake from a deep, untroubled sleep, accepted handshakes, claps on the back, the voices mixed and fragmented like the chatter of birds. I did not look back at the grave site for fear I might see dirt being shoveled in, hear the grind of gears lowering the casket into the rough wooden crate waiting in the hole's bottom.

China Mae Mullins came close to say, "You come back to the house with me in Coleman's car, we have food for everyone. The house will be nicely cooled," she said.

Speaking into my ear, our secret, T. C. Green said, "Get us that taste," cackled, slapped my shoulder. Faylennete Saucier kissed me a last time. I think it was the driver led me back to his limo, nudged me in beside my sister-in-law for the excruciating ride back to Roddy's brick ranch, mourners following for the . . . in Boston we would have called it the wake, but only the old Irish still do that in Boston.

The house was deliciously cooled, drying the sweat on my skin to an itching crust, but filled to its walls with mourners who piled plates with the heavy, starchy food spread on the long dining room table, filled glasses and cups with iced tea and soda and coffee. I talked to no one, shut my ears to their easy conversations, their laughter and rolling eyes, heads shaken as though in disbelief of what created this chummy gathering. I wondered if I dared simply leave, slip through the crush, out the door, into my rental Olds, away.

I think I started toward the door when T. C. Green put his hand on me, said, "Jus' follow on me. These old Baptists won't give you nothing you needs to drink here."

So I followed him out, into the burden of heat and light again, out the gravel drive—I looked back with yearning at my Oldsmobile—across the narrow asphalt road to the built-on porch of his double-wide trailer, took the deck chair he pointed to. "It be somewhat cool here on the porch," he said, then turned to his trailer's screen door, called out, "Tisha! Say, Tisha!" turned back to me, said, "Tisha my lady, bring us that taste." Very slowly, I felt my dizziness shrink, my vision and hearing a little keener.

Tisha was a striking woman, though her fine hair looked uncombed, wearing an open housecoat with what might have been a shiny slip beneath it, barefoot, her toenails painted gold, a shade only a little lighter than her honey skin. She had large, dreamy eyes, a sullen mouth, could have, I thought, passed for white. "Tisha, this be Roddy's bro you heard him talk about," T. C. said. Her hand was cool and dry in mine, her scent sweetly musky, taking my hand before I could rise from my deck chair.

"Hey," is all she said, like someone still half-asleep. Her painted nails matched her toes, her lips a glossed pink.

"Now get us," T. C. Green said, "some of that *special,* huh?" She smirked at him, smiled at me, turned, strolled inside. "What you *needs,*" T. C. said to me. Now I felt fully awake, alert. I could hear birdsong, the small breeze soughing in the nearby pines, even a dribble of loud, cheerful talk from Roddy's house across the road.

"It feels cooler all of a sudden," I said.

"If it ain't, it gon' feel like it is!" T. C. said. Tisha opened the screen door with a thrust of her rounded hip, handed glasses of what looked like water to T. C. and me, walked to the railing where T. C. squatted, perched herself there, smiling at us like we were her foolish but lovable children. "For Roddy," he said, raised his glass.

"Roddy," I said, raised mine, and we drank. It was cool on the tongue, then a little flash of fire in my throat, then a delightful glow expanding in my stomach and chest like an inflating balloon. "God," I said, and, "What's this? It's not vodka or gin."

"That from the stump," T. C. said. "Little something me and Roddy did on the side, make us some spare monies. Son," he said, "you gots the bes' Mississippi lightnin' in this and two more counties besides!"

"Roddy bootlegged?" I said, drank again—now I could look at Roddy's house, the mourners' cars and pickups in his yard, pastures and fields beyond, the pine woods—I could look at T. C. Green grinning, at Tisha posing on the porch railing, I could know my brother was dead and buried in the tiny cemetery of The Church Without Spot or Wrinkle, and I could feel, believe this was a good time and place to be.

"Roddy one more time," he said, toasted, drained his glass.

"Roddy," I said, emptied mine. He handed his glass to Tisha. She slithered off her perch, took mine, carried them inside, returned in seconds with them refilled. "I've got to be able to drive to Jackson," I said, wet my lips with the pure, clear, wonderful stump whiskey.

"You feel like the wind with this in you," he said, laughed loud.

"Your Roddy and T. C. make that, it's *good,*" Tisha said, remounted her perch.

So we sat, drank, talked, I am not sure how long before I left.

I think Tisha refilled our glasses at least twice more while T. C. and I talked away the afternoon on his double-wide's porch. I do not think I felt drunk, just a deep, total easing of body and mind, a fine sense of exhausted peace that came of his strong stump whiskey, the view of fields and woods, a tangible cooling of the air as the sky sprouted high, boiling clouds, a perceptible dimming of the harsh light. The jam of cars and pickups in Roddy's yard seemed to belong there, the glad bits of talk and laughter that floated across the road to us somehow appropriate.

"Is it threatening rain?" I asked.

"Like as not, this season," T. C. said.

"Mos' every day," Tisha said, her hair trembling in a stronger breeze.

"What did Roddy *do* here? Besides bootleg this stuff."

"Oh, Roddy!" he said, and, "Make the juice, sell off some of all that land China Mae gets from her peoples, buy some more land to be selling, play some cards for *big* monies sometimes. Oh, you Roddy," he said, "he like to *do* all the time!"

"Roddy," Tisha said, giggled.

"So he was happy? Here. This," I said, meant the whole of it, Mississippi, living among these people, this weather and landscape.

"I believes," T. C. Green said, "happy whatever." Tisha giggled again, covered her mouth with her honey-gold hand to stifle it.

"That is so strange," I said. "He had a pretty crappy life of it, what I knew of it."

"Never hear him say," he said. "Always easy to laugh, tell the joke, like to party, like being married to Miss China Mae, like *doing.*"

"I think my sister-in-law disapproves of me," I said.

"She disproves lots, but she approves Roddy for sure."

"You know her well?"

"China Mae my cousin," he said. "She been gone long to Chicago before she come back with her Roddy and all this land, builded them that good house."

"How'd they meet? I mean, I can't imagine Roddy getting to know her, it's so unlikely."

"Race track," T. C. said. "Washington Park. Roddy say they went to bet the exact same horse, got to talking. Chicago," he said, and, "I been in Chicago once, did *not* like that winter none."

Tisha said, "I likes Chicago."

I said, "I've never actually been there. Boston's always been home for me and mine."

"Roddy say Boston okay if you likes a old city place to live."

"I ain't been to no Boston," Tisha said.

Clouds mushroomed higher and higher, the wind picked up, the first thunder thumped. Across the road, mourners began to leave Roddy's house, two, three, four at a time, their talk and laughter loud on the rising wind. Their cars and pickups pulled out, down the narrow road. I finished my last drink, sat back, thought I might try to put it in some final perspective. But I could not, or did not want to think clearly of the past, conjured no vision of a future. There was only this sense of peace like a comforting warmth within me, and without, even though the crack and snap of thunder and lightning were nearer, the wind gusting strongly now, it seemed peaceful. I said, "It's going to be a drencher."

"Make things grow," T. C. Green said.

"Lightning fraids me," Tisha said, hopped off the railing, pulled her housecoat tightly closed, went inside.

"Tell me," I said to T. C. Green, "what Roddy said about me. You said he talked about me." He set his empty glass on the porch floor, looked down at it a moment, then up at me.

He said, "He say you his brother, only family he gots. He say you disproves most everything. He say you a scared little boy since you was a child. He say he loves you no matter. He say he don't get along good with you because you a worry wart. *Worry wart* is what he say about you. That's what Roddy say I remember about you."

When I could say something, I said, "Everybody has his own opinion on everything." T. C. Green chuckled, shook his head at me like I was dimwitted, stood. "I need to head out for Jackson," I said, and shook his hand. "Thanks for the hooch," I said, and, "Thanks for being my brother's friend here."

"Roddy," he said, "gots *lots* of friends in this place."

Thunder exploded overhead, the clouds opened, and I ran through the hard, straight rain to my rental Olds, soaked to the skin. I could see lights on in Roddy's house—there were still a few vehicles around me in the yard, but all I heard was the rain. I had nothing to say to my brother's widow, did not want to say the usual things that mean nothing, did not want to hear the usual things said again, so I pulled out carefully, wipers flapping, headlights on bright. I suppose I should have waited for the rain to slacken, but did not.

I retraced the funeral procession's route to The Church Without Spot or Wrinkle, paused there to see if the canopy was down, if I could spot the fresh mound of earth, but the rain was too thick to see anything. So I drove on, slowly, searched my way back into the town, past the Ramada to the freeway entrance.

I drove on despite the slippery pavement, the poor vision, away from this place I would never visit again in this life, toward Jackson, toward Boston, toward the world I knew, only a little sad for my brother's death, only a little glad I was still alive, certain only that I had a place to go to, work and wife and children I wanted to hope would make their meaning clear and certain to me when I rejoined them.

I drove through the rain, and then it slackened, ceased, and I drove on, trying to decide what exactly I felt, but that eluded me.

The Divorced Men's Mall Walkers Club

Though he well knew this wasn't for him, Leichtfuss, a retired millwright recently divorced by his wife of thirty-two years, was at the mall by six each morning because he had nowhere else to go, because he needed to go somewhere, *be* somewhere.

The halogen lights were still on, the vast parking lots like an empty desert at this hour, the cluster of cars close to the main entrance an oasis; he parked, got out, walked up to the huge glass doors, the gathering of walkers huddled against the chill mist in the air, waiting for Security to unlock and let them in. Leichtfuss said, "Good morning" to his group, to whoever might want to answer. It was, as he expected, Nesbitt, always maddeningly cheerful.

"Good morning to you, sir," Nesbitt said, Leichtfuss joining him and his bunch to one side. Nesbitt grinned like he'd said something funny, and Swidwa, the poor-mouth, nodded to him, but the others—Prinslow, Chapman, Schwarz, Sillars, Hitler (his real name, but Leichtfuss still wasn't sure he believed that!)—gave no sign they knew him, shivered, stomped their feet, stared through the enormous glass doors for the first glimpse of Security—Bostic—coming with the keys to let them in.

"Good turnout," Leichtfuss said to Nesbitt for something to say, tipped his head at the whole of the small crowd.

Nesbitt smiled, said, "Better than average," and, "Can't let a little cool weather put a stopper on you," and smiled again like it was wit. Leichtfuss, unable to think of anything he wanted to say, unwilling to give Nesbitt an excuse to say something else optimistic, positive, pretended to clear his throat, scan the crowd as if it interested him.

Like always, they had separated into their groups. In addition to a few solitaries, athletic young men and women utterly unattached, lean and muscular, speed-walkers whose skin looked weathered from outdoor sport, grimly disciplined in demeanor, the married couples held the ground closest to the doors, gabbing, laughing, smiling in pairs as if each husband and wife were there by themselves, but they were a group, a gang, the marrieds. Some of them wore matching outfits, like fraternal twins, wholly sufficient to themselves, as if they alone came at opening time to walk the mall.

Behind them, as if keeping close to one another for warmth or moral support, were the single women—widows and divorcées, the eligibles—earphones already clamped to their heads, already secure in their music or inspirational tapes; they dressed for this with care, an eye to fashion, Leichtfuss saw. Gleaming spandex, bright-colored sweats, kerchiefs at their ropy throats or flaring back over their shoulders, expensive brand-name shoes, much dyed hair too black or red or garish platinum. If he got far enough away, where he couldn't see their wrinkles and wattles and the raised dark veins in the backs of their bony hands—they were all lean, in shape—they looked like much younger women, bouncy, excessive makeup effective at a distance. They made Leichtfuss think of a tiny flock of sheep, nervous, on the brink of scattering in panic.

And on their flanks, roaming like guard dogs or wolves, were the eligible singles, widowers all, a dull, aged gang that hovered, if only out of remembered instincts, close enough to sniff the heavy perfumes rising like an aura from the single women. Every so often one of the prowling eligibles broke free from his pack, advanced, pretended to check the doors for Security, Bostic with his keys, passed a remark or two. It caused a flutter among the women, a sort of vulnerable bleating, until the eligible darted back to his gang, the women subsided to continue waiting again for Security.

Prinslow, the lech, sidled close to Leichtfuss, covered his mouth with his hand before he spoke, as if lip-readers might be present, said, "Look who's looking to score!" They watched a stubby man with a white mane and ruddy face skip back to his place with the eligibles.

Leichtfuss said, "Poor bastard's probably just cold and lonely. Where the hell's Bostic?"

"I got my eye on what he's lonesome for," Prinslow said, leered, sidled away.

Here to one side, a rogue group, eight of them when at full strength, was Leichtfuss's gang, the divorced men. Outcasts, losers, the eligible widowers shunned them because, Leichtfuss figured, he and his peers were held responsible for what they'd become; the eligibles were victims of nature, rendered solitaries by their deceased mates' excusable mortality—you couldn't fault anyone for dying, right?

"Here comes shit-heel Bostic!" Swidwa near-shouted. Talk and mock-cheering erupted all around. "Late again!" Swidwa snarled.

The widows and divorcées avoided them, Leichtfuss thought, because they were legally defined failures, expelled from the institution of marriage, unlikely to have any money left in the ashes of their disgrace. If they did, would they be here, walking the mall each early morning, rain or shine? They were right to stay away from them—him—Leichtfuss thought. His gang, the divorced men, belonged off by themselves, pariahs burdened with emotional and financial baggage so heavy they barely managed to carry it themselves, without the right or temerity to ask anyone to lend a hand.

Then Bostic's keys were clicking and snapping in the large locks, chains removed, doors opening, and the walkers streamed into the mall, the distinct groups merging only for the ritual of entrance before separating again to begin the day's exercise they all believed would let them live healthier, happier, longer lives.

Slipping in, Leichtfuss brushed against Bostic, who refused to move out of the way, forced the flow of walkers to divide around him on their rush in. "Pardon," Leichtfuss said.

"I'd say," Bostic growled, and, "They got a screw loose letting you all in early, I got plenty enough to do more important."

"I empathize," Leichtfuss said. Bostic glared at him, blew out his breath in a show of exasperation, turned his back on him. There was no point being polite to Bostic. A large man gone fat and soft, at least near retirement age, rumor had him an ex-cop double-dipping until he could grab Social Security. He hounded the walkers, flitting from tier to tier on the staff elevator, striking poses—arms folded, gut sucked up, cap visor just above his small eyes, glowering. Obviously proud of his generic uniform, walkie-talkie, and holstered Glock, he clearly disliked walkers, watched them like they fit shoplifters' profiles, lurked behind kiosks and decorative pillars, in shop entrances like a state trooper manning a speed trap.

"Let's hit it, boys!" cheerful Nesbitt called out, and Leichtfuss followed his gang of divorced men to their starting point at the central fountain, couples hopping the closest escalator for the third tier, eligibles and single women riding up to the second.

"One day right soon," Prinslow muttered, "yours truly is going up one tier where all the nookie lives."

"I'd like to see that," Hitler said.

Fat Charlie Chapman said, "Those bitches walk too fast for me."

"We walk too fast for you, Charlie," Swidwa said.

"Let Bostic see you annoy just one of them," know-it-all Schwarz, a lawyer, said, "he'll get you cited and barred for life."

Greg Hitler said, "Effing Bostic wisecracks to me on my name just once, I'm reporting him to management."

Leichtfuss said, "Let's walk, okay?"

Out of place, displaced as he felt every morning with this crew, Leichtfuss confessed to himself he liked, *really* liked the mall at this hour, before the shops opened, before staff straggled in to open, before the first shopper even dreamed of hitting the parking lots. There was something about it, the half-lighting, floors and display windows gleaming clean, potted plants and ornamental shrubbery motionless in shadow, the faint hint of cleaning compounds and disinfectant in the recycled air—it felt *new* to him, untouched by human hands despite the custodial crews just packing up to leave, despite Bostic and his cohorts dogging them with suspicious looks, despite the bitching and whining of his peers . . . it was pristine, made Leichtfuss feel new, unsullied, a newborn in a perfect world created entirely for him.

At the ground floor's central fountain, blinking lights circling the pool came on, and, with a geyser's gush, the fountain came to life, a silver spear of water leaping up, flowering at its peak, splashing back down to dimple the pool as if with gentle, persistent rain. And the music started, an organ's trilling in the higher ranges seeming to burst out of all the glass and stone—it felt like energy to Leichtfuss, insinuated itself into his muscles and bones, made him hop and stretch and shake out the kinks of his troubled night's sleep. "Let's get walking!" he said.

"Hold your horses," Hitler said, setting the meter clipped to his belt to measure each day's distance; he kept a log.

"What's playing today?" Schwarz asked Sillars as the semi-midget adjusted his Walkman's headphones.

"Forties big bands," Sillars said.

Leichtfuss said, "I'm ready to walk here!"

Prinslow said, "You must have your essential fluids backing up on you. You need your ashes hauled, clean out your tubes, takes care of nervousness."

"We're off!" Nesbitt said before Leichtfuss could think of a good one to shut the lecher up.

They began their day's walk.

He liked the walking well enough. Their pace, set by fat Chapman, who huffed and wheezed the whole way, sweating hard, was easy. Sillars was lost in his headphones, Hitler checking his belt meter at every lap, so the only distractions were Prinslow's unsubtle cracks about the shape, size, and probable availability of any female custodial or staff coming in to open a shop, Schwarz's pulling alongside to explain the obvious about new window displays, Swidwa now and again ranting over outrageous prices posted on the merchandise. Leichtfuss walked effortlessly, took in the varied riches of the mall's ground floor.

Window after window, shops, interiors still dark, showed their lavish wares. It encouraged, strengthened him. Here ranks and rows of men's shoes, soft leather and sturdy fabrics; here, fireplace treatments glowed gently gold; from jewelers' cases winked the highlights of precious stones, the flash of silver; fashions for all draped on stylized mannequins; blended tobaccos and exotic coffees spiced the air lightly; here floated the promise of delicatessen, bakery, cold drinks and hot meats; racks of spectacle frames looked out at him like alien eyes; automatic teller machines and coin changers tastefully announced themselves; kiosks, still locked and shuttered, stood sentinel; drugs, health foods, lingerie, greeting cards for all occasions, televisions and radios and computers and cutlery, all lay in readiness for the day's imminent commerce.

It was a cornucopia, a symbol and sign of everything good and plentiful in store for everyone, for Leichtfuss.

Prinslow dug an elbow in his side, said, "Check the can on that!" directed Leichtfuss upward to a glimpse of the file of single women striding near the second tier's railing.

"Which one?" he asked.

"Too late," Prinslow said, "you missed her," and moved away.

Looking up, squinting against the skylight, Leichtfuss caught the movement of the singles on their tier, the marrieds above them. "Keep it to the right!" Bostic barked at him. "Just like driving on the highway, got it?"

"Got it," he said, tried to sound defiant. "Officious prick!" he said to Schwarz when they were well past the security guard.

"He's within his rights on that one," Schwarz said, "even if there's no traffic coming at us."

"Let him wisecrack me just once more," Hitler said.

"He'd claim disruptive conduct, get you a fine slapped on your ass and banned besides," Swidwa said. Leichtfuss moved ahead of them, put himself back into the mall's wonders, display windows, delicious mix of odors, the organ's recorded joy, the play of light, shadow, color, and here came the end of their first lap, the fountain's perpetually magnificent play!

They walked, lap after lap, Greg Hitler calling out the mileage each time they circled the fountain. As they turned into the home stretch, the mall came alive with staff opening shops, flipping on lights, voices calling out through the organ's music, and the first shoppers entered as they halted at last at the fountain, stood still for a moment at the mall's center, lights on full everywhere, shoppers moving past and around them in twos and threes, whole families, children alongside, in buggies and strollers and slings. Leichtfuss stood, feeling his quickened breathing slacken, warm ache pulsing in his thighs and feet, film of perspiration slicking his brow, took in all this surge of life and purpose about him, glad, if only for a moment, he had come, walked.

"On the knob!" Hitler announced, recorded the distance covered in his pocket notebook log.

"I'm bushed, beat," Chapman managed to say when he caught his wind, lowered his head, hands on knees, dripped sweat on the floor tiles, face purple-flushed.

"I calculate," Nesbitt said, "I'm half my age, cardiovascularly speaking."

"Piece of ass and a bicycle ride'd kill you," Prinslow said.

"Executive session!" Sillars said, stripping off his headphones, and, "Bob Crosby was the best!"

"I can't, I forgot my wallet," Swidwa said.

Leichtfuss said, "I'll treat you for today." He figured Swidwa owed him at least ten dollars now, knew he'd never see it.

Then Bostic was on them, heel of his hand on his Glock's butt, said, "Are we congregating here? No undue congregating, which is plain English for loitering," he said, advanced a step.

"Congregating," Schwarz said, "is gathering. Loitering is remaining in place, not at all the same."

"Don't shithouse lawyer me," Bostic said, raised his walkie-talkie toward his mouth.

"We're going," Leichtfuss said.

"Executive session!" Hitler sneered, and they moved toward the nearest escalator to get to the second tier, Orange Julius, for what they called *executive session,* a drink and a snack, as much small talk as they could stand on a given morning. Bostic watched them from the foot of the escalator until they stepped off and disappeared from sight above him.

It was Orange Julius instead of French Café or one of the fast foods on the ground floor because of Prinslow. There were usually a few eligibles, widows and divorcées, at the tables there after their walk. "I'd see the point of it if you ever got up and hit on one of them, but all you do is stare, for shit's sakes," Leichtfuss said.

"Shows what you know about sexual strategy," the lecher said. "First you mark your target with care, then intimidate them, soften them up. When they're ripe, make your move!"

Hitler said, "I'd like to see that."

"Some day," Prinslow said. Leichtfuss stopped his laugh before it got out.

They ordered at the Orange Julius counter, sat at one of the big tables, had a view of the opposite side of the tier, the tip of the fountain's spire, picked up their drinks and food when their number was called. If there were any eligibles at other tables, Prinslow turned his chair toward them, fixed his gaze on them.

"I'll owe you for this," Swidwa told Leichtfuss as he took the money. "I forgot my billfold is all," he said. Seated, orange flips or crushes or swirls or coffees, croissants or danish or English muffins before them, they held executive session. What we do, Leichtfuss thought, is talk. We talk about ourselves because that's all we have to talk about. They talked until they were bored, or someone got angry, or Bostic slipped up on them to tell them they had to leave unless they were going to make additional purchases. Then they left, each off in his own direction, each to his own life, whatever it was, until the next morning's walk.

They talked, because they had nothing else to talk of, about their divorces, all of which had come late in life, at a time when wasting diseases and death were more likely events. They talked, and in a few weeks Leichtfuss learned their stories.

Only Prinslow had been married more than once. "The first wife," he said, "we were innocents. I hardly ever even think about her. This last," he said, "we were twenty-three years some odd months married, it was ugly, so naturally the kids take the bitch's side, papa's the villain naturally."

"So what caused it? After so long?" Leichtfuss asked.

"Got caught with my stinger in a honey pot on the side," Prinslow said, snickered. He said, "You notice the gal there—" he nodded at the teenager working the Orange Julius counter—"notice she left a couple buttons unbuttoned, she leans forward to hand me my change, I'm viewing all the way down to her damn navel!" Leichtfuss doubted it, didn't care enough to check it out.

He said, "You sorry? You miss your wife and kids?"

"I like the bachelor life," Prinslow said, turned away to focus his intimidating stare on two eligibles at a nearby table, engrossed in chatter, oblivious of them.

With Chapman it was his health. "She said," he said, "all I did was sit on my ass and swill beer and eat like a pig. She said I was digging my grave with my teeth. I'm still here, ain't I?"

"Did you try to change?" Leichtfuss said.

Chapman said, "I live the way's normal for me. Now suddenly I'm falling to pieces, my bowels are half-clogged, I probably got emphysema from forty years smoking before I quit, I got ringing in my ears, sunlight hurts my eyes, night sweats, my heart pounds all of a sudden for no reason, she kicks me out like I'm an Eskimo it's time to go off and die so there's no mess for her to clean up after me."

"What about your children?" Leichtfuss said.

"They got their own lives," Chapman said.

Schwarz contended he'd beaten the system. "Don't ask me what motivated her," he said. "But I can tell you I saw it coming, so I took steps to put my assets where they can't be touched. You should have seen the look on her face when she figured out her freedom was costing her an arm and a leg! She altered her tone right fast!"

"She wanted to reconcile?" Leichtfuss said.

"She did," the lawyer said.

"Why didn't you?"

"Hah!" Schwarz said, and, "You think I'm going to let her off the hook once I've sprung the trap? Let her stew in her own juice. Next time she'll think twice."

"Aren't you both a little past the age for a next time?" Leichtfuss said.

"I speak hypothetically," Schwarz said. "It's a reflex with me from my years in the legal profession. A matter of principle obtains here."

It was also money with Swidwa. "Thirty-one years I put up with it," he said. "I didn't booze, I didn't sleep around, I never laid a hand on her. I turned my paycheck over to her like clockwork. She used to give me like an allowance for little daily expenses. I carried a sack lunch to work every day to save on lunches. So she decides she wants to start some new life, which I personally think was the menopause got to her, guess who gets the short end of the stick in the settlement, right?"

"You don't look exactly homeless to me," Leichtfuss said.

"No," Swidwa said. "If I live in a barrel and eat the rain falls in it, I'm in good shape!"

Nesbitt didn't complain. "It was amicable. Amiable. Cooperative," he said. "I harbor no resentment, no guilt, we remain friends. Actually, we socialize a good deal in connection with our grandchildren."

"No misgivings? None?" Leichtfuss said.

"Tolerance. Acceptance. Hope for the best," Nesbitt said like he read the words off a wall, cut in granite on a monument.

Sillars the semi-midget said, "We were ill-matched from the start. My wife was a good foot taller than me. Our friends called us Mutt and Jeff. I was humiliated. She said she felt humiliated by me for thirty-four years. I'm glad it's over," he said, and, "Both my sons are tall like her."

With Hitler, it always came back to his name. "She said," he said, "I made her constantly nervous, which is horseshit. All I did was keep our accounts, paid the bills, I did the taxes, I asked her please to keep a record of her spending for whatall, she says I'm driving her up the wall. The real story is she was embarrassed being Mrs. Hitler. Proof of which is she took back her maiden name, after twenty-nine years, dumped my name the second we got final papers!"

Leichtfuss said, "What about your kids?"

Hitler said, "They took the same abuse I did when I was a kid, which was worse because the damn war's just over in those days. The girls got married, so they're past that. The real proof is my boy Harold legally changed to his middle name Thayer. Goddamnit!" he said, slapped the table, "I'm no goddamn relation in the slightest to the goddamn Nazi!"

"I believe you," Leichtfuss said.

Schwarz said, "You ought to research, there has to be *some* connection no matter how tenuous," which broke up executive session that day, Hitler calling Schwarz a shyster, stalking off, down the escalator, out of the mall.

They made Leichtfuss talk about himself, and he tried over the course of those several weeks, hoped it would lead to answers to his own questions, but it did not.

He had never cheated on his wife, thought their sex life was okay, what there was of it in recent years. "Maybe *she* had something on the side," Prinslow said. Leichtfuss doubted that, no evidence either way. Nor was he as dull a companion, he thought, as Chapman, no couch potato, no glutton.

"You complain a lot about your health to her?" the fat man asked. Leichtfuss had not, certainly not often. She did accuse him of not paying attention, not hearing her the first time she spoke. He had the usual to be expected at his age, stiff joints, minor chronic backache, irregularity, teeth requiring crowns, thinning hair, cold feet in all weathers, but seldom complained of anything.

"She gut you in your settlement?" Schwarz asked. She had not. With an even split of assets after the house, which she got and sold at once, with half his millwright's pension, Social Security and Medicare and Medicaid and veteran's health benefits if it came to something lingering and terminal, he was covered.

"Count yourself lucky," Swidwa said. No, Leichtfuss and his ex-wife never argued over money except when she spent foolishly.

"She humiliate you in public?" Sillars said. Leichtfuss did not think so, certainly never seriously.

"So she just ups and tosses you out on your behind," Greg Hitler said.

Leichtfuss said, "It wasn't like that. She sat down one night right after dinner and announced she was leaving, divorce, not just separation. She packed and she moved. The oddest thing of all is our kids, we have four, two of each, all married, two grandchildren, they seem to think it must be my fault, or maybe they don't seem to think anything of it, like it's normal. I'm suddenly very detached from my children, like I'm dead and forgotten or something. Only family I've got left is one brother, but we've been out of touch since our folks died way back." His fellow members of this divorced men's mall walkers club, seated in executive session at Orange Julius, shook their heads, clucked tongues, smirked and smiled at him.

"What," Schwarz asked, as if summing up the weeks of executive session on this morning, "would be your most concise definition of probable cause or causes?"

"If I thought I knew that," Leichtfuss told them, "then I probably wouldn't be sitting here with you, getting up in the wee hours to walk around a damn mall like one of those horses on a merry-go-round, would I? I'm not like you people, there's no simple explanation." That broke up this day's executive session, the seven of them hardening their expressions, sliding their chairs back from the table at Orange Julius, walking off like they heard a command in a range above Leichtfuss's hearing, left him alone there, wondering why he did this, walked, talked about an insoluble mystery—his divorce—as though a solution were just beyond his grasp.

So when he left this day, got up at last, rode the escalator to the ground floor, the mall crowd thickening all around him, he walked through them as if he was invisible, firmly resolved to give it up, leave and never return, find a life, any life, somewhere else, somehow—this was a dead end, like his marriage.

Bostic jumped him as he passed the sparkling fountain, said, "You're not contemplating walking here some more at this late hour of the morning I hope."

"I'm on my way out," Leichtfuss told him, and, "Don't look for me in future. There, did I make your day for you?"

"I don't believe in miracles," Bostic said, and shadowed him all the way to the main entrance, as if he looked like trouble, a possible shoplifter or teenage cut-up or loiterer, a drunk liable to get rowdy, create a disturbance.

For the first week, Leichtfuss shut himself in the one-bedroom efficiency he moved to when his home of twenty-two years was sold as part of his divorce settlement. It was small and spare, but met his basic needs, and he had cable TV.

At first he watched local, national, and international news broadcasts, hoping to educate himself, but there were so many natural disasters, wars, and homicides, along with the nauseating play of politics and political commentary and analysis that he switched to sports, but developed no interest in any team or superstar. He tried movies, the black-and-white classics of his childhood, the Technicolor epics of his youth, the frontal nudity and filthy speech of contemporary films shown on pay-per-view, but they failed to distract, much less amuse. He was too proud to descend to the soaps or talk shows. *Books!* he thought.

The branch public library was inhospitable. He was intimidated by the computer stations he had to consult, the desk clerks were brusque, even rude, and the closest to peers he found in reading areas were semi-doddering codgers who never spoke, never noticed him, or homeless types pretending to peruse periodicals as a ploy to gain shelter from the mean streets they roamed. When he was panhandled twice for spare change in one afternoon, he thought to patronize the nearest bookstore, but that seemed as much upscale coffee shop as store, the patrons mostly smug buyers of best-sellers and self-help manuals and New Age twaddle. There were evening programs offered, poetry readings and chamber music and great ideas discussion groups, but Leichtfuss knew better than to try to join that coterie.

He bought some books, biographies of people famous in the generation before his, but when he sat to read in his efficiency the pages swam before his eyes, his kitchenette clock ticking too loudly in his ears for him to concentrate. When he was able to focus for brief periods, the revisionist biographies shattered his illusions about the once-celebrated movers and shakers of civilization.

A new life—a life—Leichtfuss decided, meant *People!* But where was he to meet people? The couples he and his wife knew dropped them—him at least—when they divorced; he never saw them, heard from them. The few co-workers he liked evaporated, as he had, in retirement, gone to warmer climes or off on unending travel in motor homes, on discount cruises, not a few dying earlier than mortuary tables predicted. The closest Leichtfuss came to weeping was when he thought back to his millwright's trade; he was good at it, could fix any machine, set up for any new job run, had a knack for it, as if mechanical solutions lay in his hands like instincts—he choked back a need to weep, cleared his throat, set his jaw.

Where to go to meet people? How meet people in this last phase of his life?

Churches and bars were possibilities, he figured. But churches were out. He'd seen the worst of that on cable TV, remembered the vague Protestantism of his long-gone parents with apathy. So he tried a few neighborhood bars.

A social drinker all his adult life, he found he'd lost his taste for alcohol. Beer bloated his stomach, mixed drinks left him queasy, and the prices were confiscatory. Bartenders and waitresses were too young, too busy, too artificially friendly to imagine real conversation with, and the clientele he observed were either in pairs who whispered and nuzzled in the semi-dark or bunches of men who hooted and roared, swore, or cliques of women, also too young, who smoked and cackled and also swore like soldiers on furlough.

In desperation, he read the in-search-of columns of an alternative newspaper, but the only women in his age range—forty-five to sixty he thought reasonable—seemed to seek, often explicitly, sometimes by reliance on palpable euphemisms, casual or kinky sex. Ashamed of himself for even considering the possibility, he again verged on weeping until he steeled himself to telephone family.

His oldest daughter, in a suburb ninety miles away, said, "Dad, this is not a good time, okay?" She sounded on the brink of tears herself.

His oldest son, halfway across the continent, his voice flat and clipped, said, "I see where you're coming from, Dad, but I'm just not equipped to give you direction. When you think of it," his son said, "doesn't everyone suffer this sort of thing from time to time?"

Leichtfuss, because he knew nothing else to say, said, "How's that grandson of mine doing?"

His son said, "Fine. Everyone's fine."

His younger son, on the other side of town, had a voice message accompanied by music so loud it was difficult to distinguish the words.

His baby girl's phone was never not busy, the signal a taunting buzz that infuriated him.

When he called his ex-wife, she said, "Let's keep this correct."

Leichtfuss said, "I thought we agreed to remain friends?"

"Friend*ly*. At least not *un*friendly," she said. She said, "Cordial is the word I prefer."

He wondered if he dared call his only brother, retired to live in semi-luxury in Mexico; they quarreled bitterly over their parents' estate. He did call, said hello, spoke his name, and his brother said, "We're too far down the road, too much water under the bridge," and hung up his receiver with a sharp click.

To relieve his growing cabin fever, he took long walks into strange neighborhoods, but found no one willing to make eye contact, noticed, in the nicer parts of town, police patrol cars slowed, cops giving him the once-over, reminding him of Bostic, the mall.

And so he returned to the mall, set his alarm, rose in the predawn, dressed in sweats and walking shoes, was at the main entrance at six sharp, joined his peers huddling near the glass, peering in, bitching because Bostic was late as usual.

He expected worse than he got from them.

Prinslow said, "Look who's here all of a sudden! We thought maybe you got yourself shacked up and maybe died on the downstroke!"

Chapman said, "You look like you lost some weight, Leichtfuss. I wish I had your metabolism."

Schwarz said, "Someone after you with a summons, you had to lie low?"

Swidwa said, "The ex's threatening to take me to court over some legal fees from way back she claims I should be good for. Like you can only squeeze so much blood from a turnip, right?"

Nesbitt clapped him on the back, said, "We've missed your cheery presence, chum!"

Sillars said, "Watch yourself, Bostic's on a rampage, the big overgrown fuck!"

Hitler looked into his notebook log, said, "You screwed up our totals big time, man."

Leichtfuss was ready with lies—he'd had a bad bout with the flu, vomiting, the runs, killer headaches, burning joints—but didn't need them. Bostic opened the doors and they followed in behind the marrieds, the eligible widows and divorcées, the few solitaries leading the pack. As he passed him, Bostic said, "I knew it! What I need," he said, "back again just when I started believing you died or they put you in a home for safekeeping."

Leichtfuss said, "Someday you'll cross a line, Bostic, you and me'll have a conference with mall management you won't like."

"I double dare you, you old fart!" he heard the security guard call after him. He might have said more, but now they were in the mall, headed for the fountain to begin the day's walk.

It was wonderful! The mall was perfect, spanking clean, like new, all glass and tile and brushed metal trim and fixtures, dimmed shop windows, soft lights, and then the fountain spurting, the pool's ring of lights, the recorded organ's generic trill. He stretched, mini-jogged in place to loosen his legs, felt his blood churn, lungs expand, squared his shoulders, lifted his chin, stepped out at the head of his gang.

The walk was wonderful, like always, absolutely as it had always been. Semi-midget Sillars lost himself in his headphones, Hitler called out the increments they covered at the end of each lap, Nesbitt kept pace with Leichtfuss, his face lit with a benevolent smile for the departing custodials, staff and first shoppers trickling in. Swidwa came close to say, "Orange Julius hiked some of its prices."

"I'll cover you if you're short today," Leichtfuss promised him.

Prinslow directed his attention to an anorexic-looking solitary whose spandex pants defined the crack between her shrunken buttocks with precision. "That one," the lecher said, "couldn't throw a piece to a mouse with no more ass than that!" Leichtfuss, suffused with good feeling for all, agreed with him. Schwarz gave him a detailed summary of the progress of renovations at the Hallmark outlet. Chapman, he noticed, seemed to be keeping up a little better than usual.

Done, Leichtfuss, glowing with profound satisfaction, went up the escalator with them to Orange Julius for executive session. There were no women present for Prinslow to lock his eyes on, nothing to divert them from their talk as they ate and drank their post-walk snacks.

Leichtfuss said, "Tell me why you guys do this. The walking. I'm just curious," he said.

Prinslow said, "Are you kidding? You jest. It's the great American meat market!"

Chapman said, "For my health. I'm down nearly two pounds this past month."

"A sound body for the sound mind to reside in," Schwarz said.

Nesbitt said, "Would I be embarrassed if I said I enjoy such good company?"

Sillars said, "I don't know, I like listening to my music, it lets me forget myself for at least that long."

"I'm keeping track," Hitler said, waved his notebook log, said, "I plot the miles on a big map I have, a person could walk the equivalent of around the equator. It's a challenge I like."

Leichtfuss said, "I'm not sure why I like it. I know I've decided I like it a lot." Prinslow told him to confess he enjoyed checking out the gash. Nesbitt said good company for its own sake was sufficient reason for anyone. Chapman asked after his health. Sillars suggested he buy a Walkman. Hitler said he should keep a chart of how far he walked in a week, a month, a year—it added up. Schwarz assumed he needed regular psychological cleansing like everyone else, and Swidwa wanted to know if he knew what a workout gym membership cost these days.

Leichtfuss said, "You men know me as well as anyone I can talk to. Why do you think my wife divorced me here when my life's practically over?"

"Sex," Prinslow said. "It's always doing the nasty at the heart of it. You couldn't cut the mustard," he said.

"Stop torturing yourself," Schwarz advised.

"Get on with your life," Nesbitt said.

"Why not admit you squabbled over money?" Swidwa asked.

Chapman put his vote down for mental cruelty, Sillars seconded the motion, and Hitler said either Leichtfuss or his wife suffered from low self-esteem.

"I've got to work on this if it kills me," Leichtfuss said, and they all got a laugh out of that—Schwarz said look out, it just might.

The executive session broke up. The last to leave, Leichtfuss scanned the mall's ground floor for Bostic from the escalator as he descended, hoped for a chance to say something, but he was nowhere to be seen.

Then, just as he was set to push open the big glass door at the main entrance, the security guard caught him by surprise, said, "And no doubt I can count on you again tomorrow, huh?"

Leichtfuss turned, smiled his best smile into the teeth of this large, armed man who frightened him, said "Bank on it!" and opened the door with his shoulder, left the mall, knew he was no wiser than when he entered, but hopeful, buoyed by some almost tangible hope everything would clear up for him, make sound sense to him, sooner or later. If not soon, then better later than never. When he was a working millwright, a machine's problem meant a solution existed.

Questions, Leichtfuss believed, meant answers.

On Watch for Big Red

Major Willis is asking me numerous things about my life, such as how I spend all my free time, do I masturbate much, etcetera, and I'm telling him only a little about various things such as watching Big Red, my loaded pistol, waiting on the mail delivery, and so on. He says to me, "Get a damn life, Kendler!"

Since I don't like telling the major very much, back in my apartment I say to myself, "Get a life, Kendler!"

I talk out loud to myself a lot—it feels more real if I actually say the words, discovered this soon after I moved in. If I only think things, words, they don't last very long, sort of evaporate until I wonder if I've been thinking anything at all. Then where am I? So I speak the words, and even though it's only me here to hear them, they're heard, and I'm at least sure I had something on my mind worth thinking about, being constructive, positive.

And I answer myself: "You've got a life! This *is* a life, your life!" Okay—and this I happen only to think, no words hanging in the air around me inside here—this is a start. I think: be specific.

Big Red. I don't know her name, checked the mailboxes down in the lobby entrance, but there's no name on the #1 box, hers, so I simply refer to her in my thoughts as that, Big Red. *Big Red.* Sweet jumping Jesus! She's got to be damn near six feet if she's an inch. All legs, I think when I see her, start with her bare feet—*always* barefoot, even when it's chilly in the morning, dew on the grass. Showgirl legs. Then moving up, ample hips, pinched waist, and—Lord's mercy on me!—a set of knockers would do Hooters proud! Long swan-neck, long arms, large hands, a face admittedly not textbook beautiful, but nice cheekbones and biggish lips, large eyes. And red hair. Big Red. Her hair's not the bright red a stripper or a starlet gets out of the henna bottle, which when natural only goes with the milky-pale skin always strikes me as a little sickly looking. Which Big Red is not. Her skin is either naturally darkish, possibly tanned, her hair a dark red, just on the edge of what's called auburn.

I see her from my small balcony, where I can go pretending to want to only smoke outdoors, get a longer or shorter show depending if she's out to water all her potted plants on her patio—she has to bend over a lot to do this!—or just checking them out, appreciating, I suppose. The rare occasion is her taking a slow stroll out through the front hedges into the mowed complex greenbelt. Once she walked all the way, barefoot in the dew, over to under the apple tree, pulled down a low branch, put her face right into the blossoms for a deep whiff. I'm surmising.

I see her daily if lucky, a few times a week if not. I don't know her name, don't want to, don't know if she has the #1 apartment all to herself—never seen a man, husband, child. When I see her I say things aloud, whispering because I don't dare be heard, of course. I whisper, "Oh you are fine!" or, "Thank you whatever powers that be for Big Red!" or, "Look up, look up, Big Red, I'll wave, we'll possibly exchange greetings, words!" She's never looked up yet. I'm surprised she doesn't *feel* me watching her. I watch, pretend to be on my balcony for the sake of smoking outdoors.

Big Red, I grant, is not enough to make a life. But an ingredient, something to build on.

"A life," I say, "exists in a particular time and place at any given moment, Kendler." So it follows I have one. Life.

The time is *now,* always, right? The place is *here,* #4 unit, Building 2. Two bedrooms, one of which I sleep in, the other for an overnight guest if I should ever have one. Or could be an office or study if I had any work or interest requiring space. Small but adequate bathroom, no inconvenience because I can, living alone, leave the door open, making for more roominess when I use the commode. The shower's a gem, spray strong and hot enough it feels like it could strip flesh off the bones. Very restorative after a poor night's sleep or bad dreams or bad hangover from my occasional big drunk. That's the upstairs of this bi-level.

Downstairs—only half-a-flight, actually—is my almost tiny kitchen, but adequate because I never cook, new and semi-new appliances part of my lease when I signed. My only table sits in a sort of nook. I can see the TV from there, but usually camp out in the recliner for that. Cathedral ceiling, some hooks I could hang flowerpots from if I so desired, but don't. I have a good-size end table next to my chair. This holds my big glass ashtray. I do my real smoking in this chair.

The patio doors are a prize, not only for the balcony they open onto, from where I go to pretend-smoke and watch for Big Red, but also the view of the complex greenbelt, mowed smooth as a golf course fairway, and the apple tree in bloom, and then the beechwood trees, a kind of mini-forest in which I regularly spot birds, rabbits, one big gray squirrel. When there's wind, even a decent breeze, I like to watch the beechwoods sway, listen to the leaves sigh. The patio doors are my personal window on the world.

So. Now. Here. A life, right? As far as time and place go.

I say, "A life is interaction with other people. On this count I also have one. Life."

Start with Big Red, who I count as one even though I only watch her.

Then Costa, just across the hall in #3. I don't see him often, because he's often out jogging and riding a fancy bike for which he wears a yellow helmet and spandex when he's not at work in his strictly standard suit, white shirt, and solid-color tie, but we've spoken several times. He frankly puts me off. Younger than me, maybe forty, but looks older, fairly fat in spite of his jogging and biking, red-faced, always sweating through the armpits of his shirt, heaving and blowing from the walk up from the lobby if not running and biking. What puts me off Costa is he does all the talking, going through an ugly divorce after fifteen years, luckily no kids, says the wife's trying to nail him, gut him, always changing the terms through her lawyer, who Costa says is a mean-assed shyster, the source of prolonged wranglings eating up Costa's money. I did learn he does something with data for a bank.

He's never asked what I do. He's got to know I'm too young to be retired, but never asks, which I find quite off-putting. Still, he counts as a person, right? Although he won't last long on the list, as he's here month-to-month only until he gets his decree, means to buy a house to replace the one his wife's taking if her lawyer has his way.

Another is Kendra Cluck—what kind of a name is a *Cluck?* She manages the complex from the ground-floor in Building 1 she gets rent-free for the job. So I knew her first, applying, negotiating the lease. If I liked blondes, which I don't especially, she'd be in a class possibly with Big Red for looks, but for my taste she talks too much too fast, possibly coming from her memorized sales pitch she makes for the complex. I'm currently irritated with her for not getting maintenance over here fast enough when I call. A leak in the supposedly new fridge. The lock on the door jams, locked me out twice. I know her mostly from the telephone calling for maintenance, also for advice, where's a good barber, which is the best supermarket, recommend a dentist. She's quick with advice, very fake-cheerful, super-polite telephone manner, but talks too fast for me to make a note, write directions I forget as soon as I hang up. I end up finding my own way most of the time. Still, perfectly correct to count Kendra Cluck, right?

So counting Big Red, that's three. And I count the checkout woman at Piggly Wiggly, which I decided to patronize even though Kendra Cluck touted IGA. All I know is her name's Mattie, which is on the name tag she wears, along with a Smiley Face and the slogan *Shop The Pig!* She's at least my age, pretty worn-looking to be frank, bad bleach job, and has a tattoo fading on her one forearm—I surmise she could have been a biker moll or some such in early life? I count her both because she's always the one checks me out, and because she always makes the same joke, "Sure you're of age?" when I buy cigarettes or liquor, which is almost daily.

I always say, "I think so, but I can show you a picture ID if you want," at which she laughs, and I do too. That's certainly interaction. So with Mattie of Piggly Wiggly, counting Big Red in, that's four. I don't count the maintenance man Kendra Cluck finally gets around to sending over as he's only been twice, for the lock and the leak, and only speaks in a kind of grunting when I say hello and good-bye.

I wonder about counting the rest, if I need a special category.

Because Major Willis at the V.A. is a purely professional contact, relationship. He's the doctor, therapist, I'm the patient, so no matter how personal the conversation, questions and answers I try to give as honestly as I can, it's only technically interaction. In addition to which I don't trust him, think he'll recommend pulling my disability.

And because my former wife Ellen refuses to talk when I phone. She says hello, I say hello, she says, "I do not need this, Ronald!" or,

"Give it up, Ron!" or, "Don't you have anything better to do with yourself?" Once she said, "Please be informed I contemplate obtaining a restraining order to put *finito* to this harassment." She hangs up on me. I take vows not to call ever again, break them when talking to the walls and the TV don't work, or Big Red's nowhere to be seen for a couple of days. When her new husband Al answers the phone, I hang up without speaking.

And because our daughter Laurie, though she will usually speak a little when I call long-distance, which I can scarce afford these days, is always the one to cut it short. I tell her about her mother threatening a legal restraining order, she says, "Deal with it, Dad." I tell her Major Willis all but predicts they'll take away my disability—after which it's the streets for me!—she says, "Handle it, okay?" I tell her how it's no picnic trying to make a new life at my age, she says, "Cope, for Christ's sakes!"

I don't take offense due to her having her own problems. A live-in who rides in motorcycle races, possibly peddles dope, and I suspect abuses her, verbally if not physically. Laurie makes me think of Mattie, and vice-versa, because Laurie was very foolish at one time, from which period she has multiple tattoos—and several piercings, nose, navel, tongue, eyebrows—she lacks the money to have removed by laser surgery. Ellen has the money from her new marriage to Al, but won't extend help. I would, but lack the money, which I suppose my daughter resents.

That's three in this category, total of seven. Major Willis says stop whining over no friends, so little human interaction, count yourself fortunate for seven if that's all there are. Most of the time that's what I do. When I'm able, I conclude seven qualifies as a life. Here. Now. People.

I spoke to Big Red today! I was in the basement, the laundry facility—one washer, one dryer, two dollars a load in each, quarters—just taking my wash from the washer, stuffing it in the dryer, and here she comes, carrying a basket of her laundry, stops dead in the doorway, surprised the facility's occupied, startled. She was barefoot. Jesus. I spoke fast, saw she was startled, might think for a second I was some intruder, dangerous.

I said, "I'm just getting my stuff in the dryer, I'll be out of here in a minute, you can start your wash."

She said, "What?" and with just the one word I caught an accent, European of some variety. I kept my wits long enough to introduce myself.

I said, ""My name's Kendler. Ronald. I just moved in, number four, upstairs, I'll be out of your way in no time."

She said, "That's okay. You can wash." A definite accent. And she stepped back out of the doorway, retreats, and I'm still concerned I startled her.

I said, "I'm Ronald Kendler."

She said, "Hello, Ronald Kendler," and definitely I saw a small smile on her face, though she kept on backwards, turned, went up the stairs carrying her white plastic laundry basket. And didn't give her name in return.

So she's still Big Red to me. Barefoot on that cold, damp cement basement floor. What if she'd come on in, did her wash while mine dried in the dryer? Jesus. I still call that a *good* day!

A life starts at birth, goes on all the way until death, basically speaking. So *everybody* who's alive has a life in that sense. Everybody has a life in the terms of starting, the time and place, the people involved. Family. Up to the given moment, which in my case is now. So I qualify on these grounds alone.

I was born in 1947, postwar baby boom. My dad was a WWII vet, married my mom right after he rotated home from England, where he met my mom, brought her over, a war bride, and married her, and then they had me.

It's not easy telling about my family origins and all, because truth is I proved rather a disappointment to my mom and dad, I think. They certainly never told me the contrary. I've thought for some time they wished they'd had more, other kids, seeing I didn't turn out any whiz.

Maybe we were all just pretty ordinary, all of my family.

As for example, the only special thing about my mom was her English accent. And words she used. She said *lorry* for *truck,* and *lift* instead of *elevator,* and *rashers* for strips of bacon, and also she drank pots of strong tea, lots of sugar and milk in it, all day long. I think she was a good enough mom to me, though I'd get embarrassed for her accent and her English words when I had a friend with me, which wasn't so often.

My dad was a postman from as soon as he got discharged until the day he collapsed from a fatal aneurysm and died out on his route the first winter after I went to Vietnam. If there was anything special about him, it was my dad wore his mail carrier uniform even when he wasn't on the job. That, and he wouldn't talk about his time in WWII in England except once to say a buzz bomb hit a hotel where he was billeted, he was in the toilet and ran out in the street in his skivvies because he was afraid the building was coming down on top of him. He said he was never so embarrassed, and my mom said it wasn't a thing to be telling me. I surmise that's all the action he ever saw, which can be considered prophetic about my Vietnam tour.

I knew Ellen some from high school, where I was the average so-so student. I was surprised she said yes to marrying when I was home on furlough from Fort Bliss before I went to Vietnam. Possibly it was the uniform.

My mom said, "Oh, I take a dim view of the prospects for this in this situation, Master Ronald!"

My dad said, "You sure you're ready to take on a wife and responsibility still wet behind the ears? You're a kid, Ronnie." I was in fact nineteen.

We didn't know when I left for Vietnam, but Ellen was pregnant with the baby who became our only child Laurie, born in 1967 before I came home again.

So, to this extent, there's my life from birth up to after Vietnam. Birth to then, people, places, ordinary enough. I've said how my dad passed away delivering the mail, and add to that my mom did the same, sitting up in a chair in her living room, got up out of bed in the wee hours, distressed, sat in her chair in front of the TV, though didn't turn it on, suffered a massive stroke it was determined.

This was in 1972, by which time I was already experiencing the difficulties resulting later in my VA disability which is now in jeopardy. My daughter Laurie was five or six, and my wife Ellen was already the primary breadwinner, selling real estate for the agency owned and operated by Al, who became ultimately her next and present husband. This didn't happen for some years to come, but I surmise they were probably having their longtime affair already. Though I have no proof, and Ellen won't tell me a thing on the topic no matter how nicely I inquire.

But, birth to whatever point in time, my life as it qualified in this regard.

Major Willis says, "Post-traumatic stress with regards to you is close to a bad joke, Kendler."

I say, "I don't see why."

He says, "You were a goddamn R.E.M.F., goddamnit! You were never in harm's way. You didn't handle Agent Orange, you never left Long Binh, you didn't succumb to drugs, not even pot, that's by your own admission."

I say, "We got mortared pretty close by. I worked alongside men snorting heroin daily. I was separated from my wife and daughter, my dad dies and I'm denied compassionate leave."

Major Willis says, "You operated a forklift in a warehouse. Show me the stress, Kendler."

I say, "What else could explain the position I'm in today?"

He says, "Lack of will power. Basic character flaws. Inadequate personality. No inner resources." Major Willis closes his eyes like he can't take the sight of me any longer today. In truth, he looks far more stressed than me. He looks too old to be only a major. Maybe he's just not very good at his work. Or it's possible promotions are slow in the service nowadays. Or he's only prematurely aged, younger than his appearance. I'd like to ask him if he was in Vietnam, but refrain for fear it would prejudice him against me even more than he is.

The worst times are also oddly the best. The worst time is when I can't think of a single thing to do. I've got nothing I need to go to Piggly Wiggly to buy from Mattie, the mail won't be delivered for hours, besides which I don't expect anything, my disability check not due for days yet, the phone won't ring, and I don't dare call Ellen or Laurie for a while, having been told expressly not to call the last time I did. The worst times.

Which is what I do. Nothing. I could always drink, but somehow don't want to when these times come. I sit in my recliner, the TV off because there's only soaps and stupid talk shows and old movies on. I sit in my recliner, wonder how I'll get through this nothing, how long it'll last. And it often turns into the best time.

I'm sitting, looking at nothing, thinking nothing except that I have nothing to think much less say, and then I happen to look out the patio door, my balcony, and I see the beechwoods moving in the wind. Then I'm listening, hearing the wind in the leaves, which is like breathing, or applause, or a crowd far away roaring, cheering, if the wind is strong enough. I get fixed on that, watching and listening, and then I'm imagining all the creatures living in the beechwoods, birds, rabbits, the one big gray squirrel, all alive and running around, flying, scurrying, in that small woods.

That's *doing* something. A perfect something to be doing because I'm sort of part of it, but no effort on my part, looking, listening. There've been times this goes on pretty long, through daylight into dusk, even dark, after which I'm only hearing, can't see the trees shake and sway. It's strange, but my worst and best times are all at once. I never think to get up, go out on the balcony, check for a glimpse of Big Red.

I seriously doubt anyone else would derive the same pleasure.

Major Willis says, "I can get you job training, Kendler. What kind of work appeals to you? Computers? Clerical? Manual labor? Give us a hint, Kendler."

I say, "Do they have anything where you don't have to interface with people? I don't feel up to interpersonal relations yet. If you could get me something where I work alone, sort of in isolation from others?"

He says, "Think you'd like stuffing envelopes at home?" He's jesting, sarcastic, which I don't mind. He says, "How about night security? Except you'd have to carry a firearm, and I wouldn't care to entrust you with a weapon."

Major Willis is sarcastic, makes fun of my weapon. A .22 Saturday Night Special. Loaded. I keep it by my bed, but in a box, and don't take it out. But I feel better knowing it's there. There's a lot of crime and general danger in the world today.

"Too bad," says Major Willis, "nobody'd pay for somebody to sit around and fret feeling sorry for himself, you'd be a lock for the position."

Sarcastic. I'm tempted to tell him I know how to use a variety of weapons, but only say, "I was qualified Marksman on the rifle in the military, but probably I've forgotten most of that."

I call Kendra Cluck, say, "I'd like to test out the air-conditioning in advance of the season. Can you send your man over to sort of supervise?"

She says, "Mr. Kendler, it's not hot enough to air condition."

I say, "I just want to be prepared."

She says, "When it gets hot, if it doesn't cool to satisfaction, call and we'll look at it."

I call Piggly Wiggly, say, "Is Mattie working today?"

Whoever, manager-type, says, "May I ask who is this calling?" so I hang up.

I call the VA, say, "My name's Kendler, Ronald. I have an appointment with Major Willis. Doctor Willis. Thursday, three in the P.M." It takes this person a while to verify.

Then she—nurse or clerk—says, "Yes. I have that here."

I say, "Just confirming."

I call Ellen, say, "Would you please tell me precisely when it was, what year even, you started having your affair with Al, and also if there were others along the way in addition?"

Ellen says, "If you do not cease and desist I promise you you'll wish you had." Then Al, who I didn't know was on an extension, pipes up.

He says, "How would you like me or my designated representative to kick your ass up between your shoulder blades?" I can't think of a proper retort, plus he may be serious, so hang up.

I call Laurie, say, "So how's your live-in biker Walter these days?"

My daughter says, "Will you fucking get off our case, Dad?"

I say, "Laurie, when I pass away, everything I have goes to you."

My daughter says, "Big whoop!" I start to say, be serious, this is costing me long-distance, but she hangs up before I can get it out.

Jesus. I went out onto my balcony late this morning. I was there to truly smoke, not pretend, felt like watching the beechwoods to see if I could spot any rabbits, the squirrel, pick out birds in the branches. Big Red was there! Barefoot. Wearing shorts! Jesus.

She was just walking, skimming her bare feet through the greenbelt grass, sort of half-dancing. I think she hummed something to herself, a tune I couldn't make out. I froze, set my head like I was looking at the beechwoods beyond her, followed her with my eyes until they hurt. Then she turned, saw me.

She said, "Hello today, Ronald Kendler!" The accent. She waved.

I hope I put something like a friendly smile on my face. I did wave, lifted my arm, waggled my hand. She laughed, said something I couldn't hear because all I could hear was blood pounding in my ears. She waved again, then walked back to her patio, skimming her bare feet through the grass, humming, disappeared beneath my balcony. I heard her close her patio door. Wearing shorts.

Jesus.

The drinking, I confess, is a problem. I minimize it to Major Willis, as this could land me in some VA rehab I don't relish the idea of, group talk sessions and such. Tattooed Mattie where I shop the Pig is the only one in a position to know my quantities, and I doubt she keeps track, just jokingly asks always if I'm old enough for liquor and my smokes. I drink daily, but once in a while get really shit-faced. It's a problem, but also a relief.

I set up in my recliner, turn on the TV, it doesn't matter what's on. I use a glass, but don't bother with ice or mix. I know what I'm doing.

It's a little like the bad-good times when I stare out the patio door at my beechwoods. At first I'm drinking, feeling the burn in my gut, then the buzz all over, and then I'm sort of gone away. I get to the state I don't care about where I am, my situation, former wife and estranged daughter, Major Willis, disability at risk, this time and place, whether I have a life, and if so, what's its quality. It can get fairly grim.

I kind of imagine doing things. Calling up important people like Ellen and Laurie, Major Willis, even Piggly Wiggly Mattie or divorcing Costa across the hall, shout and scream at them, but never do because by this stage I'm far enough gone I couldn't punch the right phone buttons. I only imagine doing this. I have also imagined going downstairs, knock on Big Red's door, invite her up for a drink, which is absurd because I'd break my neck on those stairs if I dared try that, the shape I'm in at this stage.

I have reached the point, if rarely, of considering climbing up the half-flight of steps to my bedroom, taking my pistol out of its box, but never have actually done that yet.

I pass out in my recliner, wake up feeling so bad I wish I was dead. But always get on my feet, make coffee, get juice. I get busy, and this phase ends, though I do some daily drinking in any case. It's not a *big* problem.

I speculate the average life leads to the accumulation of things. Property. Money. Mementos. I'm no exception.

I own some things. A bed, with linens. Towels and such. Cookware I seldom use. A Joe DiMaggio coffee maker. Glassware. Kitchen nook table and chairs. My recliner. Clothing, some of it presentable enough. The TV. My old Toyota I trust only to get me to the VA and back, Piggly Wiggly. Official documentation relating to my military service and disability. Personal mementos in the form of two photo albums, old snaps of my mom and dad, some taken in Vietnam, Long Binh, men I worked beside in the warehouse whose names I can't remember. Laurie's baby pics, some of her, Ellen, me, as a family.

A .22 Saturday Night Special. Loaded. But in a box from which I don't remove it.

Sure, less than most, but possibly more than some. Notice, I don't mention money, am not at all a materialistic person. There's surely more, but I don't see the need of an inventory. Accumulated things.

I catch Costa on the stairs, coming up all sweated, heaving and blowing from his bike ride, pudgy face all blotched pink from that and the stairs. I'm on my way down with garbage in separate bags for the recycling bins. I say, "So how's the divorce coming?"

He says, "Great, just great. Her shyster made mine an offer I can live with."

I say, "That's great!"

Costa says, "Yeah, I can live with it if I take a vow to swear off eating and drinking!"

I say, "Oh. I'm sorry. What's she want now?"

Costa stops there on the stairs, looks me over, the garbage bags in my hands, says, "Butt out, okay?" and stomps on up the stairs to his apartment across the hall from mine. I hear him slam his door shut, stand there a while before I head on down to the recycling bins. I suppose I somehow offended.

Mattie at Piggly Wiggly says, "Got any proof of age on you?"

I say, "I must have left it in my other pants." We laugh. So I say, "Mattie, would you mind telling me how you got that tattoo?"

She looks at me like I exposed myself there at her checkout station. She says, "Get the hell out of my damn face, creep-o!" Drops my change on the counter instead of handing it to me.

* * *

Major Willis says, "I've got amputees, single and multiple, I've got addicts, I've got confirmed alcoholics and clinical psychoses up the ying-yang, I've got borderline illiterates and pure-dee sociopaths. Where do you fit in, Kendler?"

I say, "I'm no malingerer."

He says, "That's all for today. Go on, remove yourself from my office, I'm sick of the sight of you!"

When I call Ellen all she says is, "You've been warned!" Yells it in my ear.

I call Laurie, say, "If I were to pass away, it's possible there'd be enough after the VA buries me to pay for your laser surgery, honey."

She says, "You are such a total asshole."

When I dial Kendra Cluck, I can't think of an excuse to ask her to send maintenance, but it doesn't matter because she's out, just her answering machine, which I do not leave a message on, remembering it's after office hours. What I thought of saying was asking if she could tell me the ethnic derivation of the name *Cluck,* but would never do such a personal thing.

Most people have what can be called a life's work. I regret I don't. When I rotated home from Vietnam, was discharged, I had some money saved from monthly allotments to Ellen, who was already working part-time as a legal secretary, where she learned to do computers. For some months I was kind of a house husband, keeping the house clean, caring for Laurie. When Ellen got on me about finding work, contributing, getting a career, I was enthusiastic at first. I saw myself in an office, suit and tie, had a little ambition. I suppose I should have gone back to school on my vet's benefits, which Ellen urged, but I was a pretty punk student in high school, so I joined the general labor force. I did a lot of things.

I pumped gas until the station went total self-service. I was a mover, moved people's belongings who were moving only short-distance. I did nights at a quick-stop, had hopes of being a manager-trainee, but this didn't happen because this quick-stop was operated by a Pakistani person who selected a great-nephew just migrated to America for the position, so I quit, angry, in protest of the injustice. I shelved books at the main public library, and for a time was a great reader of books on all topics, but finally got bored with that. I took the exam for the U.S. Post Office, but didn't score high enough to be called for employment except as holiday temp, which I did several Christmases. It's possible I saw myself following in my dad's footsteps to some degree.

I had too much pride to work fast-food, but confess to selling my blood platelets to a clinic at one especially low point.

This is largely why Ellen went ultimately into real estate sales and management with the Al she began a long affair with and finally married after divorcing me. Laurie's bad teenage and early adulthood years complicated my efforts and desire to catch on at something.

I once had visions of an office, suit and tie, good money, a career as something, but this vision faded away. I'm doubtless guilty of lack of adequate ambition. I certainly do not blame my condition on Vietnam, where I was never in fear and didn't get so much as a scratch. The disability is just a ploy I initiated when there was nowhere else to turn.

I'm about positive Major Willis is going to derail that. And soon. Then where am I?

It's a stretch calling this a life's work.

Coincidentally, seeing as my dad's career was the postal system, mail's also a large part of my life. When the time comes for my disability check to arrive, I sort of camp out by the mail boxes in the downstairs lobby. This is just half a flight of stairs below Big Red's apartment, #1. Even if the check's not due, I get my mail the second I see the postman walk out, watching from my balcony.

Besides usual bills, which make me a little frantic, given my finances, I also get flyers from Piggly Wiggly and other supermarkets, and shopper throwaways, and also periodically those little postcard-size things with pictures of abducted children and teenagers. I read everything comes in the mail to me. Bills due cause me some minor panic, and all the advertising stuff is at least colorfully done. The abducted children's pictures cause me sadness. I can get depressed, thinking of how many are out there, lost or dead or held against their wills. I study their pictures on the little cards, like postcards, addressed *Occupant,* and I could almost weep for sadness.

I get few phone calls. Long-distance companies call with deals to lower my rates. I listen politely to the pitches, say good-bye before I hang up. A meat company in Nebraska calls fairly often with deals on boxes of frozen corn-fed beef cuts, and I listen and decline politely. For a time after I first moved in, various persons male and female kept calling for someone named Marv who had this phone number before me. I explained each time, suggested directory assistance, but never any conversation beyond this politeness.

It's check day, a good day, maybe two days due, so I'm naturally at the mailboxes when the postman comes. I'm always glad again Big Red has no name on her mailbox, so I can keep calling her Big Red in my mind. The postman's a youngish man, wears shorts with knee-high socks and a sun helmet, the same big leather bag like my dad toted for years. I say, "Something for Kendler today?" All the while he talks he's unlocking mailboxes, stuffing them with letters, locking them back up, lots of first-class mail—I'd like to scrutinize more closely to see what Big Red gets, but don't want to know her name from an envelope, can see Costa gets thick envelopes I presume come from his wife's lawyer or his.

The postman says, "Not today."

I say, "I've got money coming should have been here yesterday at the latest."

He looks at me like I insulted, says, "I just deliver."

I say, "Is there a way we could maybe check?" Again a look like I was rude.

He says, "Mister, I've a long day here, okay? Okay?" When I don't speak for fear of further offending, he leaves. I wait a few minutes on the chance Big Red'll come out with her mailbox key, but she doesn't. I unlock my box, take out the one thing he could as easily have directly handed me, another one of those abducted kids cards.

Costa and I exit our apartments, face to face in the hall. Before I can say hello, he wheels away from me like I'm contagious, down the stairs, Nike bike riding shoes thumping on the carpeted steps. Not a word. Not a glance.

I show up punctually for my appointment with Major Willis, stand in his office doorway. I say, "Major?"

He looks at me, whooshes air out between his teeth, says, "The hell with it. You're canceled. I red-lined you in my appointment log. Something's in the works'll come to you via certified mail, Kendler."

I shop The Pig, head for Mattie's register with my smokes and liquor and some few staples. She sees me, unties her apron, tosses it on the counter, shouts out, "On break!" and trots off toward somewhere Pig employees go for their breaks, fast, like she has to go to the toilet. I have to line up at the next register, a girl maybe sixteen, name tag saying *Peg* and *Shop The Pig!* who checks me out without making eye contact.

Kendra Cluck's phone rings and rings, no answering machine message. I give up after seventeen rings.

I know better than to dial Ellen or Laurie.

It was hard to believe. I almost still don't believe it. Jesus.

I was in my recliner, not exactly watching what was on TV, late afternoon, doing only a small amount of my drinking, not intending a big one. For a second I thought it was a voice from the television show, but the accent was there. Jesus.

She said, "Ronald Kendler? Ronald Kendler!" I got up, put my glass down so she wouldn't know I was starting drinking so early in the day. I went out the patio screen door, looked down over the railing at Big Red looking up at me, grinning like I'd told her a joke. She said, "Hello, Ronald Kendler." Jesus. She was of course barefoot, and wearing her shorts, and what's called a halter top which reveals basically all there is.

I said, "Hello."

She said, "Ronald Kendler, I'm tonight going to cook some chicken grilled on the grill with charcoal on my patio. Will you like to eat a supper with me, Ronald Kendler?" Jesus.

I thought a lot of things in a big hurry while she stood there, bare feet, shorts, skimpy tight top, dark red hair almost auburn. I thought: smile at her! I thought: I'll bring my bottle and ice and two clean glasses, we can drink while her chicken grills. I thought I'd tell her she could call me Ron or Ronnie instead of Ronald, and I'd ask her actual name. I thought we could play a game, me guessing what accent that was she had.

She said, "Will you like to eat chicken here outside on the patio, Ronald Kendler?"

I said, "No. I can't. I'm real busy." And I went inside my apartment before she could speak again, shut the glass patio door so I wouldn't hear anything, so I wouldn't smell charcoal burning if she cooked her chicken to eat alone. I did one of my very heavy drinking times the rest of the day and most the night.

* * *

I'm sure my thoughts were greatly affected by the drinking. But I'm clear on how I thought I'd go upstairs, take my pistol from the box, bring it back downstairs, just sit with it, open up to the balcony and listen in the dark to whatever I could hear. I thought I'd sit up all night in my recliner, not drink so much as to pass out. And I'd just hold the pistol, which I keep loaded, feel it in my hands. This scared me.

So to show courage I did get my pistol from its box, did sit with it. About all I felt was how hard and cool it felt in my hands. Then I was realizing I was drunk enough to no longer be scared, and then I did pass out.

When I woke up it was just dawn showing above the beechwood trees, and the pistol felt colder from the night air in my hands. Waking up, for a minute I thought about doing something with that pistol. But I didn't. I put it away in the box upstairs again, and then I revived myself with my gem of a hard shower spray like needles, drank orange juice, made coffee in the Joe DiMaggio.

I didn't do much the rest of the day except go out on the balcony now and then to check for Big Red, keep a watch, but she never came outside all that day. But I stay on watch. Sooner or later, she'll show, inevitably, barefoot if not in shorts and that revealing top.

It's a life.

Jesus.

Long Odds

Once a month, Kleczka had a night out with his pals. Night Out, his wife called it. She thought it was good for him to get one night a month to meet his old neighborhood pals, hoist a few brews, play some cards or cribbage for small stakes at Mickey's All Sports over in the old neighborhood, watch whatever games were on the big-screen TVs. He only half-enjoyed it anymore, thought maybe he was finally outgrowing Mickey's, his pals from high school days, would just as soon make it another good night home after a long day's work, watch his own Sony, talk with Ceely, be with his kids.

"It ain't like I'm stressed I need relief," he told her.

"Everybody's got stress," she said.

"You?"

"I guess a little."

"You ever sorry you quit work?" he said. His wife worked telephone marketing the first two years they were married, before Stan Jr. was born, was good at it, made bonuses.

"Not so's I notice," Ceely said, laughed. And she said, "After I clean up from dinner I got a laundry to do, you need a shirt for work tomorrow, I'll probably call my ma later if it's not so late." She called Stan Jr. and Kimmie into the kitchen for dinner. Night Out, she and the kids ate in the kitchen instead of the dining nook.

Stan Jr. said, "How's come we eat in here when dad's gone?" Ceely said, "It's cozier for just the three of us." Kleczka thought that's what he'd said too.

Kimmie said, "I bet you don't know I'm painting you a birthday picture for your birthday."

"I do now, but I promise to pretend I don't," Kleczka said, and reached out, gently touched her hair. "You guys be good," he said to his children, who had already begun to eat the second Ceely dished it up—a casserole, looked good to him. "I'd almost rather eat here than Mickey's x-ray cooked brats," he said to his wife.

She smiled at him, said, "Don't get all schnockered."

"I never do," Kleczka said.

"I was kidding," his wife said.

"I know," he said. He stood beside his son's chair, touched him on the shoulder.

"What?" Stan Jr. said.

"Be good," he said.

"You'll be late, they'll start in calling me, where's Stan, we're all waiting on him," Ceely said.

"I'm on my way out," Kleczka said. He got to the kitchen door, stopped, looked back at his family. He had a great family. His wife sat down, the three of them eating hearty, like not a care in the world, like nobody else was in the room with them. "Ceely," he said. She looked up, fork in front of her mouth. She still looked good, put on a few pounds from having kids, but good still. She was the best-looking girl at St. Casimer's except maybe for Sharon Murdoch, who had to get married to Knees Gazapian when he knocked her up. Kleczka and Ceely waited until married, the best way to make a family start right. "Guess," he said, "what Marvin said to me today, I was logging off the computer, just before I left, right?"

"Tell me," she said. His children looked up from their plates at him, chewing politely, mouths closed like Ceely insisted.

"I'm logging off the shift," Kleczka said, "Marvin's just happening to pass by on his way into the showroom floor, I think he had a client maybe, I says to him I'm logging off, I'll see him bright and early, right?"

"And?" Ceely said. Kleczka looked at his great family having dinner in this great kitchen of their great house they'd been in two years almost now, but still looking like new because they worked at keeping it up. He wanted to tell them because they should know it, feel as good about it as he did.

"Marvin says to me, his exact words, `Stan, my man, you're a pure whiz and a jewel in my crown.' His words exactly," Kleczka said.

"I could have told him that," his wife said. His kids went back to eating their dinner.

"And you think I need relief from stress," he said.

She said, "You don't go, Wheezie or Jimmy C. or somebody's gonna be calling me where's Stan, it's our night for Mickey's."

"I'm gone," he said, and left.

Backing his Saturn out the drive, he flipped on his lights, stopped a moment at the end of the drive to look at his great house, the lawn like barbered. He and Ceely worked Sundays sometimes hours on the lawn and flowerbeds, decorative shrubs, started that routine the week they moved in. They gave up going to Mass because they agreed a family's house was more important to being a strong family than going to Mass regular. Kleczka didn't believe his faith from the time he was a wise-guy high school kid, even when he tried, getting married in the church, his kids baptized.

He had everything he could have wanted, he thought, passing out through the big limestone Christobel addition arch onto the freeway access road.

Driving to Mickey's All Sports, the old neighborhood, he suddenly felt very glad to be out. It gave him some time to think, feel really good for the life he had, family, house, job. Night Out was mostly boring now, but it gave him this chance to think about things.

Lucky to graduate high school, he was such a rotten student, wise-guy, sheer dumb luck he took the industrial arts instead of something wouldn't have prepared him, commercial or, much less, college prep. Here he was, Saturn service manager, wore a white shirt, clip-on bow tie, red Saturn Family team smock, worked a computer as easy as if it was a plain typewriter, dealt with the public constantly all day, phone and in person, in addition supervising mechanics and mechanics helpers and the custodials who cleaned up inside and kept vehicles on the lot looking clean as new.

This was a *good* day, Marvin the director of customer relations his immediate supervisor, a college grad of course, telling he was a whiz and a jewel in his crown. He was glad he told Ceely. It wasn't a thing he could say to anyone else, his Night Out pals. What Marvin said, and his family finishing their cozy dinner in the kitchen, Kleczka felt like singing, turned on the radio, but it was talk, not singing, and he felt silly.

He stopped at a quick-trip for cigs. He was working on quitting smoking, didn't smoke in his house or his car, Saturn was naturally a smoke-free workplace. He smoked—Camel Lights only—in restaurants where he went for lunches, in his back yard if his kids weren't around to see it, and once a month smoked all he wanted at Mickey's.

He bought his cigs, then bought a scratch-off lottery ticket. Putting his change away, he saw a dollar bill in his wallet, faded like it went through the wash in somebody's pants so he took it out, bought this scratch-off, some golf game thing. He never golfed in his life.

He scratched it off with a penny, saw his score was below par or whatever. "I think I'm a winner here," he said to the clerk, a guy looked Arab or Mexican.

"Yes," the guy said, then scratched off another part on the ticket with his thumbnail, said, "Plus you have a double birdie bonus, eagle. Twenty dollars," he said, and, "Will you have cash or more tickets?"

"I'll take the dough," Kleczka said. "I never gamble except on cards and cribbage and sports pools." He wondered if he should tip the guy, like a bartender or waitress, for selling him the winner, but didn't. The Arab or Mexican smiled, showed big totally white teeth, handed him two crisp new tenners from his register. "It must be my day," Kleczka said.

The old neighborhood was more run-down-looking than ever, houses sagging and dingy, yards growing up like hay fields or else the grass worn off showing bare dirt, crummy little stores, lots of them closed, trash in the gutters, the cars parked curbside mostly junkers with rusted panels. The coloreds were moving closer all the time, they'd take over if they ever got in.

Not like when Kleczka was coming up a kid, families like his took care of property, had pride, almost no street crime. The ones with pride, like Kleczka, moved up and out, scattered to the suburbs and new developments out on the freeway in what was the boonies when he was a kid.

But he still knew some people, geezers his pa's age still kicking on their brewery and foundry and factory pensions and the Social Security, still one service each Sunday in Polish at St. Casimer's where he married Ceely, his kids baptized, still the old Polonia Hall where they played dartball and had wedding receptions, little pockets of the Polish and Irish from the old days, the odd few like Knees Gazapian, who was Armenian. And Mickey's All Sports that was Rourke's Tap when Kleczka was a kid, where his pa did what drinking he did, where his pa and ma took him right along, a family place, for Friday fish fries in the old days.

He'd done good, starting all the way from part-time pumping gas for B. S. Wisniewski's Mobile station to mechanic for Ryan Ford, to Saturn now, come a long way up. If he'd had any voice for singing, Kleczka would have been singing when he pulled into Mickey's lot, even if the run-down old neighborhood was sort of sad.

He wasn't late. Wheezie O'Brien and Jimmy Champion were still at the bar having the first one, gassing with Mickey, and Knees Gazapian still hadn't showed.

"What ho!" Mickey said.

"It's the Stan Man," Jimmy Champion said.

"Tidings," Kleczka said, and, "Gazapian's in the john or he ain't showed yet?" He was glad to see them, but it was still pretty boring to see them once a month here. And Wheezie looked bad, death warmed over, and Jimmy C. was fatter every time. Mickey looked older than his age.

"He'll be here," Jimmy Champion said. "I called just in case, he says he'll be here. He's going through some serious shit you probably didn't know, it came up sudden."

"His turn in the barrel, I had my share plus already," Wheezie said. Wheezie O'Brien bitched, but had cause. First his wife dumped him for the Wop Enea who sold new Fords at Ryan when Kleczka worked there—Marice Miller she was when Kleczka knew her, when they were both kids back at St. Casimer's parochial, a sweet girl he'd never dreamed would pull that on her husband—which Wheezie took very hard, got drinking seriously, lost his brewery job, union, working now no more than clerking, selling across the counter at Chinski's Liquor three years now, plus his health always shaky, the asthma since he was a kid, and he still smoked like a chimney.

Wheezie looked bad, skinny, skin pale grayish, circles under his eyes, needed a haircut, old clothes like only a few cuts above homeless, like the few old winos Kleczka remembered from his kid days.

"What shit is that? With Knees," he said.

"I get depressed hearing this," Mickey said, "people out of the blue get hit with a ton of bricks," went away down the bar to refill the gang at the far end.

Jimmy Champion said, "What it is, he's losing the store, he's for certain got to go bankrupt. Also his wife's suing for a divorce, plus some troubles with the one daughter." Knees Gazapian had three daughters.

Wheezie O'Brien said, "Welcome to the club," and, "All the time big-shot Gazapian, he overextended trying to keep up with the big discounts and fancy malls, serves his ass right."

"That's cold," Jimmy said. "You are one cold customer, Wheezie."

"I didn't hear nobody sobbing when I get it in the ass," Wheezie said.

"That's kind of hard to believe, Gazapian," Kleczka said. He shook his head, waved for Mickey to come down and give them a round, thought about Gazapian, who they called Knees because he was a hot-shot sports star in high school at St. Casimer's, was supposed to go to college on scholarship but his knees blew out playing football senior year so he went into his pa's business, Persian rugs, a famous old company three generations with regular rich customers, got it all when his pa died, married Sharon Murdoch because he knocked her up, about the most beautiful girl at St. Casimer, made a mint, Kleczka had figured. "I'd never of believed Knees taking bankrupt suddenly with no warning of all people," he said.

"Believe," Mickey said. And he said, "Your own business can be the shits, I can testify. You," he said to Kleczka, "you're the smart type, you got it knocked with Saturn, let the corporations do the worrying for you."

"Him?" Jimmy Champion said. "What am I, your step-child?" Jimmy Champion was shift foreman at Ladish Box, lived in a home new as Kleczka's, Cedar Creek, the development just over from Kleczka's Christobel.

"Give us a round here," Kleczka said, reached for his wallet.

"Give us the dice cup, I feel suddenly charmed," Wheezie said. They rolled liar's dice for taps and schnapps hookers alongside. Kleczka won. "Figures," Wheezie said, and, "I should of shut up and let Stan moneybags pop."

They drank, and Kleczka said, "Give you a chance to get even," smacked the bar with the leather cup, slid it at Wheezie.

"Give me a break, God," Wheezie said, and they rolled and Kleczka won again. "I'm snake-bit," Wheezie said.

"Every dog got its day," Jimmy Champion said.

"Which reminds me," Mickey said, taking Wheezie's and Jimmy's money. He said, "Stan the man's our big winner here."

"Of what?" Kleczka said, still thinking about Knees Gazapian of all people having a sudden disaster.

"Month's pool," Mickey said, turned to get the cigar box with the pool receipts.

"Ain't this a pisser?" Jimmy Champion said. "I had myself figured for close on that, what with the Bills and Miami last week."

"Give me a goddamn break once in my life!" Wheezie said, scooped up the dice, rattled the cup beside his ear for another game which Kleczka won. Wheezie put his face in his hands, elbows on the bar, moaned like he hurt bad.

"Two twenty-six," Mickey said, counted out the bills for him, tens and fivers, a single, a twenty. "I think that's the record except for two years ago one time, Eddie Czerwinski was two forty-one or two I think it was. Old Eddie, the one worked railroad, not young Eddie's a school teacher," he said.

"The rich get richer," Jimmy said.

"And some of us are cursed to get it where the sun don't shine," Wheezie said, sucked on his medicine puffer, lit a new cigarette.

Kleczka said, "It's ironic. I never win this kind of stuff. Except I stopped off for cigs, I won twenty on the scratch-off lottery just now coming here on my way."

"Is it your birthday maybe?" Mickey said.

Wheezie said, "You're just saying to make me feel bad, right?"

"Leave me buy a round," Kleczka said, but Wheezie wanted one more roll, so they did, and Kleczka won again.

"I give up rolling against you," Jimmy said.

Wheezie said, "Mickey, do me a tab, I'm short for cash here, okay?"

Then they let Kleczka buy a round, were nursing that when Knees Gazapian finally showed up. "Better late than never," Jimmy said.

"Knees," Wheezie said, "don't bet nothing against this big Polish fuck tonight, he's blessed or something."

Mickey said, "What ho, Mr. Knees!"

Kleczka said, "Knees, you look good." He did. Knees Gazapian always looked good, since high school days. He was big, black-haired, looking tanned permanent from being Armenian. The girls and women always went for Knees Gazapian, he had his pick. He always had the clothes to look good because his pa had a Persian rug business was a famous old firm in the city. Plus he could talk a line. And if it was true he'd had a surprise financial disaster and being sued for divorce from his wife who was probably the most beautiful girl at St. Casimer, and also a problem kid, it didn't show in his looks. Except he didn't right off flash the big smile showing all his good teeth like he was about to bite, the way he did when he was talking a line to some woman, always made you think he was always on the make.

Knees Gazapian said, "Let's get a fucking table, I think I can clean all your clocks at cribbage if you got balls for it."

"You're on," Jimmy Champion said.

"I'm game, all I can lose is what I won already. You're talking to the man won this month's pool," Kleczka said. It sounded like bragging the way it came out, but he didn't mean it that way exactly, just wanted to tell the news. He was sorry he said it, seeing Knees was having unexpected financial and personal disasters.

"Dumb luck," Knees said.

"Take my marker, Knees?" Wheezie O'Brien said. Mickey brought a fresh deck and the cribbage board from behind the bar.

And Kleczka won at cribbage. The cards came to him like his personal guardian angel was dealing, his pegs marching up and down the board like they were a parade band. Jimmy Champion fired up one of his stinkpot cigars, sat back, clucked his tongue, blew smoke rings like there was no point crying over his losings. Wheezie coughed on his cigarette, said, "May you choke on it, you big Polack fuck," wrote out markers for Kleczka, who knew he was not good for them, would never dun Wheezie O'Brien for money he didn't have.

Knees Gazapian didn't show any feelings at losing, just smiled his small smile, shelled out when he lost, stared off sometimes, looked up at the ceiling like there were answers to this maybe hiding up above the cigar and cigarette smoke.

"I have to say this is my best night in I don't know how long," Kleczka said, stacking his winnings neat in front of him. "In fact," he said, "if you count the lottery ticket twenty bucks at the stop-and-go plus this month's pool, it's the absolute best I can remember."

"Did you forget liar's dice you rolled like you were not conscious?" Wheezie said.

"You must be living clean," Jimmy said.

Knees Gazapian said, "Even a dumb fuck Polack gets lucky streaks if he lives long enough." He said it like he wasn't kidding, so Kleczka looked at him. Knees just looked right back at him, as if he did mean it, and then at the last second smiled one of his big on-the-make smiles showing his teeth. Kleczka bought a round. He was feeling possibly half in the bag from all the schnapps, so switched to just taps, noticed Knees was putting away rock and rye like it was soda pop.

"I say we switch to poker so's I can get mine back fast," Wheezie said, but they stayed with cribbage, and Kleczka kept on winning. It was getting to be a considerable amount he was ahead now. He chuckled, thinking how he'd tell Ceely all about the scratch-off ticket, liar's dice, the pool, cribbage when he got home tonight.

"Laugh," Wheezie said, "make me feel bad."

"You got the world by the bag, right, Stanley?" Knees said.

"Leave me enjoy my one night of my life, okay, guys?" he said.

But he *did* feel like he had the world by the shorts. It wasn't the lottery and pool and cribbage money, it was his whole life, he realized. He'd come up out of the old neighborhood, no special education, no special breaks or ins he could think of. His pa was brewery union, the best he could have done for Kleczka was get him in the union, like Wheezie O'Brien was until his wife dumped him for that Wop Enea, ruined his life, and he crapped it all by drinking as a result.

He looked at Wheezie, skinny, sickly, coughing, sucking on the medicine puffer to get his breathing every so often, smoking his brains out, looking like one step away from homeless wino. Wheezie had been a good kid, jolly and joking, wise guy, good little football player, look at him now. And Jimmy. So Jimmy came out okay, shift foreman at Ladish Box, big deal. But no way he'd go above that, no way he was in line for plant manager, for instance. And Jimmy Champion was getting very fat, big beer gut and jowls, and his hair premature snow white, all styled and sprayed like he was a rock singer or something, a long way from when they played football together on the line for St. Casimer's.

"I'm cleaned," Jimmy said when Kleczka won again.

"You ain't got the faintest inkling what *cleaned* is!" Wheezie said.

"Knees?" Kleczka said. Knees shook his head no, he'd had enough cards for one night. "In which case drinks are on the big winner," Kleczka said, yelled for Mickey to set them up.

"I knew there must be some reason I liked you once," Wheezie said.

"Here's to Stan, may your pud drop off in the urinal next time you take a leak," Jimmy said.

"I thank you all," Kleczka said when Knees didn't say anything. He folded his winnings into his pocket because his wallet was too full to put any more in. He laughed, toasted them all before sipping the foam off his fresh tap, then saw the way Knees Gazapian was looking at him.

For a second he thought Knees was drunker than he looked, or he'd offended him, but then Knees smiled his on-the-make smile again. He looked at Knees. Knees Gazapian was the one had it made, big and sleek, good-looking, star athlete until injured, his pa's Persian rug business to take over like a gift, a mint, knocked up and married Sharon Murdoch the best looker at St. Casimer's. But look what happened to Knees, several disasters coming on from out of nowhere.

Knees said, "Stanley here thinks he's got the universe by the nuts, boys. Look at him, he's grinning, swelling up to burst."

Kleczka said, "I never said that, Knees," felt bad because that was just how he did feel at this very moment, half in the bag, feeling his full wallet like a stone on his hip, feeling the lump of bills folded against his leg, thinking in a flash about Saturn and his home in Christobel, Ceely and Stan Jr. and Kimmie. He said, "Don't be pissed if a person enjoys a little run, okay, Knees?"

Knees said, "Are you not aware my life is going down the porcelain convenience, you dumb Polack?"

"Do you mean that personal, Knees?" he said.

"Are you aware, Stanley, that a family business for generations is set to crash? Did you not hear my middle daughter eloped suddenly because she got herself impregnated by a scum I wouldn't let in the back door of my home to use the toilet if he begged me? Are you aware my life is turning to dogshit even as we speak, Stanley?"

"I only just heard some rumor," Kleczka said. He was going to get up, pay Mickey for the drinks, maybe go to the john, tear up

Wheezie O'Brien's markers and flush them, drive home to Christobel, tell Ceely the run he had, check on his kids sleeping in their bedrooms, go to bed, sleep, forget all this, never go out for Night Out ever again, never come back to Mickey's, the old neighborhood.

"And you can sit there and gloat in my face because you win a few fucking dollars playing fucking cribbage, you made lucky bets on a sports pool?" Knees Gazapian said.

"He didn't mean nothing by it, Knees," Jimmy said.

"I didn't mean nothing by it," Kleczka said, and he said, "I don't need shit from you, Knees," started to get up to go. "Fuck your Persian rugs, you never earned it to start with, it was your pa's and his pa's before," he said.

"Sit," Knees said, "just a minute more. Something I forgot to tell you I should have ages back." Kleczka sat down. He was deciding if he should punch Knees's lights out or just hear him and go.

Wheezie said, "This place is getting too bad for me, I'll be at the bar," got up, went to talk to Mickey, run his tab.

Jimmy said, "Me for home," but Knees asked him to stay, said he needed him to verify something. "Can't we just end friendly, Knees?" he said, but he stayed. All the time he talked, Kleczka wasn't sure how many minutes it all took, Knees Gazapian smiled his little smile, played with his glass. He had big, hairy-backed hands, a large diamond ring instead of a wedding ring, a big digital watch on his hairy wrist, talking like it was ordinary small talk.

He said, "What burns my butt is a person like you, Stanley. Dumb Polack. Ever since I knew you at St. Casimer's you are such a dipshit."

"Knees," Jimmy Champion said.

Kleczka said, "Leave him spit it out, it don't make me no matter. This night out once a month's been getting old a long time now. Leave him finish."

Knees said, "You think you're really farting through silk, get to wear a white shirt for Saturn, don't get grease on you these days, not like at B. S. Wisniewski's, huh?"

"I like it," Kleczka said. "It's got a future."

"Live out in the burbs now, where is it?"

"Christobel," Kleczka said, "not so far from Jimmy at Cedar Creek. I like that too," he said.

"You got the two kids, boy and girl, king's choice," Knees said.

"You mad 'cause you got only daughters, your middle one knocked up, Knees?" he said.

"How's Ceely these days? Ceely Dumbrowski she was once upon a time. She still a looker?" Knees said. In just that second, Kleczka had a flash of what was coming. He should have stood up, walked. Or he should have stood, jumped Knees Gazapian, cleaned his clock royally for him. But it was like he was paralyzed, like he was in a dream where something was coming for him he couldn't move to fight back or escape. He couldn't even speak.

Knees said, "In case you didn't know, which I'll lay odds you don't, Jimmy here can verify, did you know I got real friendly let's call it with Miss Ceely D. once?" When Kleczka said nothing, he said, "It was when I think I'm pretty sure you were already engaged. At least I know you were steadies at the time. The circumstance was Jimmy and I ran into her one evening, I don't know where in hell's half acre you were, off dicking off. We had some beer. End of story. Did you know that, Stanley?"

For a few seconds, or a minute, Kleczka just sat and looked at him, Knees's smile getting bigger, like he discovered he won a prize. Then he was able to say, "You fucking lie." Knees shook his head no. Kleczka said, "You're a greasy-ass Persian rug seller crapped his pa's good business you never earned in the first place, your daughter's a pig and you had to knock up Sharon Murdoch to get married to her, I'm glad you wrecked your knees. I hope you get cancer or some disease rots your ass to death," Kleczka said.

Knees Gazapian smiled his biggest smile, said, "Dream on, Stanley," and stood up, waited a beat as if he waited to see if Kleczka was coming for him, then turned out and walked out of Mickey's, shouted, "Losers!" as he went out the door.

Kleczka sat with Jimmy Champion, silent. They could hear Wheezie O'Brien getting noisy over at the bar with Mickey, until Jimmy said, "Me for home."

"One sec," Kleczka said. He knew what he was going to say, knew he should not say it, but he had to, and he already knew the answer. "He lies, right, Jimmy?" he said.

Jimmy said, "Shit, I don't like mixing in ancient business."

"He lies?" he asked again.

"Nope," Jimmy said, and said, "Don't ask me more, Stan, okay? Just how I was only in a position to know it's truth is all. I can say she was really sorry it happened. She told me that herself. She told me never to say about it to anyone ever. Okay?"

"Okay," Kleczka said, and then Jimmy Champion got up and left without speaking to anyone at the bar. Then Kleczka got up, gathered the cards and board, carried them to the bar, handed them across to Mickey.

"The big winner," Mickey said.

"Come on," Wheezie said, grabbed the dice cup, banged it on the bar, "give me one last shot at your lucky ass!"

"I'll probably not see you guys maybe ever again," Kleczka said to them, to anyone could hear, and left Mickey's All Sports.

On the drive home to Christobel, totally sobered after all the brew and schnapps he put away, Kleczka expected to explode, but didn't. He kept waiting to suddenly do something wild, lean on the Saturn's horn, speed, punch the dash, swear, scream. Instead he was thinking very clear, how he'd tell Ceely exactly what happened, get her to confess, and it would be settled, behind them, because they had a whole life left to live, God knows how many years while Stan Jr. and Kimmie grew up, he had a good and important job, a position, they had a huge new house to pay off the mortgage, a whole life.

He pulled into Christobel, through the big limestone arch entrance. It was floodlit, but now it looked dark, ugly, the ironwork letters saying *Christobel* like something foreign he couldn't read. The big houses on the curving streets, in cul-de-sacs, were dark, like big mounds of dirt or stone, looked empty in the light of the halogen streetlights. His own house was another dark, empty mound, but Ceely had the porch carriage lamps on for him, and he parked, let himself in, felt totally sober, thinking clear.

She was in the dining nook, looking in a mail-order catalogue, like she was shopping bargain clothes for the kids, ballpoint pen and paper to write things down. She looked up at him, said, "This was a late one." He walked past her to the kitchen, took a beer from the fridge, popped the tab, came and sat down across from her. "Another on top of all you probably had?" she said.

"I never get schnockered," he said, drank, sighed loud.

"I didn't say you was. So how was it?"

He said, "How's it ever?" He took another swig of his beer to give himself time to think of what to say, how.

"Who all was there?"

"The usual," he said. "Wheezie, Jimmy C.," he said. Then he said, "Knees Gazapian." Nothing showed in her face. Why should it? It was ancient to her. He said, "Wheezie's like to die with his breathing and still smoking. He already looks half-dead. He might as well be dead. Jimmy's fatter. He uses a ton of hairspray on his hair like he's on TV or something." When she said nothing, still looking at him, he said, "Gazapian's going bankruptcy in his pa's rug business, plus one of his kids had to get married shotgun to some creep is what the story is. This all hit him all at once. The neighborhood's going to hell," he said, and, "I bet coloreds take it over in no time. I'm never going Night Out no more I think."

"Some good time you had," his wife said, flopped her big mail-order catalogue shut.

"I won a lot of money, the pool and cards," he said, "not to mention liar's dice for drinks, plus a lottery worth twenty beans on the way stopping for smokes."

"So you *did* have a good time!" she said, stood.

"That's sad, about Knees, huh?" he said.

She said, "Everybody's got some sadness in life, I think, Stanley. He can probably work out of it if he tries," she said.

"Yeah he could maybe," was all Kleczka could find to say, wanting to ask her if she had any sadness in her life, what it was. There was nothing showing in her face. Why should it, or was she just a good actor?

Ceely said, "You for bed now? Finish your beer." His wife always waited up for him when he had Night Out, and they went up to bed together, stayed awake a while in the dark, talked some about the kids, Saturn, what she had planned for the next day for herself, what her ma had to say on the phone if they talked.

"I'll be up in a little," he said. "Go on ahead." Then his wife looked at him for a second like she knew something was wrong or funny, but said nothing. She left her catalogue, paper and ballpoint, on the table, left, and he listened to her footsteps on the carpeted stairs going up to their bedroom.

Kleczka sat with his can of beer in front of him. He tried to think what to do. He thought about some possibilities.

He thought he might just get up, leave the house, drive off away, drive as far as he could, never come back. What would Ceely and the kids do? What would they do at Saturn, him never showing up, just gone? Then he thought he could go down in the basement, get the shotgun that was his pa's, who liked duck hunting, get it out of the cabinet where he kept it locked away from his kids. He didn't remember if he had any shells for it. If there were shells, he thought he might load it, lean his forehead on the end of the barrel, take off his shoe and pull the trigger with his toe if he couldn't reach with his arm that way. Thinking this made him shiver. He tasted his beer, like cold, wet metal from the can.

Then he thought if there were shells he'd load it, go upstairs, shoot his wife, then himself. He waited to see if he shivered, but did not. No, he thought, first he would shoot his kids, then Ceely, then himself. He would go to Kimmie's room, shoot her, then Stan Jr., then his wife, who would be coming from the master bedroom because she heard the shots. Then he would shoot her, then himself.

"No," Kleczka said aloud to himself in the dining nook. He fumbled in his shirt pocket, found his Camel Lights, was about to smoke one when he remembered he did not smoke in his house. He wondered why he didn't fire one up now, but he didn't.

Then his wife called from upstairs, "You coming up or what, Stan?" He stood up. He wondered if he was heading outside to his Saturn, or if he was heading for the basement door off the kitchen. "Stanley, it's late!" his wife called from upstairs. She could wake the kids, calling out so loud.

He said, "Okay!" hoping he did not wake them.

Then Kleczka knew he wasn't going to do anything. He was going upstairs to bed with his wife. And he would never say anything, ever, to her about Knees Gazapian. He would go to work at Saturn in the morning, prove to Marvin he was a true whiz of a service manager, like usual. They would have their usual life. He would not forget what he knew, not ever until he died whenever, but never say anything about it to Ceely, his kids, not anyone, just always know it.

All he had to do was not ever go on his Night Out once a month, ever again, and it would otherwise be like usual except for what only he knew. Knees Gazapian and Jimmy Champion would never say anything to anyone, he was sure.

"I'm coming!" he called up to his waiting wife. If she wanted to talk, he could tell her details about the lottery ticket, the month's tavern pool, liar's dice, cribbage money. What was the odds on all that?

He would talk to her like usual, and he could be thinking of all he had, coming from pumping B. S. Wisniewski's gas and fixing Ryan Ford's cars, now Saturn. And his kids. And a very good wife. And this great new house better than anything anybody ever had in the old neighborhood, where he'd never go again. He could think about Wheezie O'Brien almost as good as dead, Jimmy C. fatter every day, Knees Gazapian with business and personal disasters wrecking his life. He thought he could think about all that and be talking usual talk at the same time, forever if he had to.

What to do, Kleczka told himself as he went upstairs, shaking enough he had to hold the banister as he climbed, was to count blessings and try not to think otherwise, think of the bad things happening to other people if he needed something to keep him going. That could probably, he thought, make a usual enough life.

Gilded Quill:
The Story of Jones

I wrote and I wrote . . . The creative process released me into another dimension. At the same time, the things I wrote reminded me of who I truly was . . . It was a comfort, a distraction, and a joy to write. Just to write.
—Joseph "Joe Bananas" Bonanno

Jones, frustrated because he believed he had been born to write, but did not write, yearned for something, anything, to happen that might change his life.

His occupation, desk clerk (nonprofessional status) at one of the city's branch libraries, provided only a meager living; while he had medical insurance and the distant promise of a modest pension, he could not afford an automobile, travel, or a social life beyond dinner out—alone—twice a month. His furnished flat was adequate, but his strict budget precluded even cable channels. Besides, he hated television.

His only interest was literature; he read voraciously, his taste in serious poetry, fiction, and other belles lettres a matter of some pride to him. He stayed au courant by being the first to withdraw volumes displayed on the rack devoted to new acquisitions.

Beyond this, he had a great concern for his health. In this regard, he ate only vegetables (which troubled his bowels) and qualified as a serious jogger, though he lacked the sporting impulse that might have set him training hard for the cross country and marathon competitions abounding in his city.

He was also vain of his appearance, which kept him fashionably slender and accounted for his sole vice, tinting his prematurely gray long hair (no longer fashionable) a rich chestnut. When he jogged, he cut something of a figure in spandex, outrageously expensive running shoes, and headband. Otherwise, at home and on the job, he affected something of a uniform: loafers or sneakers, stone-washed jeans, form-fitting turtlenecks, and a pale tan corduroy jacket, elbows adorned with large, purely decorative leather patches.

In rare lucid moments of reflection, daring to fantasize, he thought of his attire as his *writer's garb* . . . for Jones, in his heart of hearts, considered himself a *Writer.* He was a Writer as he sat alone in a moderately pricey restaurant, snatching covert looks at less attractive men dining with very attractive women; he was a Writer as he checked books (almost all of them trash—how-to, technical manuals, pop psychology, spiritual uplift, genre novels, and other non-Literature) in and out at his library counter station; he was a Writer as he let his eyes drift over the rack of new acquisitions on display in all their colors; he was a Writer as he walked his neighborhood or rode the municipal transit bus—even as he raced through the streets, dawn beginning to light his path for another day, splendid in spandex, he was a Writer.

And though Jones had never written anything, not put pen or pencil (he disliked computers, could not touch-type) to paper with artistic intent since graduating college with a worthless degree in humanistic studies, he *knew* he was a *Writer!* Yes, beneath the placid facade with which he confronted Reality in all its manifestations, words bubbled and popped! On and off the job, inspirations for poems, stories, novels coalesced into vague shapes as teasing with potential as the vivid, if chaotic and sometimes disturbingly erotic dreams he knew he should record daily in a journal.

When Jones performed his morning ablutions, admiring his good teeth, unlined skin, and luxuriant hair, he saw a Writer in the mirror . . . which was all, really, preventing his collapse in despair at the dull, deplorable circumstances of his existence. Did he not carry, in the breast pocket of his corduroy writer's jacket, a pen and small notebook in which to jot random observations, striking locutions, and eavesdropped bits of street, restaurant, and even library shoptalk dialogue?

Jones might have continued this way ad infinitum were it not for the notice published in a weekly shopper he picked up in the supermarket where he, each payday, purchased his month's groceries.

Born to write? Dying to write? Are you a poet and don't know it? Budding novelist? Gilded Quill could be the answer to your dreams! said the small boxed announcement; there was a telephone number.

Jones, feeling an electric quiver—what the Muse's tickle might have felt like if he had a Muse—called the number. Digits trembling, mouth dry as parchment, he dialed, stood semi-paralyzed as the answering voice said, "Hello?"

"Hello," croaked Jones, and, "I'm trying to call Gilded Quill?"

"You got it," said the female, officious, faintly impatient, a touch irritated. But Jones steeled himself, told of reading the notice, of his irresistible desire to become the writer he *knew* he was born to be, and the voice gave him an address and meeting time and date. "Dues," concluded the voice, "are twenty-five dollars a year for probationers, cash preferred, checks on local banks only." Before he could ask about *probationers,* the voice hung up on him.

The address turned out to be a fast-food restaurant; Jones inquired at the counter, was directed by a kid wearing an apron and paper hat to a meeting room just off the corridor leading to the rest rooms. He entered without knocking, closed the door, the smell of deep frying and fetid toilets, sounds of pans clattering, muffled shouts from the kitchen following him in. Counting himself, there were twelve in the room. To the faces—indifferent, even a tad hostile?—turning to him, he said, "Gilded Quill? I'm Jones? I called about joining?"

"Be seated," said the aged woman who stood, supported by her aluminum walker, at the group's head, "we'll get to you shortly." He found a metal folding chair against the back wall, unfolded it—its joints screeched, embarrassing him—and sat far enough back to allow him to take it all in.

Eleven—twelve counting himself—Jones counted. The aged woman gripping her walker was addressed as "Madam President" by the membership. Her pink, mottled scalp shone through her thinning hair under the fluorescents. Her mouth made a masticating motion even as she spoke, as if she chewed a small cud of gum. Around her neck hung a large medallion, a little like a squash-blossom necklace, her chain of office, he later learned. She swayed often, to the brink of toppling, but did not, held fast to her walker with claw-like hands, fingers beringed, purple veins bulging.

She conducted business very efficiently. A square-built woman with a mannish haircut, approximately Jones's age, submitted the treasurer's report, barking numbers like a drill sergeant; Gilded Quill appeared to be quite solvent, even prosperous. The newsletter's editor, a benign, motherly woman, appealed to the membership to get items of interest for publication to her at their earliest possible convenience.

None of them, Jones thought, looked at all like writers. There was a very pale, emaciated woman of vague age; her skin was almost translucent, her jet-black hair too obviously dyed; a very old man, absolutely hairless—chemotherapy? Jones wondered—who sat very straight in his folding chair; a grossly fat man, oily gray-streaked hair, in a rumpled suit who smiled very broadly to himself; a black man, impeccably attired; another middle-aged man, asleep in his chair—he snorted, perhaps dreaming?—utterly ignored by the others; a cadaverous man, younger than Jones, his long hair in a tight ponytail, large gold hoop in one ear; a woman, also younger than Jones, an absolute stunner, tight sweater, long legs crossed to reveal just a tiny flash of sleek thigh, her perfume strong enough to penetrate the fast-food kitchen's cooking grease and the toilets' acidic stench . . .

Jones, Jones concluded with satisfaction, was the only writer-looking person there!

"First on the agenda," said Madam President, mouth and jaws working hard, "the awarding of the Bard's Hat," and she loosed one hand from her walker to reach into a plain box on the table beside her, withdrew what looked to Jones like a Revolutionary era tricorn. A hush fell on the room; the pots and pans and shouted orders came up a notch from the kitchen, along with a muted flushing noise. "The Hat of the Bard this month," she said, waving it over her head, unsteady on her feet, "is awarded to . . . Major Otto Deurwachter, United States Army, Retired!"

Jones politely joined in the applause for the hairless man who exhibited such excellent posture. He rose from his chair, snapped to attention, strode to the front, accepted the hat, placed it solemnly on his bald head, did a neat about-face, strode to his chair, about-faced, seated himself, back ramrod straight.

"Major Deurwachter is awarded our Hat for his annual self-published *State of the Nation's Moral Culture,* copies of which you all received at last month's meeting." There was another, briefer round of clapping Jones pretended to join in.

"And now," said Madam President, wobbling, "to Mr. Jones, who presents himself for consideration for membership in G.Q." Jones feared she would ask him to stand, speak, but she instead requested the membership to introduce themselves. "I," she said to begin, "am Gwendolyn Burris. My current project is a family chronicle, focused on my great-grandfather, one of the pioneer founders, much neglected, of our state. I have more than three thousand pages in rough draft," she added, "and do not foresee a completion date at this time." And in turn, they rose, faced Jones or their president, or the ceiling, or the nearest wall, pronounced their names, proclaimed their writing interests, their credits.

"I'm Agnes Snook," said the pale lady with too-black dyed hair, "and I write steamy romances, bodice rippers, under the pen name of Andrea Solange. My twenty-seventh paperback original comes out next month. And I expect to get that hat from the major for it!" she added, provoking titters.

"I'm Major Otto Deurwachter," said the major, tricorn on his head, at rigid attention. "I compose, publish, and distribute widely a yearly critique of this country's moral condition, and I don't mind saying I give it to them with both barrels right smack between the eyes!" There were knowing looks and more titters.

"My name is Orson Beadle," said the obese rumpled man, rising with difficulty. "I presume you know my regular column on the arts, literary and otherwise, in the Sunday supplement?" Jones did not, but smiled, nodded as if he did. He sensed reverence in the room for Orson Beadle, who eased his bulk carefully back into his chair.

"Elsie Rossman," said Elsie Rossman. "I edit my church's bulletin, so it's sort of natural for me to edit *Gilded Quill,* our newsletter, and I'll urge everyone again to get your items for inclusion to me before the deadline. I have a sample copy I'll give you later, during Social," she said to Jones in an aside. He smiled again, nodded, felt like a trick horse counting on command.

The stunner was even more stunning when she got to her feet, a fresh wave of her heady perfume wafting over Jones like a sweet mist. She said, "I'm Clarice McMahon, and I'm a poet, and I write poems about nature, and my first poem was just published in Orson's column last Sunday, for which I'm eternally grateful." And she gave Orson Beadle a smile that rendered Jones grateful to be alive. As she sat down, he filled his lungs with her scent, held his breath as long as he could before exhaling as quietly as possible.

"Jane Peplinski," said Jane Peplinski, and "Everyone calls me Pep for short. I write devotionals. Some of my better ones have been syndicated in newspapers, thanks to Orson, and religious publications." She spoke with a serenity Jones could only envy.

The kid with the ponytail and hoop earring stood, smiling directly at Jones, said in a soprano Jones might have expected from stunning McMahon, "Kyle Cox. I too pursue the muse Calliope, with, I add, however immodestly, at least a smidgen of success, though most people don't know the journals I publish in," and he smiled again at Jones, who tried not to respond, winked, and resumed his seat. Crossing one leg over the other, he bobbed his foot rapidly.

The treasurer stood, squared her broad shoulders into a posture the equal of Major Deurwachter's, said, "Bernice Bosworth. I'm active in the Marine Corps Reserve—" Major Deurwachter guffawed; Bernice gave him a look that frightened Jones. "As I was saying," she said, "U.S.M.C. Reserve. I'm my unit's official historian, and I'm interested in the historical role of women in the military, which I'm researching with an eye toward a long essay breaking down the Amazon myth I've already begun to outline." She did not look at Jones, sat down.

The dapper black man possessed a radio-quality voice. "I am Antoine Robinson," he said. "My work is of a scholarly nature, which is in keeping with my profession as a teacher of junior high school English. I would describe my literary bent as eclectic, not having yet settled on a specific genre or topic, though reincarnation begins to seem to me a rich vein worthy of exploring, at least in some point in my studies." Jones wished he had the money and confidence to dress like Antoine Robinson.

None of them looked like writers to Jones, but each, he saw, sported a large gold quill-shaped pin; McMahon the stunner wore hers on her hip.

The sleeper remained unnamed, undisturbed, snoring lightly in the brief silence before President Burris said to Jones, "And will you be so good as to introduce yourself?"

His palms suddenly damp, a thin film of sweat glossing his brow, rash of heat in the armpits and crotch of his clothes, stomach a-flutter, Jones forced himself up. All but the sleeper twisted in their chairs to look at him. He tried to find saliva to lick his lips, but he was dry as sand, mind blank and buzzing.

"Jones," Jones was able to say, and, "I just feel like I was born to be a writer." Almost in unison, the members of Gilded Quill turned back to face their president. Jones's legs almost deserted him as he eased back onto the hard seat of his folding chair.

President Burris reminded everyone it was custom to appoint a mentor to assist probationary members in any way possible, asked for a volunteer to liaison with Jones—Jones closed his eyes, prayed McMahon the stunner would put herself forth, but when he opened them it was Pep Peplinski, at least a decade his senior and plain as mud, who had her hand raised.

The meeting adjourned, the kid in the fast-food paper hat entered pushing a refreshment cart, all but the sleeper rose to begin the Social, and Pep Peplinski took his arm. Bitter coffees in hand, she nudged him into a corner where she bent his ear to the point he had to bite his lip to keep from screaming.

"Let me give you some pointers for your own good if you want to make it through probation," Pep Peplinski whispered to him; her breath was nasty.

"Is it that hard to join?" he asked.

"We're reasonably exclusive," she said. And she gave Jones a rundown of the membership. "Orson," she said, "is a power to be reckoned with." Jones watched the Sunday supplement columnist inhale bakery with both hands, his bulk teetering over the refreshment cart. "He publishes who he wants in that column. If he takes a shine to you, you're in. If not, he has the rudest form rejection slips."

Of Major Deurwachter, USA Retired, she said, "He's harmless unless you ask him about his service career, then he's a crashing bore. Nobody reads that annual diatribe of his, but he gets the Bard's Hat once a year to keep him happy. He was on vacation in Mexico once, his wife had some kind of seizure? He wouldn't take her to a doctor there, he stuffed her in the car and drove a thousand miles to the nearest veterans' hospital in Texas so she could be treated for free."

"Agnes," she said of the author of bodice rippers, "thinks she's so wonderful just because she makes tons of royalties."

"What about—what's her name?" Jones said, pretending to have forgotten. "Clarice something?"

"I suppose her poems are nice enough," Pep Peplinski said, her breath a rank rush in his face, "but she's so shameless the way she flirts with Orson to get in his column." Jones wondered what he might offer in exchange for her attention, could come up with nothing. Did she maybe jog?

"Is she married?" he asked.

"I really wouldn't know," said the author of devotionals. "Kyle," she said of the poet who wore the hoop earring and leered a lot, "is, frankly, to my mind a little strange, but he does have lovely manners. Bernice," she said, darting her eyes, enlarged by thick spectacles, "is an excellent treasurer, I'll grant her that."

"I think I recognized her voice from the telephone," Jones said.

"Antoine," Pep Peplinski said, nudging Jones to look at the marvelously groomed black man who talked with animation to Clarice McMahon, "is the most nicely dressed man I've ever known. I've made notes on some of his color combinations for my nephew, who doesn't know the first thing about dressing to advantage." Jones experienced a momentary dissatisfaction with his corduroy and turtle necks, felt relieved when it passed; Antoine Robinson did *not* look like a writer!

"I noticed," Jones said, jealous of the teacher-scholar for his proximity to the nature poet, who seemed to enjoy his conversation inordinately. "What about him?" Jones asked, nodding at the sleeping man.

Pep Peplinski made a dismissive sound with her bloodless lips. "We pay him not the slightest mind," she said, and, "His name is Volkayvich, something like that, Polish or Serbian or the like. He sleeps all the time, so we ignore him. He hasn't written anything in ages." Jones felt both fatigue and shame creep through his bones. "Elsie Rossman," she said without prompting, an edge in her voice, "I consider my rival. I'm just as qualified to edit *Gilded Quill* as she is!" Jones agreed.

"Your president seems a little fragile," he said as they watched Gwendolyn Burris try to manage coffee and a jelly doughnut while maintaining balance inside her walker's rails.

"She'll outlive us all," Pep Peplinski said, almost sadly. "But she can't succeed herself in office after this term. You just watch the politics break out when that time comes!" she added, her voice brightening. Jones assured her he would. "Your reading will be at the top of the agenda for us next month, you know," she said.

"Read?"

"You have to bring a manuscript and read it aloud to us. That's how you get off probation for full membership," she said.

"Read?" Jones repeated. "Out loud?"

"Your manuscript. Anything of your choice," she said, and, "The membership committee recommends to the membership sitting as a committee of the whole, and then we vote on you. In or out," she said. Jones felt suddenly giddy.

"Who's the membership committee?"

"Antoine," she said, "Bernice and Clarice." Jones felt his heart lift, just a bit. "I must circulate," she said, and left him with his bitter, now tepid cardboard cup of fast-food coffee. He mimed sipping, found a spot to abandon it, was about to slip out the door, prepared to say he needed to go to the lavatory if asked his destination, was stopped by the steely grip of Bernice Bosworth on his bicep.

"Dues," she said. "Due now if you plan on reading next month," her eyes locking his. He wrote her a check. At the door, he looked back at the membership of Gilded Quill, set to wave a cheerful good-bye if necessary. But no one seemed to notice: Clarice McMahon was now head-to-head with Orson Beadle. The sleeper did appear to stir, barely perceptibly, and as Jones exited, he caught Kyle Cox giving him a warm smile of farewell.

The first week, Jones felt charged with energy, brimming with enthusiasm, rock solid with confidence. Bursting with anticipation, he laid in a stock of supplies: a heavy loose-leaf binder for notes, outlines, and occasional commonplace observations, a ream of second sheets for his holograph drafts, a box of pencils and one of roll-ball pens, a fresh typewriter ribbon—a computer was out of the question on his budget—a ream of hammered bond for final clean copies. He did spring for a sturdy card table, his escritoire in this new life unfolding for him.

The second week, Jones established a work schedule he posted on his refrigerator door: he would write for four hours each evening after his daily stint at the branch library, reserving weekends for revision and close copyediting.

As the third week dawned, however, the bottom fell out of his life. He sat at his table per schedule, but nothing, absolutely nothing, happened. What was he to write *about?* Write about what you *know,* he reminded himself. But what *did* he know? Library procedures and routines. Dining out. Serious running. These topics, he saw at once, were totally sterile as sources of inspiration.

When he tried to recall his past, childhood, adolescence, college years, he was struck by amnesia. He tried to experiment with free association—something viable might emerge from his subconscious—but his amnesia transformed into aphasia. By the end of the third week, after trying to record his dreams immediately upon awakening, the only notes of substance, written in the aftermath of sleep's semi-fog, appeared to sketch an episode in which he spied from afar on Clarice McMahon as she engaged in some overtly suggestive pantomime. This so shamed him he threw it out with the week's garbage.

Jones knew what to call it: he was *Blocked!*

The second day of the fourth week, by an act of sheer will he had not imagined himself capable of, he sat at his table and scrawled, trembling like the flame of a sputtering candle, a pedestrian description of the sights, sounds, and smells he knew on routes he ran, spandex-clad, each morning. The third day was a limbo of almost clinical depression. The fourth, he typed the manuscript, a paltry six pages, double-spaced with wide margins, augmenting the draft with what he prayed would pass for delicate, even sensuous reflections—how it *felt* to run through the streets in dawn's light.

The fifth day, his mail included the new issue of *Gilded Quill;* there, on the first of its four pages, blared the announcement of his imminent reading—how large, he wondered in near-panic, was their mailing list? *Jones Probation Reading,* it began. *Don't miss this important and exciting event!* it concluded. Nauseous, he had no desire to read of the membership's recent accomplishments under the heading, *Publications, Awards, Professional Recognition.*

The day upon him—how time flew!—he called in sick, alternated between lethargy, short bursts of rage, and practicing the delivery of his text before his bathroom mirror. As the hour approached, Jones, exhausted, dressed in his writer's garb, having attained a state of resignation; he felt the way he imagined a convicted felon awaiting sentencing might.

He did falter, but only for an instant. They were all there in their folding chairs, President Burris under a pale halo of light from a single ceiling fluorescent, facing him, in her walker, across their heads; no one turned to look at him. The room seemed darker, dimmed for his presentation, but the odor of deep-frying and the toilets seeped in from behind him. His manuscript crackled in his hands.

But then he looked at each of them in turn. The membership committee, Agnes Snook, Antoine Robinson, and the stunning poet of nature, sat up front, pads and pens at the ready to take running notes—Snook's too-black hair gleamed in the halo's aura; Robinson's absurdly snappy blazer was set off by a garish ascot at his throat; Clarice McMahon's too-dense perfume assaulted his nostrils. In the second row, the retired major was ridiculous, tricorn Bard's Hat perched on his hairless skull. To his right, Kyle Cox smirked, legs crossed, at some private joke. To the major's left, Orson Beadle was a heap of excess flesh wrapped in a shabby suit. Behind them were the editor of *Gilded Quill,* clutching a narrow reporter's notebook, Bernice Bosworth, her shoulders broader than Jones's, and his mentor, Pep Peplinski, who did turn to him, offering a wan smile—of encouragement? Last, directly in front of Jones, the Polish or Serbian sleeper slept his deep sleep.

None of them, Jones thought with satisfaction, look at all like *writers!* Despite, he thought, their membership pins.

"We await your words, Mr. Jones," said the president, and Jones marched to her side like a soldier, wheeled to face them as Gwendolyn Burris slid to one side, the rubber tips of walker squealing on the floor's tiles. "Give us," she said, "anything by way of introduction you care to."

Jones, resolute, took a breath, held it a beat, fixed his eyes on Clarice McMahon's exquisite knee, glistening in hose, exhaled, said, "I'm not sure what to call this. I don't even have a title," and read his six pages describing the experience of running the streets of his neighborhood in dawn's light.

It was the supreme humiliation of his life to date. He had hoped for expressions of interest—perhaps even delight?—to form on their faces. He had feared there would be hoots, catcalls, jeers, heckling.

There was nothing; the membership of Gilded Quill, their badges winking like doubloons in a twilight, simply sat there, perfectly deadpanned. No one budged, no one blinked, not a yawn or a sneer among them. The sleeper did not snore or snort or wheeze.

Finished, his mouth so dry his lips were glued to his teeth, he stood in a silence so total it echoed until President Burris said, "Thank you. We request that you excuse yourself now so the membership committee can make its recommendation and we can discuss with candor before we vote. I'm sure you understand," she said, and, "You will be informed of our decision."

Jones somehow found his way around the still silent, immobile seated bodies, found the door, left the fast-food restaurant, disposing of his manuscript in a trash receptacle on his way outside. Home, he stayed up far beyond his usual bedtime, waiting for a phone call that did not come.

Nor did he hear from Gilded Quill the next day, nor the next. It was nearly a month, on the eve of the next meeting, that Pep Peplinski telephoned. He had, however, received the new issue of *Gilded Quill;* he read, filled with loathing, that Major Deurwachter graciously passed the Bard's Hat to Agnes Snook, and that Orson Beadle had accepted half a dozen new nature lyrics by Clarice McMahon for publication in his Sunday column. Jones's reading was noted in strictly neutral terms.

"You don't have to say it, I already know," Jones said.

"It was a difficult decision. We agonized," Pep Peplinski said.

"I could tell all the time I was reading," he said. "Rejected," he said, and, "You people probably think you know everything about everything. I just sometimes wonder what's the point of anything," he said, and wondered what point there was to his life, to anything at all.

"But we *didn't* reject you," Pep Peplinski said. Jones felt his heart rise up, his head clear, a surge through his limbs.

"I'm in?"

"Basically," Pep Peplinski said, and explained it to him. As he listened, Jones felt his joy drain slowly, his spirits deflate like a balloon with a slow leak.

The membership had deadlocked, five for admitting him to membership, five against, one abstaining. "Of course I can't reveal who voted how, that's strictly confidential," she said, and, "I suppose it's what they call a hung jury?" A compromise motion to grant Jones an extended probation—final dispensation to be resolved at some indefinite date—passed unanimously with one abstention. "The one abstention doesn't affect it at all. The thinking was to let you choose when you're ready to read for us again," she said.

"But I can come to the meetings?" he said.

"Indeed," she said. "Of course we can't give you your Gilded Quill pin or membership card, but you do enjoy all other benefits. You'll receive the monthly newsletter, for example, and you're free to participate fully in all activities. I do hope this is acceptable to you?" Pep Peplinski said.

"Can I think about it?" he asked, and was told the membership would like an answer not later than tomorrow's regularly scheduled meeting. "I have to think about it," Jones said.

And he did, alternating between fits of anger, despair, and hope. Who were they, that cranky gang of eccentrics, Jones thought, to reject *him!* What, Jones asked himself, ever made him think he was a *writer?* Didn't this mean, he wondered, they saw promise in his writing? Shouldn't he be encouraged?

So Jones accepted an extended, indefinite probationary status with Gilded Quill.

For the first six months, he sat, mute, beside Volkayvich, the always-sleeping Pole or Serb, listened, observed, tried to learn. He paid rapt attention to the treasurer's reports, strained not to miss a word as members read and critiqued new work, discussed projects in progress, and announced successes big and small, nodded judiciously during noisy—sometimes acrimonious—workshop sessions, took notes when marketing strategies were debated.

Jones found it all wonderfully stimulating, found his appetite keen, his sleep deeper and more restorative, his hours on the job at the branch library seemingly shorter and more fulfilling, his running efficiency honed. He did not find it odd that he was not provoked to attempt any writing, but no one ever alluded to the terms of his probation. He would very much have liked to display the gilded pin on the lapel of his corduroy jacket, but not enough to put words on paper.

He happily joined in the refreshment cart Socials, worked at being affable, friendly, developed a taste for the stale bakery and lukewarm coffee.

Six months under his belt, he felt confident enough to suggest a new activity, an idea that came to him in a dream one night, recorded upon awakening, developed as he ran that morning.

Recognized and given the floor by President Burris, he said, "Working in a library, I naturally see all the new acquisitions that come in. We have a special rack where they're displayed. What I thought was, if the membership was at all interested, I'd be more than happy to sort of present a sort of report on new books that might be of interest. I'd enjoy the reading, and it could be helpful if people were kept up on new things coming out—fiction, poetry, whatever—for their own work. I know," he said, "it can possibly be inspiring to see what's being done on the national literary scene, as it were?"

A motion to this effect, instituting a monthly agenda activity, *New and Notable on the National Scene,* put by Pep Peplinski, seconded by Antoine Robinson, passed unanimously—the sleeper recorded as abstaining—after only perfunctory discussion.

And so Jones created his niche in the ranks of Gilded Quill. The selection of new books, the reading, proved arduous, but he discovered a great untapped capacity for discipline deep within himself, and the members' response to his monthly presentations was unfailingly warm. "I must tell you how much everyone just *lives* for your little book reports!" Pep Peplinski confided.

And Jones discovered he truly enjoyed the fellowship of each Social.

He commiserated with Gwen Burris when she lamented the bylaws precluding a run for reelection to another term of office. "Oh," she said, "I'll pass the gavel with grace, but it galls me no end inside!"

He heard Agnes Snook's talk of her agent, sales, subsidiary rights, and royalties with no trace of envy. "Hollywood," Agnes said, "is the target of this new one. I'm putting in so much sex and violence they won't dare pass when we shop it on the coast."

Major Deurwachter had fascinating war stories to tell when Jones was able to get him off politics and the decay of the nation's soul. "So I put my carbine muzzle up under this gook's chin, told him he'd answer what we asked or I'd blow what he used for brains all over the bunker's ceiling," the retired major said, describing his role as a young draftee in the Great October Push of 1952.

"I'd like to see something of yours to consider for my column if the spirit ever moves you," Orson Beadle offered, speaking through a mouth full of day-old cruller.

Elsie Rossman always asked him for something she could use in the newsletter. Jones suggested a comprehensive list of recommended reading titles; she said she would give the matter serious thought, but space was a problem.

Pep Peplinski shared her campaign strategies with him. "Gwen won't support me. She won't support anyone trying for *her* job! Dog in the manger. But I've counted noses, I think I'm close to a lock. Do you think you have any influence with Kyle Cox?" she asked. Jones said he didn't know, but promised her his vote. "Oh, you can't *vote*, dear," she said. "Only full members can vote. Which makes me think we must find a way to get you off probation. By hook or by crook," she said.

Kyle Cox seemed receptive to Jones's appeal on behalf of Pep; as long as he kept his hands to himself, Jones didn't mind Kyle's innuendoes.

Antoine Robinson was always a pleasure; Jones made notes on his attire, even though he preferred his corduroy and turtlenecks, even though he couldn't afford a new wardrobe.

And he liked Bernice Bosworth, admired the precision of her bookkeeping; when Bernice, who always greeted him with a handshake, squeezed too hard, Jones gave as good as he got.

Clarice McMahon was a treat he always saved for the end of the Socials. Just as they were about to go their separate ways, the refreshment cart reduced to crumbs too small for even Orson Beadle, the coffee urn yielding only a last sour dribble, Jones always approached her, breathed deep of her pungent flowery aromas, said something like, "Any new poems hot off the press, Clarice?" And Clarice always rewarded him: a show of her snowy teeth, the arch of a delicately drawn eyebrow, the shift of her urgent bosom in his general direction. Life, Jones thought, could be good!

The culmination was Jones's election to full membership, engineered by Pep Peplinski. Writers, Pep argued, were by definition also readers. Reading was as vital to their respective crafts as quiet solitude or epiphanies. Did not Jones, then, serve a vital purpose in Gilded Quill with his monthly presentations of the new and notable? The vote was close, the motion carried by Volkayvich, the sleeping Pole or Serb, roused from slumber by Jones to cast his ballot, the first time in collective memory he had not been recorded as abstaining.

Jones went on to swing the presidency for Pep Peplinski in a close vote over Elsie Rossman. Pep's first act in office was to present Jones with his gilded membership pin.

And, ever after, Jones wore it on the lapel of his jacket, one evening a month at meetings, but also daily, on the job, where he was sure his co-workers noticed it, though none presumed to ask what it was, what it represented. And he wore his gilded quill on his spandex as he ran through the streets each dawn, aware how it twinkled, catching the first rays of the new day's sun.

Q: Questing

Quaid answers to his name, but likes to be called Q, which is how he addresses himself in moments of what he considers profound introspection. *Q,* thinks Q, *for queries.* As in: *How'd you get where you are, Q?* And: *And just exactly where is it you think you are, Q?* And, more to the point: *Where, Q, do you think you're headed?* These questions pose themselves most often when he's flying the freeways. Such answers as have come to him so far are unsatisfactory, but he persists. He thinks of his existence as something on the order of a mission, a search, seeking.

Q, thinks Q, *for quest.*

Monday through Friday, he maintains a soothing illusion of confidence. Monday through Friday, Q flies the freeways. To and from the four classes he teaches, one each at four schools located in the far four corners of this sprawling megalopolis. The four part-time teaching gigs at four schools generate a near poverty-level income, a most spare living. Q doesn't, can't, won't call it a life, not just yet.

Monday through Friday, Q flies the freeways to and from the four women he courts without, to date, success. Of these four women, only one is alluring, one has apparent psychological problems, one makes him feel intellectually inadequate, one may be less than wholly female in orientation. None has been willing to engage in sex with him.

But on the freeways, Monday through Friday, driving defensively against the relentless high-speed, seemingly suicidally reckless traffic, Q takes heart from the mere fact of motion, mobility, movement. Flying the freeways, to and from, Q is encouraged by the concept, however only theoretical, of direction, destination, of implied goal.

It is the weekend, Saturdays and Sundays, Q dreads, fears. Because weekends are stasis; Q is in stasis, going nowhere. Weekends are forty-eight hours of potentially devastating considerations. In stasis, Q might be compelled to truly, seriously think. Sometimes he cannot avoid it.

He thinks of his four part-time teaching gigs at four schools: City U., remedial composition; Martin Luther College, expository prose; Pere Marquette College; introductory rhetoric; St. Mary's College, Shakespeare's Major Plays. He thinks of the total of seventy-six students he neither likes nor respects, most of whom exhibit for Q only indifference and disdain.

He thinks of the four women he pursues in seeming vain: Marinelle, who is fat and mannish; Vonda, who is sexy, but ignorant; Patti, who is intelligent and professionally focused, but moderately androgynous in appearance; Belle, who is the most compliant, but so moody he suspects she's maybe chemically out of balance.

He contemplates the stacks of student essays he should read and grade. He thinks of reading he has assigned, but not yet read himself. He broods about lectures and exercises he should prepare.

And he worries for the condition of his vehicle, a 1980 Honda: knocking rod, balding tires, broken exhaust pipe, loose steering, screeching brakes, rusted panels, tentative ignition. His Honda worries him most of all, for if it should fail, he will be immobile, in stasis, unable to fly the freeways, going nowhere.

In an effort to escape such weekend musings, Q resorts to alcohol, marijuana, and televised sports. Q will even watch golf. When he succeeds by these devices, his weekends are a kind of only semi-static blur. Booze or weed or television, or the combination of any two, sometimes all three, make for such peace as Q can know over a weekend.

There is no comfort in his cramped apartment, no haven. Though the rent is low, the neighborhood is bad. There is no solace in flaked paint, cracking plaster, and gurgling plumbing, no ease in the faint, pervasive stench of the worn carpeting that suggests the previous tenant kept cats, only infrequent relief from his fellow-tenants' raucous lives, no refuge from the thick cooking odors hanging in the building's hallways.

The sole mercy mitigating Q's oppressive weekend is the simple certainty of its limited duration, in the promise of Monday coming, when he can rise to its new light to hit the freeways for another week. He has not prepared his classes, does not believe any breakthrough with any of his four women is imminent, but at least, provided his 1980 Honda cranks, he will be on the move again. And he sets forth, Honda roaring and belching, pinging and clattering, on the road to somewhere, flying the freeways.

Monday is City U., English 101-Remedial, twenty-one of the least qualified of the poorly qualified, since City is open enrollment. Q has not graded the batch of essays he promised to return today, so must, negotiating the morning freeway rush, come up with a ploy. Q has a quiver full of ploys to fall back on when he needs to cover his incompetence or neglect.

There is a family emergency ploy, but Q has already killed off a parent—both of his are long deceased—put a nonexistent sibling in intensive care with life-threatening trauma, already conjured two bouts of serious flu out of thin air. Mentally sorting his stock, he discards the blatant no-show due to fictional car trouble; he's pulled that twice already this semester. He passes over the weak assertion that he has lost-then-only-this-morning-found his briefcase, and elects the story that he became so engrossed in close reading and extensive commentary that he simply could not finish the work, which he'll promise on his honor to return at Wednesday's meeting. Q wonders how many, if any, of his remedial comp students will buy into that one.

And Monday is the freeway, his mental fancy footwork complicating and increasing the risks on all sides of his wheezing Honda. Q brakes to allow a Yuppie's Volvo to dart off the entry ramp in front of him, driver's ear glued to a cell phone. Q spots a gap, pulls out and floors the accelerator to pass an oblivious soccer mom in a van traveling a dozen miles below the speed limit. Q hunches at the wheel, eyes darting to his tilted rearview mirror, in terror of the growling semi tailgating him. Back in the slow lane, his Honda rocks in the wakes of a stream of commuters blowing by on his left. A crick forms and deepens between his shoulders, his knuckles ache from his death-grip, his calf cramps, his lumbar region throbs. But he's moving!

How'd you get where you are, Q? Oh, thinks Q, it's a chain of events acting upon a nature ripe from birth for aimless, mindless response to unseen, unexpected ur-forces! He doesn't like to get into this in any detail. He's diverted, in any case, by the fact of Monday, the freeways to City U., his remedial comp class, the reassurance of routine. *Q,* thinks Q, *for quotidian.*

With luck, he finds a parking space, sprints across campus to the Humanities Building, a massive concrete bunker-like structure he thinks suitable to be adequate shelter against missile bombardment. Then up four flights of ringing metal stairs, into his classroom just in time; were he even a minute late, at least half those present would have walked. It had happened. He would not have minded.

Q faces his remedials.

They're a motley lot, their attitudes toward him expressed dramatically by their choices of seats to the back and sides of the room, as far from Q as possible. They sprawl, slump, slouch, the only eye contact made by a trio of glowering African Americans. The dominant mode of attire is grunge and head-shop chic. One acne-scarred girl sports garish tattoos and a gold nose-ring. One thug, T shirt and farmer's overalls, is barefoot. A bearded, pony-tailed man Q's age could pass for a reclusive survivalist, complete with camouflage battle dress, is probably a Viet vet. Q prays he never asks about *his* time in country; Q spent his tour in Nam at Long Binh, assigned to the stockade's laundry, a R.E.M.F. never once in harm's way, but lies about his service whenever he thinks he can get by with it. Q sighs. His remedials sigh a collective response.

He kills as much time as he can with a slow roll call, comments banally on the weather and freeway traffic, tells a bad political joke, then gives the spiel on the papers he has not finished grading, his utter absorption in the task, rattling off a number of encouraging elements emerging in their prose, all this from whole cloth. He promises to have them in hand come Wednesday, and as a salve for their disappointment, which is not evident, dismisses class very early. Nothing mitigates the choral sense of relief that rises toward him, after which, like water running swiftly downhill, his remedials exit the classroom in smug, appeased silence.

Except for Salvatore, Q's connection. Salvatore is the perfect type of an urban street-rat, wraith-thin, sallow skin, lank, greasy hair, black garb set off with chrome studs, bad teeth, chewed nails, broken shoes. Q has an arrangement with Sal.

"You looking to cop, Prof?" asks Sal.

"If and what I can," says Q, adding, "And you the man," in an effort to sound suitably hip. He scores a dime baggie, good stuff, though less potent than what Q learned to enjoy, along with binge boozing, in the Nam.

In exchange for Sal's weed at discount, Q will give him an A for the course, having excused this slime from all assignments in the bargain. Q knows that if there were an even mildly appealing woman in the class who would offer him sex for a grade, he'd agree to that in a mini-second. He lost his virginity to a prostitute while on R & R in Bangkok, and has for the most part been frustrated in that regard since. This accounts for his playing four women at the same time—anything to up the odds in his favor!

Q, thinks Q, *for quim!*

Sal takes his money, high-fives him, slithers out of the classroom. After a quick stop at the nearest men's to wash Sal's touch off his hand and stow the baggie in his briefcase, Q is off to the student union commons. Monday is also fat, mannish Marinelle.

And there she is, awaiting Q at their customary corner table, away from the smelly cafeteria line and the clots of jabbering, loitering students. Marinelle *does* look mannish!

Her hair is cut shorter than the fashion for most men, her head a squarish block atop her near-square torso. Marinelle wears slacks and a blazer and sturdy brogans. Her hands are large, sausage-fingers blunt. She wears no makeup, no jewelry, no scent Q can detect. When he scoped out the talent in the English department office, she was the best prospect, clearly too plain—even homely—to be enmeshed in any relationship. The gal at the desk facing Marinelle's was the one took his eye, a certified stunner, all bleached coiffure, blood-red lipstick and nail polish, glittering earrings and rings and bracelets, short skirt, heels, creamy legs, one blouse button too many unbuttoned to display cleavage that halted Q's breath a full beat, her perfume a luscious redolence of lilacs in full bloom.

The stunner obviously out of his class by a mile or more, Q bypassed her to chat up Marinelle. He thinks he may have aimed too low in settling on Marinelle, but any port in a storm.

She greets him with, "You blew your class off again, didn't you, Q."

"I let them out early for a little treat. They deserve a break from the grind now and then."

"Bull fucking shit," she says.

"So are we on?" Q asks to get her off the topic.

"On for what?"

"We've talked about this before, Marinelle. My place? We could rent a video, drink a little wine, I'll roll us a couple doobies. Some good shit just came my way." He's not absolutely sure he'd like to finagle Marinelle into the sack, wonders if she has too much body hair, doesn't shave her legs or armpits, has better defined musculature than he.

"In a pig's ass, Q," says Marinelle. And she says, "You're about as subtle as a kick in the balls, you know that?"

Semi-relieved, Q says, "So, you suggest. I'm planning on working in the library all afternoon, we can take off as soon as you get off."

"Bowling?" says Marinelle. "I feel like maybe bowling a few lines. I've got a yen for some of those pickled eggs they got at Century Lanes." Q's stomach lurches.

"Doesn't much excite," he says. They have gone bowling several times; Marinelle has never lost a game or a beer frame. She crows when she wins.

"How about shoot some skeet? That gun club down by the lake lets you buy a daily membership. I haven't hoisted a shotgun since who laid the Chink."

Q says, "I had enough of guns to last me in Nam."

"Will you can that crap, Q? You sat on your butt and toked in Vietnam." At least she does not, as she has more than once, call him a rear-echelon motherfucker. They compromise on going to the batting cage at Sports-O-Rama; Marinelle says she played very competitive fast-pitch softball in her youth. Q believes her. "You probably swing like a pussy," she says. When he denies this, she says, "Loser treats," and, "Ain't got a hair on you if you don't take the bet!" He accepts the challenge, immediately regretting it.

Time for her to return to her desk, they embrace good-bye there in the corner of the commons, the rattle of metal trays and tableware, the babble of student laughter and vulgar language, cigarette smoke and steamed food smells mingling in the air. Her bearhug tests Q's spine and ribs.

He kills the rest of the day chipping away at some of his remedials' essays. He reads some all the way to the end, reads portions of some, ends up only tearing the corners off last pages; when his students question this, he'll tell them he wrote a summary comment there, then thought better of it. This ploy has worked before.

He picks Marinelle up when she clocks out, they go to the Sports-O-Rama's batting cage, where she embarrasses Q, hitting her balls farther, at higher speeds, than he can. He pays the freight. One of Marinelle's best features is her willingness to go dutch, no small consideration on Q's income, so this debacle hurts doubly. And she rubs it in, says, "How's come you're so wimpy at sports, Q?" He alibis by telling her his parents were past forty when he was born, wholly unexpected, that his father kept his distance while his mother coddled him.

"It made me the kind of a kid kept to himself a lot," he says.

To which she replies, "It shows, Q."

When he drops her off at her apartment, they do kiss a little, dryly, outside her door. When Q tries to cop a feel, she fends him off easily; she's clearly the stronger, more fit. Marinelle is many pounds overweight, but there's iron under that excess!

Depressed, disgruntled, and out the cost of the batting cage, only the freeways home soothe his withered spirits. Sal's baggie will get him through the late evening, and, Honda belching cloudy, oil-laden exhaust, weaving in and out of traffic at great risk, he's in motion!

Q, thinks Q, *for quelled again.*

Tuesday mornings in his apartment don't trouble Q. He sleeps in a little, slumber abetted by Sal's pot last night. And rises eagerly because Tuesday means Vonda, at St. Mary's. Shakespeare's Major Plays is an early evening class, so he meets Vonda on the campus in the afternoon, and this prospect is such that Q can even put in some time on paper grading if he's in the mood, doesn't turn to his TV for auto racing or co-ed body building competitions or Australian rules football.

When Q hits the freeways for St. Mary's—and Vonda—he is charged, exuberant, focused. Vonda stirs his libido like no other. She has a girlie-mag body, silky long hair, deliciously pale skin, a stripper's strut he dearly loves to observe from the rear.

Q, thinks Q, *for quarry!*

On the downside, Vonda is dumb as a post. She has betrayed to him her belief that London is a nation distinct from England, didn't know the date of Pearl Harbor, much less Hastings, and mispronounces myriad words. Because she is so much younger than Q, she knows only what he tells her of Vietnam, leaving him free to fabricate war stories that spellbind her. When she asked him what he did through the years since, he told her he was finding himself, and she was incurious enough not to request elaboration.

But there's an upside to this, because her classmates, demure Catholic girls all, are almost her peers with respect to ignorance, so Q's free to wing his lectures on the Bard.

And he's flying the freeways again, to St. Mary's, to Vonda! His Honda trembles like a wino with the shakes, but he passes with aplomb more than one junker older than his, flips the bone at an arrogant young man in a Porsche, maddeningly inscrutable behind reflecting shades, who blows his horn to clear Q from his path, tailgates a stretch limo without trepidation. Q's on the move!

Exiting the freeway, Q is thrust into a different world, one he wishes he had been born to.

St. Mary's campus is all landscaped, barbered greensward, dotted with copses, ponds, and elaborate, well-tended floral beds. When there's a breeze, the swish of freeway traffic is obscured, the air spiced with the trill and warble of songbirds. Founded by the Sisters of Golgotha well before the Great Depression, the college buildings are mini-cathedrals of dark gray granite, the hours announced by crystalline chimes. One of the few last bastions of religious higher educational tradition, as much finishing school as college, St. Mary's caters to the overly privileged daughters of solidly affluent Catholic families who still keep the Faith, or at least its forms. In addition to the conventional, non-career-oriented liberal arts, St. Mary's offers European summer travel, horsemanship, and numerous retreats to maintain and enhance the young ladies' moral fiber.

Q feels deliciously subversive when he fantasizes about Vonda.

He finds the dark interiors, all subdued tile and polished wainscoting and stained-glass windows, a tad oppressive, and the teaching sisters, who wear headgear putting him in mind of Arab terrorists, their modernized uniform frocks a pale prison-blue, detract a little from his delight. The beads at their waists clack as they walk the shadowy halls, and they seem—rightly, Q concedes—to regard him with suspicion. But he bucks up, hands out smiles and greetings all around as he picks up his junk mail and heads back outdoors to find Vonda.

And she waits for him under a massive shade tree, on a stone bench donated by the Class of 1928, legs crossed, foot bobbing in time to a fast tempo Q hopes is a sign of strong emotional desires and needs. "Hi, babe," says Q.

"Hi, Q." There is no kissing or embracing on the campus, public displays of affection discouraged, faculty-student relationships of a personal nature anathema.

"Did you think about it?" he asks. It always takes several seconds for Vonda to respond to anything, as if she must rehearse her words to arrange them in meaningful syntax before speaking.

"I did," she says at last, "but my mom always wants me home right after night class. She says it's not safe out alone at night."

"Your mother's very conservative," says Q. "You wouldn't be alone, you'd be with me." Another downside is Q's inability to maneuver Vonda into seeing him after sunset. He's contemplated the odds against her agreeing to find a custodian's closet in one of the buildings, sharing his Honda's back seat in the parking lot, crawling into a bower in one of the wooded areas; they're too great to risk any such suggestion. He frankly has no strategy, no tactic, yet, but Vonda's enough to keep him working on it.

"Can I tell you something once, Q?"

"Tell away."

"I'm not getting it. I just don't catch on to this Shakespeare stuff." He'd hoped for some intimate revelation, but, then, Vonda often converses in non sequiturs.

"You're doing fine," Q lies. He lies to Vonda with abandon. He has lied about his military service, about his age—Vonda is almost a quarter-century his junior—about Shakespeare, about her progress in the course, about the sincerity and tenderness of his regard for her. An upside is Vonda seems to believe everything he says.

"I won't be able to do the term paper," she says.

"I'll help you with it," Q says, suddenly seeing the possibilities rife in tutoring sessions in his apartment. "Don't fret over it," he says, and says, "So what else's new in your life?" He's fishing for an endearment.

"Nothing," she says, disappointing, then says, "Oh yeah. I almost forgot. I was watching this educational channel you said I should?" Q likes to think he can sophisticate Vonda, if only a little.

"And?" He waits for her to arrange her words.

"And there was this one program. About these boy singers in Italy way back, they operated on so they could sing high notes?"

"*Castrati,*" says Q, thinks this might lead to a discussion of matters he'd like to get candid about with her.

"Yeah. I was wondering. Q, did they, like, cut off their vocal chords of these little boys to make them sing like they had women's voices?"

Q says, "Something like that," and would have elaborated, informed, but it's time for their class, the bell tower's chimes calling. Walking across the greensward, Q allows himself to straggle, get an extended look at Vonda's so delectable posterior. It all but dizzies him!

Q, Q thinks, *for queasy!*

Q savors calling the roll here. The dozen females arrayed in a seminar-style half-circle make him think of a chaste harem. Each and every one embodies the rich fruit of entrenched, honorable prosperity. Their hair shines, faces bright, postures demure. Their bright eyes regard him with parentally ingrained respect. They answer cheerily to their names, flash smiles, pens poised over notebooks, at the ready to record anything he tells them is significant, might show up on an exam. Eager to follow anything he reads from the text, their books lie open to *Hamlet.* Q reads from the plays a lot, fancies they find his voice thrilling, his interpretations dramatic.

For St. Mary's, for Shakespeare's Major Plays, Q's major ploy strikes him as near-genius quality. The day he signed on for this gig, he dashed to the college's small library to check out every critical and historical study of Shakespeare. St. Mary's faculty are permitted to hold books for the semester's duration, which means his students can't get their hands on anything that would betray his lectures for the pure bunk they are. The books lie safely locked in the Honda's trunk, will be returned only after the final exam and the receipt of his last St. Mary's paycheck.

On the first day of class, already targeting Vonda, he discouraged them from reading any of the text's introductory material or appendices; these he mines for some substance to leaven his discourse, lest it sound like absolute doubletalk. Tonight, he reads the passages in *Hamlet* where the prince makes vulgar puns in dialogue with Ophelia and his mother. When he runs out of these, Q turns to the topic of theatrical production in Elizabethan times.

The highlight tonight is Vonda raising her hand—Q encourages discussion; nothing fills the time and makes students think they're learning like class discussions!

"Professor Quaid," she says—he has repeatedly cautioned her not to call him Q in the presence of others, is always happily surprised she remembers, given her short attention span. "Professor," she says, pronouncing it *perfesser,* "why did they call it The Globe I was wondering?"

"Because," says Q, pleased with his immediate riposte, "Vonda," he says, "it was globe-shaped." At once, Vonda and her classmates write this in their notebooks. *Q,* thinks Q, *for quick-witted!*

He dismisses them, as always, at least ten minutes early. Five minutes, he thinks, doesn't count, and it's no high crime to steal five more. If ever asked, he'll say he doesn't want these girls walking the campus in the dark.

The others gone, all saying good-bye, some how much they enjoyed tonight's class, Q escorts Vonda to the parking lot. She drives a sporty convertible of foreign make he is too proud to ask the brand name of. He steers her to his Honda, which looks less shabby in the fading light. When he kisses her in this falling dark, she's all tongue and writhing and snorting breathing through her delicate nose. Looks, thinks Q, and money, and an obvious potential for passion! Who needs brains?

When, without warning, she extricates herself from his arms and mouth, says, "I better go, Q," he feels like weeping.

"We could sit in my car for a while. Talk," he pleads.

"My mom'll kill me if I'm late," she says.

"Okay, but don't forget about the term paper. I'll help you. Consider it a signed contract."

"A contract?" She pronounces it *contrack.* "Oh. Okay. I get it. Maybe. If my mom says." That—mom's permission—Q thinks, will surely put the kibosh on that fantasy!

Q, thinks Q, *for quashed.*

"I'll watch until you get in your car so you'll be safe," he says. There's just enough light left to afford Q a long last vision of her exquisite rump.

Were it not for the freeway home, he'd feel cheated by life, snake-bit, but his Honda, one headlight dead, roars and rattles one-eyed through the deepening night, and this motion, his mobility, restores his equilibrium.

So ends Tuesday, St. Mary's, Shakespeare's Major Plays, Vonda. All, thinks Q, is maybe well that just might possibly still end well, as the Bard could have said. *Q,* thinks Q, *for quotable!*

Rising from his narrow, lumpy bed isn't easy for Q on Wednesday. Wednesday is City's remedials again, and fat, mannish Marinelle, and, worse, the dour, doctrinaire Lutherans of Martin Luther College, expository prose. And Martin Luther is Belle, about whose mental health Q is dubious. When his alarm clangs, he's tempted to roll over, sleep in, call in sick, but remembers he's exhausted that ploy for this semester.

Q, thinks Q, *for quota*.

But there are some saving graces. He'll cop a nickel baggie from Sal; he's closest to carnal intimacy with Belle, even if she doesn't seem to enjoy the contact much. This could be the day! And the freeways beckon, so he does rise, does wash and shave and evacuate his bladder and bowels, loads his briefcase, is off in his stuttering Honda.

Where are you, Q? he asks as he dodges morning rush traffic, maneuvering between the seemingly oblivious and the road-enraged, tires thumping ominously on the concrete's joints.

He's on the margins of contemporary urban life, living paycheck to paycheck, he confesses. He's underpaid for the nonperformance of four shit-jobs. He's strung out between four women he doesn't really care all that much for. He's of course without a clue as to his future prospects, if any. But, he reminds himself, he's moving!

At City U., his remedials, sullen as usual, don't disappoint, don't openly protest the arbitrary grades he's slapped on their essays. He kills this fifty minutes at the blackboard, chalking selected student sentences to illustrate egregiously illiterate errors in grammar, diction, and mechanics. Dismissed, they leave the room like paroled felons.

But Sal does disappoint. "Can't help you today, Prof," he says, "my stash's way down. You know," he adds, "I'm thinking of getting out of drugs totally. I mean, you know how many narcs there are on this campus? Man, it's, like, too hairy for the bread you can glom."

"How about Friday? It's a long weekend coming, Sal, I need a little help from my friend!" Sal says maybe, he can't commit.

Q spends only a short interlude in the commons with Marinelle on her break. "I'm not on for tonight," he tells her, thinking of Belle.

"Suit yourself, Q," is all Marinelle has to say. When he says he's sorry not to be up for something this evening, she says, "I'll buy that, Q. You're about the sorriest specimen I know. You really can be a peckerhead sometimes! I think your mama must have toilet trained you too early and weaned you too late, Q." Marinelle, he suspects, is a lost cause, is happily surprised to realize he couldn't care less. He'd like to know if she's ever felt lesbian tendencies, but lacks the courage to ask.

The freeway to Martin Luther doesn't lift Q's spirits much. Marinelle's ready to dump him, and despite her fat, mannish appearance, her masculine vulgarity of expression, and her perhaps inverted sexual orientation, it's no fun being shown the door. And if Sal stops dealing, where'll he find a new connection? And Belle's black moods unnerve Q, as does the ambiance of Martin Luther and his stolidly orthodox students there. He nearly loses his chugging, huffing Honda to a rusty clunker operated by a pony-tailed thug who brakes without warning in front of him.

Martin Luther is a beautiful campus, the peer of St. Mary's, but once inside the admin building, the gloomy, dim-lit atmosphere oppresses him, and Belle, propped on her elbows at the information desk, intensifies this ubiquitous miasma. She looks up as he approaches, but doesn't lift her chin from her cupped hands. "Hi, love," says Q, forcing a smile.

"Hello" is her entire response, after which she returns her mouth to its perpetual disgruntled pout.

"How're we feeling this fine day?"

"I don't know," says Belle. And says, "Sometimes I don't see the point of anything."

"You need cheering up," he says.

"If you say so."

"I do. And I'm just the one to do it! Meet you here when you get off?"

"I guess," is the best Belle can muster. Q's libido, normally sparked by Belle's potential, wilts, but he sneaks a quick kiss of her unopened lips, and affects a jaunty stride as he hurries off to his class.

Q feels like a leper, complete with bell and sign around his neck, that he should shout *unclean, unclean!* in the halls of Martin Luther, where tinted windows emit only a dingy light, and nobody speaks to him in passing, students, staff, and full-time faculty alike seeming wrapped in some profound, pessimistic introspection. And Belle's possibly seriously disturbed, and the students of expository prose he faces are rigid in their seats, expressions tighter than a bull's ass in fly-time, as though contemplating the long odds against salvation within the theology of the Missouri Synod.

But expository prose at Martin Luther is a breeze, because, while these students have no interest in nor affinity for the subject, they love to argue, orally and on paper. Leaning hard on the former, Q easily fills the time allotted by proposing a controversial topic, then sitting back and letting them jaw until the bell tolls in the hall. He goes light on written assignments, thus cutting down on the paper-grading grind. He does fear these brainwashed Lutherans would mount a collective fuss if he graded strictly, so Q always inflates by a full letter to stave that off.

Today, roll taken, he says, "If I were to state that every woman has a right, given to her by law, nature, and God, to abortion on demand, what'd be your response?" For seventy-five minutes, he nods, prods occasionally, and pretends to take seriously their shrill, Scripture-laden, simplistic and simple-minded espousals of right-to-life over choice. This is all the ploy Q needs to finesse expository prose at Martin Luther College. By class's end, he's regained his emotional equilibrium, goes to meet Belle at her information counter with tangible anticipation.

Q can hardly believe it; it looks like a sure thing! When he invites her to join him in his Honda, parked in the most remote reaches of the faculty lot with just this in mind, she merely shrugs, enters the back seat when he opens the door for her in the falling evening light. After much kissy-face and tonsil hockey, after a spate of frenzied groping and clutching, his breath labored, when he asks if he can unhook her brassiere, he takes her silence as tantamount to assent.

"Do you like it when I do that?" Q asks after releasing her nonerect nipple from his teeth.

"It's okay," Belle says.

"Do you like this?" he asks, reaching inside her waistband.

"I don't care," she says. That's when Q stops.

He leans away from her to get a look at her face, her eyes; she looks asleep on her feet, tranced, wholly without appropriate affect. She's dead-weight in his arms. "Are you okay, Belle?" Q asks.

"I don't know. I don't know anything," she says, staring back at him as if under hypnosis.

"What are you thinking about? Seriously, tell me."

"Nothing. Stuff," she says.

"Not sex?"

"Some. I guess," Belle says.

Q. ponders, realizes he's at a crucial juncture here. He can proceed, but it would be something like an act of necrophilia. He can stop, hook up her bra for her, rebutton her blouse, take her home, and suffer the freeway to his apartment with a likely case of aching stones. In the pondering, Q finds himself thoroughly detumid.

"I think I better take you home, Belle," he croaks. She sits, silent, statue-like, as he gets her rehooked, buttoned, zipped. She's so clearly stunned by whatever ails her he doesn't even ask her to move to the front seat with him. Stasis! he thinks. He drives her chauffeur-like to her efficiency, his Honda a battered ambulance. Q sees her to her door, says, "Belle, maybe you should, like, get some counseling or something?" before she closes her door in his face.

Flying the freeways home in full night, he wonders, torn, if he's committed an act of gallantry or just failed to grab the main chance.

Q, thinks Q, *for qualms.*

Thursday begins with Q's mega-hangover. No weed to be had last night, he hit the vodka bottle way too hard in an effort to forget both Marinelle and Belle. Good riddance, he told himself. Best, he reminded himself, not to sleep with anyone who's as screwed up as he is! He doses his splitting head with aspirins, slakes his parched throat with tap water, regards his hands, fluttering like a dog trying to pass a peach pit, with horrified contrition.

Q, thinks Q, *for quaffer.*

By the time he's on the freeways toward Pere Marquette, toward Patti, his headache's subsided to a muted hammering, his tongue's no longer sandpaper, his hands occupied with the steering wheel. It beats stasis!

Pere Marquette College, the all-male counterpart to St. Mary's, isn't a cheery prospect. Were it not for Patti, even if she does look slightly androgynous, there'd be no joy, no hope at all in Pere Marquette. His students there, Introduction to Rhetorical Modes, a euphemism for freshman comp, are only a shade keener than City's remedials, though cut from cleaner cloth. They're mostly diligent, but lack the deference toward him he enjoys from St. Mary's girls. The faculty's about half Jesuit priests, sternly serious men in black, dog-collared, who always seem to be watching him for evidences of intellectual or moral heresy. Q avoids them for fear his guilt will be revealed in even innocuous small-talk.

And he treads carefully in conversation with Patti, who's way out ahead of him, finishing her dissertation, groomed for a Pere Marquette tenure-track slot, and tangibly brighter than Q. She's also way too direct for his taste. The first time he invited her for coffee, she looked him straight in the eye and told him she wanted him to know in no uncertain terms, for starters, that she wasn't currently sexually active. He finessed that one by telling her they were a match, then, because he was currently lying fallow in that regard, which seemed to break the ice nicely.

Q, Q thought, *for quipster.*

Introduction to Rhetorical Modes meets but once a week, a hundred and fifty minutes; Q almost never keeps them the full period. Today he drones just over an hour, then, prompted by plain tedium and the residue of his hangover, looks up at the crucifix on the classroom wall for forgiveness—he finds none—takes a deep breath, says, "That's all for today."

Before he can get out ahead of them, he's accosted by Farhat, a Bangladeshi exchange student Q means to flunk because his written English sucks, and he doesn't like his oily looks or his brown-nosing demeanor either. Farhat says, "Please, sir, why are we not having always all the time in class meeting?"

Q comes up with a pretty good one, he thinks, given his hangover remainder, which now seems to have settled in his stomach. "I'm conducting an experiment here. I'm doing a study to determine the optimum number of minutes a class should run. I correlate the length of a given class period with student performance on exams and writing assignments. It's too complicated to explain, but you get the idea, right?" Farhat assures him he does, grins stupidly, half-bows, departs. Q prays the little turd doesn't mention it to anyone; the Jesuits would have his head instanter!

After a stop in the men's, where he debates inducing regurgitation to quiet his gut, thinks better of it, and resorts to gulping more cold tap water instead, he heads for Patti's office on the second floor, utterly without confidence in anything.

Where are you, Q? he queries.

About, he concludes as he climbs the stairs, to go down the porcelain facility! Marinelle and Belle are total losses, strikeouts. If she needs her mom's permission, Vonda's an astronomical long shot. If Farhat repeats that last baloney, he'll be out on his ear here. Sal's a shaky source now. His Honda could give up the ghost at any moment. And Patti's too hip to fall for any line he's capable of stringing.

Q, Q thinks, *for quite*—doomed, that is.

But he's wrong! Patti, wholly contrary to all conceivable expectations, offers herself!

When he enters her tiny office, Patti gets up from her desk, closes the door, turns, puts her small hands on his shoulders, says, "You look terrible, Q? Are you feeling ill?"

"Not particularly," he allows.

"I've made life difficult for you, emotionally speaking, haven't I, Q."

"No. I mean, not really. I mean, you have your principles, I guess. I mean, I'm not sure what you mean, Patti."

"Q," she says, gives him a provocative peck on the nose, "do you think you're ready to take this relationship to the next level?"

"Um," is all Q can utter.

"I am if you are, Q," Patti says. And says, "I think I'm ready for intimacy. We're two consenting adults, Q. Are you ready for this, Q?"

For a second, he's not at all sure. Does she mean here and now, on the floor, atop her desk? "Am I going to get an answer, Q?"

Q, thinks Q, *for quizzed.*

"Yes. Of course. Most certainly!" he barks. She smiles, kisses his nose again, and they arrange for her to come to his apartment on Saturday, stay the night. Q's ecstatic; the looming weekend holds no terror now!

Q splurges, takes her to lunch off campus, the last of his hangover dissolving into blissful bewilderment at this absolutely serendipitous windfall. She's no Vonda for looks, has no discernible breasts, hips narrower than her shoulders, a boyish face under bobbed hair, but Q believes his world has changed, become wonderful, rich with possibilities. Sex is sex, he reasons, and where else might that lead? Maybe things are breaking his way at last?

When she turns the talk to his career status, he lies with enthusiasm. What Patti doesn't know won't hurt her. He blames his situation on his Vietnam experience, which unsuited him for conventional vocations, on too many years knocking about from job to job, on a bad attitude toward his schooling when he finally availed himself of the G.I. Bill, on a hostile major professor who derailed his dissertation. Truth told, Q failed his doctoral prelims twice, was put out of his graduate program on his ear. Now he knows he's too old to find a secure academic niche without the terminal degree, and even if he had it, he'd never rack up the publishing credentials a phenom like Patti already boasted. Truth told, Q knows he's going nowhere in the academic racket.

"What made you decide to study literature, Q?" she asks. He tells her he always liked a good read, likes interaction with students' minds, thinks education a noble enterprise. Patti suggests that's pretty vague, and not a little innocent. He doggedly disputes this until she lets it go.

Q, thinks Q, *for quibbler.*

Buoyant, he leaves her for the freeways, Shakespeare and St. Mary's and Vonda. But Vonda doesn't much matter now, he's got Patti on his dance card for this weekend. Oh, life is looking good!

Shakespeare is no sweat at St. Mary's. Q natters a good three-fourths of the scheduled period on the topic of humors, tossing in what he vaguely remembers about The Great Chain of Being, and, pleading exhaustion, dismisses them early.

Vonda is as easy on the eyes as always, but there's still too much light left in the evening to consider luring her into the Honda. Anyway, with Patti locked in for the weekend, he's not significantly disappointed by this. After a few deep kisses, she says, "I'm still thinking about it, Q."

"Thinking about what?" he asks, preoccupied with Patti.

"About coming to see you this weekend, helping me with my term paper, etcetera." She pronounces it *eckcetera.*

"Etcetera," he corrects her, imagining their coupling, adding, "We can always do this another time, it doesn't have to be this weekend." Q feels a cold rush at the remote possibility of two women converging on his apartment; he's relieved when she notes she still feels she needs her mother's okay. Given that, he's able to fully enjoy the vista of her voluptuous gait as she goes to her foreign-made sports car. Is it in any way abnormal, he wonders, to so exult in this voyeurism?

Q, thinks Q, for quirk.

And he flies the freeways home, ecstatic with growing anticipation.

Friday's equally without problems. His Honda sputters and balks, but he's on time for his City U. remedials, and holds them nearly the full period with a spontaneous spiel about sentence combining as a means of achieving a distinctive individual style; this comes to him like a gift, no effort, no hesitation, no backing and filling or audible pauses marring this effortless gush of hokum. His remedials are glum as ever, but seem to pay at least a perfunctory attention to his words.

A Friday bonus is Sal coming up, after class, with a dime baggie. "I thought you were getting out of the lifestyle, Salvatore," Q says.

"I still might," says Sal. "I'm not for certain sure yet, Prof."

"You the man, Sal!" Q says as they make the exchange, and would, were Sal's hygiene not so revolting, have hugged him.

He meets Marinelle at their commons table, having decided on a ceremonial kiss-off to salvage his pride, which he thinks should be hurt. "Marinelle," he announces, "I've come to the irrevocable conclusion we're not well suited, you and me."

"You're breaking my heart, Q," she says, breaks out in a gruff cackle.

"Okay," Q says, "you've made your point. I just thought it'd be the responsible thing to do to make it formal, sort of, okay?"

"Don't do me no damn favors, Q," she says, and, "Don't let the door hit you in the ass on your way out."

"No hard feelings?"

"For shit's sakes, Q," she near-shouts, "will you the fuck please just fuck off!" He does, deciding there's no loss of pride in losing fat, mannish, possibly-dyke Marinelle.

That done, the freeways to Martin Luther are a walk in the park, though he feels a bit skittish about seeing Belle again.

But there's another Friday bonus. Belle's not at the information desk, the woman in her place a snowy-haired granny who, when Q asks after Belle, says, "I understand she's not well."

Feeling freed of Belle—he hopes she isn't truly clinical—he fills the class period by provoking his dour Lutherans with a statement, qualified as hypothetical of course, denying the existence of God. So he sits it out as they wax eloquent, outraged, for seventy-five minutes, in response. This clears the decks for the weekend, for Patti.

Might it not come to pass, if he plays it cooly, he speculates, that after this weekend with Patti he could arrange it with Vonda for the following? He could, he projects, alternate them on succeeding weekends! Such thoughts take his mind off the hazards of freeway travel and the varied ominous sounds his Honda generates.

Q's euphoria endures until nearly midnight, enhanced by Sal's good grass and not a little vodka. Just before the witching hour, Q happy as a sultan with an inexhaustible seraglio from which to choose as whim dictated, Vonda telephones. Mother, it happens, has given her permission to receive some out-of-class tutoring on Q's turf. She wants to come over Saturday evening. She pronounces it *Satiday*.

He's too shocked to figure a way around this snafu, only fleetingly indulges a fantasy *a trois*. Q mumbles he'll get back to her in the morning, evades the implications of this impasse via an extra-large joint and another pint of vodka that leave him senseless.

Q, is Q's last coherent thought in the wee hours of Saturday morning, *for queered!*

Saturday, the weekend, finds Q hung over to the max again, spaced out in his cannabis aftermath, semi-paralyzed with pain and generalized angst. Unable to focus, he shifts mentally from foot to foot like a child in need of a toilet, his thoughts a jumble coalescing into one persistent whimper, psyche racked by emotional whining.

Is there any possibility of getting Vonda in and out before Patti's at his door? What excuse might suffice to delay Patti until Sunday, run Vonda through this evening, an assembly line mode? Flummoxed, Q's caught his ass in a crack, between a rock and a hard spot, up the proverbial creek without a paddle.

Q, thinks Q, *for quandary!*

His genius for ploys deserting him, he sees that canceling the entire operation is the only viable solution.

After all, Patti's less than voluptuous, her androgyny a mild turnoff. And what delight would there be in yoking himself to a woman his emotional, intellectual, and professional better? He can imagine himself a house-husband, cooking and cleaning while Patti rose through the academic ranks. Q pictures himself playing perpetual second fiddle to Patti's maturity of character and record of accomplishment. Okay, scratch Patti!

Vonda? Vonda's a veritable feast of the flesh, but how long would that be good for when she comes off like an inarticulate juvenile? There was money, the ring of security, in Vonda's high-bourgeois lineage, to be sure. But what chance he'd be in any respect acceptable to her family? And the difference in their ages amounted to a generation gap. No, drop Vonda! Wipe the slate, start anew!

It surprises him how easy it proves, how minimal is his regret, as he dials first one, then the other.

Q, thinks Q, *for quitter.*

"I'm not ready," he tells Patti, "for the next level."

"You are such a child, Q!"

"We can still be friends, right?"

"Grow up, Q!" she says, hangs up on him.

"We're just not compatible spirits," he tells Vonda, who begins to cry.

"I bet you never even really liked me, Q!" she says. And says, "You just played with my afflictions!" He presumes she means *affections.* He promises to help her with her research paper—on-campus of course—promises he'll see her through the morass of Shakespeare, but doubts he's heard through her blubbering. He hangs up on her.

Only briefly does Q revel in a surge of relief. Only briefly does this respite obliterate the facts of where this leaves him. Too soon, these reemerge, descend on him there in his rat-trap of an apartment like a poisonous cloud.

He has stacks of student writing he can't bear to read. He has hosts of lectures and lesson plans to formulate he knows he won't attend to. He has no booze left, and only crumbs remain in Sal's baggie. He has four part-time teaching gigs without a scintilla of certainty they will be there next semester. He has no women, no woman, in his life.

Where are you going, Q?

Well, no law of man or cosmos says something can't break his way! A distant relative—he doesn't know of any—could die somewhere, leave him closets of money in the will. He could buy a lottery ticket, win zillions! He could apply to the VA, claim post-traumatic stress syndrome, be awarded total disability for life! He could meet a new woman, one who was intelligent and well read, enjoyed inherited wealth, was deliciously feminine and psychologically healthy, sexually innovative and responsive! He could, he believes, by sheer act of will create a new and admirable character for himself, a vivacious personality, kick his dependence on alcohol and hemp!

He could, just now, get outdoors, crank his fragile Honda, just fly the freeways for a while?

And then it comes to Q that it's only late morning of this Saturday, that Sunday waits in line to swallow him like a black hole.

Q, thinks Q, *for quark!*

And then he's no longer thinking. He hears nothing, sees only the drab featureless and mundane particulars of his cell-like apartment, aware only of the irrefutable fact of this weekend in which he's stuck like a man mired chin-deep in a swamp.

Q, thinks Q, *for quiet*—the absolute quiet of interminable stasis.

Imagining the Structure of Free Space on Pioneer Road

My marriage is very solid, very enduring. Margaret and I will always be married, with our daughter Laurel always be a family.

After ten years of marriage, there is either something present that binds husband and wife, that will keep them together—richer or poorer, in sickness and in health, as the traditional ceremony puts it—or there is not. Without this something that binds, unites, I suppose it is still possible a husband and wife will continue together, but that is marriage only in an empty, deadening, mutually destructive form. Truly lasting marriages are like a well-built home, structures with firm foundations and strong walls. A true marriage has a kind of almost tangible shape, the result of potentially damaging forces rendered harmless by the dynamics of its design.

Margaret and I are married a decade, and there is a something present that means we will never part. I am grateful for this, but will never, I suppose, cease wishing it were something else joining us—not rich, but affluent, in perfect health.

What seals Margaret to me, me to her, has since the third year after we married, is of course Laurel, our only child, now just seven. She was born blind.

I am in my two-car garage, dressed for the hard winter cold that seeps in, sorting lights, wires. Margaret says, "I don't pretend to understand you in this."

I say, "What's to understand? It's Christmas. Half the homes on Pioneer Road put up displays."

"And for whose benefit do we put on this show?" she asks. And repeats the question when I am slow to answer.

"Whoever," I say. And I say, "People driving by. Pioneer Road's a showcase every Christmas."

"So you're spreading general peace on earth and joy etcetera for the casual commuter, is that it?"

"You could put it like that," I say when I have waited as long as I dare to answer her.

"And we can afford this ostentation," she says. This is a statement, not a question; she knows we can. The garage is cold enough to put a shiver in her voice.

I say to my wife, "If I don't stop nattering the matter to death it'll be Christmas before I get it all the way up and running the way I designed." She understands I have told her to stop, to leave me alone in the cold garage with my strings of varicolored lights, my connectors and transformers and timers and bolts and clips, my ladder and tools; I have told my wife to leave me alone in our garage where it is cold enough my breath shows, cold enough to numb my fingers and toes. And she does, not slamming the door to the laundry room, but closing it very sharply, her last word on the subject.

I stand still for a bit in the cold garage—it is a very bitter winter this year, perhaps a record-setter. I look at the heaps of wire, the varicolored bulbs in their boxes, my tools and ladder. For a moment I feel lost, no sense of what to do next, where to turn. And then I turn to my workbench, to the design I have created, carefully, slowly, for the elaborate display of Christmas lights with which I will adorn our home here on Pioneer Road. My home, mine and Margaret's, Laurel's.

I say she—my daughter Laurel, our only child, now just seven years old—was blind from birth. That is not accurate. When she was born, she was normal in every respect, sighted. The hospital where she was born was one of the few that still put silver nitrate in the eyes of newborns; the practice had been abandoned by most obstetric and pediatric professions for the very reason that there was a risk of blinding the infant. My Laurel was blinded, totally, irrevocably, by silver nitrate. That hospital's obstetric and pediatric services ceased the practice shortly after my daughter's birth. I do not—except for brief spells when I cannot help myself—blame that hospital, our obstetrician and our pediatrician.

My point is that my daughter Laurel was not born blind. For a short time, less than an hour, she was perfect in every respect, normal, sighted. For that short time she lived in, saw, the same world I and her mother did. Of course she has no memory of this, knows herself blind, forever. But I think I understand, if only faintly, why I insist on the distinction of her birth as sighted.

I used to speak of this, to my wife, others, but have not for several years now, because I know Margaret does not like, cannot bear, to hear it. Silence is as strong a bond as any words.

My wife's approach to our daughter's blindness is, once past the practical aspects of Laurel's upbringing and special education, very different from mine.

I make my living—and a pretty good one it is—sitting at a computer, fixed on the screen. There is my keyboard and mouse, the monitor's screen glowing a dull pale green, and me, eyes fastened to the letters and symbols and numbers flashing before me as fast as my brain moves my fingers. I do not feel immodest when I say I have a great talent, perhaps a near-genius, for seeing what passes before my eyes on the screen in terms that are primarily spatial, rather like the way a chess master sees the board as a near-infinite array of possible structures, a profoundly complex maze that must be fathomed to escape, to win the match.

My work demands intense, relentless imagination, and this often leaves me weary. There is much talk of the risk of damage to one's tendons in wrist, hands, fingers, but I show no symptoms. I would complain of sometimes severe spasms of eyestrain and racking headaches coming from my fixation on the glowing, pulsing, flashing screen through which, by which, I imagine the structures that evolve into elaborate, significant software programs.

I don't tell Margaret of my eyestrain and headaches. We have learned to avoid speaking about eyes, eyesight, anything of that sort. That is understandable, and it keeps us very close together in that silence.

To bedeck a large split-level house with a truly ambitious, complex display of Christmas lights is no easy task. It was not difficult for me, given my capacity to imagine space, colors, and a striking play of lights to flash and flow, surge and recede according to a precise timetable, to create my design. I had no trouble seeing, in my mind's eye, how it should, would perform when in place and charged with current.

My difficulty proves to be mere mechanics, laying out seemingly endless and easily tangled strings of bulbs, making measurements to fit the lines of windows, eaves, my roof, and then confronting the drudgery of bolting and clipping and connecting. The cold of this near-record-setting winter is a heavy, enervating presence as I walk my wires and plugs, the clinking bulbs, outdoors, then fetch my ladder and ascend to heights that alarm me, clumsy in gloves, awkward in thick coat and scarf and wool cap. The wind whistles in my muffled ears, bites at my cheeks and nose and brow, mists my eyes, shakes my ladder.

I find it odd, as I take more frequent and longer breaks to restore my circulation and rest my legs and arms inside the frigid garage, that a man justly proud of his imagination is so inept at such smaller, cruder work.

I would like to think my wife tries to watch me from one of the windows, that she describes for our daughter what I am doing, that they listen together for the sound of my footsteps on the roof as I wreath our den's fireplace chimney with a swirl of dark red bulbs, but I know Margaret will not watch me, much less offer her help. Laurel hears me on the roof, of course—her hearing is acute, one of the senses by which she knows her wholly dark world's shape and texture; she knows what I am doing, for I have told her, tell her day by day of my slow but inexorable progress. Her mother will not discuss the matter with our blind child, and this surely confuses Laurel, which saddens me, but I do not flag in my purpose.

My daughter Laurel—what can I say? Every father's daughter, only child, is lovely to look upon, or so I like to think. My Laurel is lovely. She is blond, like her mother, and slender, and delicate, very fair-skinned, but not at all wan. Her features are fine—like her mother's. She will be tall, like her mother. And graceful, there is a grace in the movement of her hands, an intricacy inherent in her long fingers. And her voice is clear, a soprano bell that peals often, almost uncontrollably, with laughter that is the only music I know or care for.

Her eyes, of course, would have matched her mother's blue-green, but are quite atrophied, shrunken, dull, semi-clouded, so she wears opaque glasses. When she walks, with or without her cane, my lovely daughter endowed with all her mother's beauty and grace, she is hesitant, her gait hinting of an impending stumble or fall, her paths, though most often true, as if guided by an electronic beam, appear uncertain, her goal a kind of guess that breaks my heart. And when she sits, to read with the tips of her fingers, or to listen to a tape or record, even sitting at the table for meals she eats with neat efficiency, there is a slight wavering of her torso, a shifting and half-nodding of her head, as though she means to rise in a rush and run away to a place she suddenly remembers and sorely misses.

This breaks my heart, but is a common thing with the blind. I do not speak of this with my wife, because I know she knows this of me; it is another silence ensuring we will remain as one in our lasting marriage.

After the chimney and the roof line and the many windows of my house are complete—I am behind schedule, slowed by this unbroken cold snap—I gain some confidence, set about ringing and draping our large yard's trees and shrubs. My ladder feels always about to slip or slide away from the tree trunk, and I want to cling to a limb as I work with nails and hammer, but need both hands. I am more confident, but must work late into each night, temperature dropping, the sky's blackness only occasionally pinpointed with stars when clouds break. I could use Margaret's help, but will not ask for it.

I feel frozen at my core when cold and fatigue finally force me indoors, where I stamp feeling into my feet, shed my bulky coat and strangling scarf, drop my gloves and blow on my stony hands.

"Laurel," I call out if she has not already gone to bed, "come hear Dad tell you what I got done tonight!" And she comes to me, very sure without her cane inside this house she knows so well by touch and sound and smell, and I tell her of the trees and shrubs I have decorated with varicolored bulbs waiting to burst forth their light when I throw—when *we* throw—the master switch called for in the intricate plan I created to make a brilliant, remarkable Christmas display to join those we see each year on Pioneer Road. I tell her what I have done that night, what I will do the next, try to make her see my complex design in her mind's eye. Of course she cannot. "Can you imagine it, Laurel?" I ask.

"Oh, Dad," she says. Sometimes I think this means yes, sometimes feel it only means I am being foolish, as she must know I am when I try to talk with her of colors, of the tones of light and dark that limn the shapes of this world I take in through my eyes, which my daughter will never do.

Pioneer Road is named for those hardy folk who settled this town nearly two hundred years ago, before statehood. They built the road to reach the city twenty miles south, and now white-flight commuters drive it to and from the freeway that will take them to their city jobs, back to their large, some lavish, small-town homes. Standing in the vicious cold after a night's work in my yard, I look at Pioneer Road, the traffic come to see all the Christmas lights in either direction, and I think what an act of faith it must have been on the part of those settlers, true pioneers, coming in wagons to carve a town out of what was wilderness, among hostile Indians—what a vision they must have had in their hearts and minds!

Margaret says to me, "What you're doing is wrong."

I say, "It's a Christmas light display, and that's all it is."

She says, "That too. Your whole approach to her is wrong-headed. You've never accepted." I think this is true, but will never confess it.

I say, "I want her to know our world as much as she can. I want to know hers."

My wife says, "If wishes were fishes."

"What then?" I say, because I must say something, will not say what I know is true, that I do not accept, that Laurel cannot know as I know, I cannot know as she does, which breaks my heart.

"Whatever," says my wife, and turns away from me, more exasperated than angry, I hope. I do not say to her that I think her approach to our daughter is as wrong as mine. I have no desire to inflict any hurt on my wife for our disagreement. I would hate to lose my wife, am grateful our only child is such that we will never, never part. I would like to call after her as she moves away from me, but do not. This exchange on the topic of our daughter, like so many in recent years, is brief, its conclusion tangible and irrevocable.

What the blind fear most is what they call *Free Space.* This refers to the situation of a blind person finding him or herself somehow in an area—a space of any sort—with no point of reference at hand. If I were to take my daughter to the middle, say, of our large lawn, take her hand away from the crook of my arm—her point of reference if she were without her cane—and step away from her, she would almost certainly freeze in place, unable, not daring to venture a single step for fear of falling, colliding, risking injury or even death by stepping into the pure void of total darkness. In this absolute dark, at just seven years of age, my Laurel would surely become hysterical.

I cannot imagine myself ever doing such a thing, of course, can only imagine how terrible this must be, this Free Space.

Yet, so intelligent is my daughter, so adapted, so skilled, I can imagine she might be able to make something of the sounds of traffic on Pioneer Road, turn toward our house, then feel the wind—if there were a wind—to locate the house, a kind of windbreak, which in turn might lead her to our driveway, and then she would no longer be lost in Free Space, but freed, would readily, easily, follow the drive's edge to the front door she would know at once with the palm of her hand, know it as exactly as she knows my face, or Margaret's, with her sensitive fingertips.

My house, the shrubs, the too many trees are done, ready for connection, illumination. Perhaps the hardest part, Christmas figures I will string on the lathe armatures I hammered together in my garage, remains. And I must hurry to meet my Christmas Eve deadline. My neighbors' houses on Pioneer Road already blaze in the black cold nights of this hard winter. There is an increase in traffic on our road, townspeople driving slowly by to see, appreciate, marvel at this once-a-year fairyland of light and color, some tooting their horns, a kind of applause.

So I must hurry, force myself to work later and later each frigid night, the work a little easier in the glow cast by my neighbors' displays, the several inches of snow cover frosted with reflected red, blue, orange, yellow, green, gold. It is hard work to set my armatures in the frozen lawn beneath the snow, and I weary so quickly in the cold, my breath short, whatever wind blows burning my cheeks and nose, the cold oozing like a liquid beneath my bulky coat, stiffening my joints, turning my feet and fingers to lead.

But I take heart at the spectacle of my neighbors' displays, already complete, alight, in both directions on Pioneer Road.

I try to know my daughter's darkness. I lie beside my sleeping wife, our breathing in synch. I try to relax, try to look at the ceiling without really seeing it. Passing traffic sweeps swaths of pale light across the textured ceiling I try not to see above our bed. I try not to see these swift sweeps of light from traffic, try not to see where the walls join the ceiling, the shape that is my bedside stand in the corner of my eye.

Then I close my eyes tightly, and try to see the absolute darkness my daughter Laurel lives in. And I fail, always.

Spots of light, varicolored, dance or loom, wheel like planets in some cosmos beyond ours. Light flashes like mini-lightning, silver-bright, from edge to edge of this darkness behind my eyelids I wish to see in its unlit essence, its totality, its unity. But varicolored lights emerge like sunrises.

And then I am thinking, knowing I have failed, and my mind swims with images, my lovely, graceful Laurel, my beautiful Margaret, our bedroom, our bed, myself lying with closed eyes, yet seeing the host of images that define my world, my cosmos. And I open my eyes. I have failed again, see the textured ceiling above me, the sudden slash of headlights from the road, the shape of my bedside stand.

At least I have tried.

My Christmas display will be the match of any on Pioneer Road. There will be a large script *Merry Xmas* just at the edge of my wide lawn, and it will flash on and off every ten seconds. Farther back toward my house, to one side, will be Santa in his loaded sleigh, four reindeer, his hands holding their reins, the whole tilted toward the black winter sky, as if he has left his bounty with us, is off into the air to continue his journey all across the earth. There will be elves, their postures signifying their dance of inexhaustible good cheer. There will be a snowman to the other side of my lawn, his top hat, pipe, stick arms, buttons down his snowy front, mouth, pointy nose, round eyes. There will be oversize lumieres lining the long drive from the road to our front door. And my chimney, my roof line, the windows, the trees and shrubs, all will be lit, will flash on and off in varicolored light.

There will be no manger, wise men, no Joseph and Mary, no child, no camel or sheep, because I am not a religious man, will not pretend a faith I do not own.

Margaret says to me, "Would you be offended if I'd suggest you see someone, professionally, about this?"

"About what?" I say because I know exactly what she refers to.

"You will not give so much as an inch, will you," she says. It is not a question.

"It's a Christmas display, Margaret," I say to her because that is all I can say when we both know it is so much more.

Imagination can be a curse. How much anguish have I inflicted on myself when I knew all the while what I imagined could never come to pass?

I have imagined my Laurel an adult, standing on a street corner, cane slung on one arm, each hand grasping a cup, one filled with pencils, the other baited with a few coins, a sign on her chest, slung on a string around her slender neck. How absurdly impossible!

I have imagined my darling Laurel an adult, seated at a long workbench, sightless peers on either side of her, the group working with precision to assemble some simple mechanism, perhaps counting beads or numbered balls into little drawstring bags, the components of some insipid board game. How utterly impossible!

At seven my daughter is far better educated than I or her mother were at that age. My daughter has had the best special education, will continue to have this education for years to come, will be qualified for any number of professions as sophisticated, or more so, than mine, when that time comes.

My daughter knows music and literature and history I never learned—yes, at age just seven! My daughter has a near-genius I.Q., certified by elaborate testing. My daughter sings beautifully, confesses to me and her mother, though we tell her she needs her rest—as we all do—that she reads late into the night, her fingers warm beneath her covers, dancing over the braille texts we provide her without limit.

My daughter Laurel is a perfect child, will be a perfect woman, except for the fact she cannot see, will never see anything, ever.

Margaret does not, will not, weep—we are years past tears for this. But her eyes do mist as she says, "Why can't we be together for this?"

I say, "We are together. We've been more together since she was born than we ever were before."

"Sometimes," my wife says, her eyes misting, though she will not dab at them because that would show me she wants to weep, "I think so. And then you go off on something like this Christmas thing."

"It's a display is all," I say because that is not true.

"It's counterproductive," Margaret says, "destructive."

"I'm just trying, Margaret," I say, and her eyes clear because she knows at least this is true.

We once took our daughter to the Fourth of July fireworks show the town puts on each year in the lakeside park. I tried to describe it for my daughter as we sat on folding chairs we brought with us to the park.

"It's a rocket," I said, excited, "it's going up—there!" as it burst. "It's a zillion little balls of fire falling, like the ribs of an umbrella, oh, and they're burning out, they're gone!"

She was too young for this, was frightened by the crash, bang, crackle, the shrill whistling of the fireworks. She startled, lurched at the explosions as if someone had grabbed her out of nowhere as she stood in a Free Space, shuddered as if she were chilled.

Laurel said, "It's too loud!" and, "I don't like the smell!" as the tang of acrid smoke came to us in the soft summer breeze.

I saw my wife stiffen in her chair, saw her clench her jaw, look anywhere but at me or our daughter or the booming succession of fireworks in the sky. And we left well before the show concluded.

At least, I think now, we tried.

I think I came closest when I tried to experience Free Space.

Laurel was gone, at her school; a minivan comes to pick her up in the morning, delivers her back to us late in the afternoon. I checked to be sure Margaret was busy in the laundry room, sorting, loading the washer, emptying the dryer, folding. I did not want her to see this.

I went to our living room. It is a big room, quite large enough for entertaining, though we have no close friends our age with small children—the reason is obvious. There is much furniture, but it is placed close to the walls, leaving a large open area. When Laurel enters, crosses, and leaves this room, she takes the long route, from chair to table to chair. Once or twice I have seen her cross the open middle, protected by her cane and the perfect sense of our house's floor plan she knows more exactly than I from her life within its darkness.

Cocking an ear for a last listen, checking on Margaret in the laundry room, I walked to the center of our big living room, stopped, stood very still an instant, and closed my eyes.

Of course I saw the colored lights slide and loom and rise and fall, as I always see them with my eyes closed. But I ignored them, stood very still, and tried to imagine I had no idea where the furniture sat all around me. I imagined a room emptied, a house abandoned, then simply a space, tried not to know there was thick carpeting beneath my shoes. I came very close, I think, to Free Space. I raised my arms, extended my fingers, and for an instant my balance faltered, I tottered, groped with my hands, began to shuffle forward, and think I almost knew, if only for that instant, what my blind Laurel knows.

And then Margaret entered our living room, said, "What are you doing?" My eyes popped open, I was in my living room, the furniture all in place, the cold sunlight of this hard winter in the picture window, my snow-covered lawn, Pioneer Road, some traffic. I looked at my wife; I am not sure what her expression meant, what she might have been thinking.

I said to her, "I was trying."

My Christmas display is complete, in place. All that remains are the last connections, tying everything to the master switch, a simple box with a button I can hold in my hand, Laurel can hold in her hand.

My wife of course strongly disapproves of these conversations, so I do not talk with my daughter about her dreams until Margaret has left the house to shop or run errands.

I say, "Laurel, darling, Dad had a crazy dream last night. I was driving somewhere in a car. It wasn't my car or Mom's, it was some strange car. I didn't know where I was going but I had to get there on time for something, the car went so slow I was afraid I'd be late."

My daughter says, "What did the car smell like, Dad?"

"I don't know," I say, "it wasn't a new car smell. I don't think it smelled like anything."

"Did you touch the seat, Dad? Was the motor loud? Did it make the brake noise Mom's used to before it got fixed? Did you play the radio or play a tape, Dad?" she asks.

"I don't think so," I say, and I say, "Do you feel my dream at all, Laurel?"

She says to me, "I know being late, and fast and slow in our cars." My heart breaks because my daughter cannot see me in my dream, driving the strange car, too slow, late for whatever, wherever.

When I get an opportunity—Margaret gone from the house—I ask Laurel what she dreamed the night before. I don't think she likes this. She often says she doesn't think she had any dreams that night, and I remind her everyone dreams lots of dreams every night. Sometimes she will tell me what she remembers of a dream.

She says, "There was a funny smell, almost like the smell from people who smoke, but it wasn't that. And there was a little buzzing noise, like Mom's mixer, but not so loud."

"Is that all?" I ask, trying to imagine a smell like tobacco on a smoker's clothes and skin, Margaret's electric mixer whirring cake batter or beating egg whites.

My Laurel says, "I was touching a flat wall. It was cold. It was more like the floor I was touching with all of me, except there was no rug on it, it wasn't wood and didn't smell like anything, and the buzzing went away, I think."

I try to imagine my daughter, arms and legs spread, her face and hands and bare feet pressed against a wall that is like a floor, but not a floor, no carpet, not wood or stone or vinyl. I cannot imagine this.

We all dream every night, lots of dreams, and we recall some, or parts of some, see ourselves in places strange or silly or terrifying, except the blind, whose dreams are only smells and sounds and textures against their sensitive skin.

I probably should not talk to my daughter about dreams, hers or mine.

I am ready, the day before Christmas Eve. I should test it, see if this great display of varicolored, flashing light will actually come to life at the press of the button on the box small enough my daughter can hold it in her small, graceful hand. But there will be no test—it will or will not work in the full dark of Christmas Eve.

There is one sort of congenital blindness science cured with one of the first practical applications of laser beams. This congenital blindness was due to a broken connection between two parts of the optic nerve. It was inoperable. But a laser beam could be directed to this place within the eye, where it performed a kind of welding operation. It was a bona fide miracle. Hundreds of sightless, blind for ten, twenty, thirty, forty years, were given perfect vision.

Not surprisingly, follow-up studies showed these people were not very happy in the world they could suddenly see with absolute clarity. They suffered disorientation, panic attacks, depression.

One study still interests me. A group of these newly sighted people were seated, one by one, at a table, hands in their laps. A knife and fork were placed before them on the table. They were asked how many objects they saw. Two, they all said. They were asked if these objects were similar or dissimilar. Dissimilar, they all said. They were asked what the objects were.

They did not know—until they were allowed to raise their hands from their laps and touch the knife and fork.

What I take from this study is that reality, things, are actually composed of words. I know my tableware when I see it; my Laurel knows hers with her fingers. Somehow this cheers me, that what we both know are the same words that make up the different worlds we live in.

Not long ago I woke from an anxiety dream I do not remember. I woke with a start, and saw a man standing in the bedroom doorway. For how many seconds did I know an intruder stood at my bedroom door? For how many seconds did I hang, paralyzed, between the urge to wake Margaret at my side and the need to leap from our bed and attack this marauder? How many seconds passed before I realized what I saw was my bathrobe, hung on a hook beside the door frame?

I pledged a college fraternity. Hazing was still in fashion. One night we were taken to the house's basement, blindfolded, told to extend both hands, palms up. In my left hand the pledgemaster placed a clump of cold spaghetti. In the other he put a small heap of finely broken eggshells. He did this to all the pledge class. He then told us we held dead night crawlers in our left hands, our frat brothers' toenail parings in our right. Then he ordered us to eat what we held. Two of my fellow pledges vomited after they swallowed the last of it; I did not vomit, but choked so hard I would have fainted if our blindfolds had not been removed, and the pledgemaster, cackling with glee, told us what we had in fact eaten.

My Laurel will never mistake a bathrobe for a burglar or rapist, but what if people lie to her, will not give her the true words that are the things of the world she must live in? Imagining this is horrible for me, so I try not to.

If I were to test my Christmas lights, and they failed, I doubt I would have the heart to search out the problem, fix it. If my lights fail to go on, perform as I have programmed them, tomorrow night, I will have failed, but at least I will have tried.

I tell Laurel, "Tell Dad about his face."

She says, "I already did before this morning."

"Tell me again," I say because I want the touch of her fingers on my skin. Seated, I rest my hands on her narrow hips as she stands between my legs, puts her so graceful hands to my face. I close my eyes, try to see what she tells me.

"You have hair that's real wavy. You washed it this morning in the shower but it already feels different than this morning after breakfast," she says.

"Dirty already?" I say.

"No, just different already. I can tell." And she says, "You have big eyes and a big nose and smooth lips, and your whiskers are already a tiny bit scratchy now," as her fingers flutter against my cheeks and chin. "You've got your eyes scrunched closed real tight," she says as I try to imagine the face she describes.

"Do you like your dad's face?" I say, unable to imagine the face she constructs with her touch—it is no face I see in my bathroom mirror.

My darling, blind Laurel says, "I like it because you're Dad." And I hug my daughter who cannot tell me if I am handsome or plain or ugly. I hug my daughter close, hard enough that she gives a little gasp of breath. I kiss her forehead, her eyelids, her nose, her mouth and chin.

When I open my eyes I see Margaret watching us. I am not certain I know what her expression means. Is she angry? Resigned? Does her heart, like mine, near-break?

* * *

I ask my wife, "Are you coming out with us, Margaret?"

"It's ten below and God knows what with the wind-chill," she says.

"There's no wind blowing," I say, and, "It won't take that long. I'll bundle Laurel up good. Just bundle up," I say.

"I'll see," she says to me, which I take to mean she will not come outside with me and our daughter to light the Christmas display. This hurts me, but I understand why she will not, cannot.

"It's Christmas Eve, Margaret," is all I can say.

"So, Merry Christmas," is all she says.

I go outside alone for a last check, trace my wires, the connections, the timers, the switchbox small enough to fit in my blind daughter's hand. It will either work or it will not.

I stand in this near-record winter cold, look up and down Pioneer Road, appraise the Christmas lights at the homes up and down each side of the road, wonder if mine—if it works—will measure up to their grandeur and good taste. Much traffic passes, families out to tour the Christmas lights of Pioneer Road, perhaps on their way to late services at our town's many churches.

In daylight, cars coming from either direction see a sign erected by the state. Five hundred yards on either side of my house stands a sign, square, large black letters on a yellow background. The signs are a warning, a caution. Each says: *Blind Child Area.* The signs are mandated by state statute, a precaution, a protection for my daughter.

As if I would ever, as if we would ever allow our beloved only child to play outdoors alone, as if we would ever turn her out into Free Space, at the mercy of this world so filled with danger to her at every turn!

I do not know where in our house my wife has gone so as not to see us go out. I bundle myself up, bundle up my daughter, take her outside. She grasps the crook of my arm as we go out the door, as the blind are trained to do—you do not take their arm, they take yours; this makes them steadier, feel more secure. It is so cold out, but there is no wind, and no stars in the black, cloud-covered sky.

She says, "It's real cold, Dad."

I say, "We won't be out long. Feel how frozen the snow is?"

"I like the crunch," she says, "but it's real cold."

"Here now," I say, stop, stoop, pick up the small switchbox. I look to left and right, the lights of my neighbors. Two cars pass.

"We're right by the road," Laurel says.

"We're right in front of the Merry Xmas one," I say. "You could touch it if you wanted to."

She says, "I don't need to."

Another car passes, but I do not care if anyone is here when we throw the switch. I look up at the black sky, shudder. "Here," I say, "you get to turn it on. You need to take off your mitten to press the button, darling."

"It's really real cold," Laurel says, but pulls off a mitten with her teeth, tucks it under her other arm.

"Hold the switchbox in your other hand, darling," I say, hand it to her, fold her mittened fingers around it. "Feel the button there?" She does.

"When should I push it?" she asks.

"Anytime. Now," I say, and have to wait only a beat. She presses the button; it works.

My Christmas display leaps into glorious being, just as I imagined! "Oh, Laurel," I say, the snow-covered yard bathed in blue and red and green and silver and gold, all flashing, Santa in his sleigh, his lead reindeer's nose a bright red, his elves, the shrubbery, my trees draped with light-umbrellas, the sole spruce a giant Christmas tree with a star on top, and *Merry Xmas* so close to us we could reach out and touch it, all blinks and flows and flashes of light! "Oh, Laurel, hon," I say, my voice hoarse with the awful cold, "if you could see, how beautiful all the colors!"

"Oh, Dad," says my daughter. "I can feel it's warm on me, on and off, I can feel the warms come and go," and lifts her hand to her face where the hot lights of *Merry Xmas* come and go on her skin. Her skin glows with reflected colors, as if she pulsed with lights within her so beautiful, graceful little seven-year-old body. "Dad," she says, "I feel the little warm come and go!" I am distracted for a second as a passing car honks, appreciating, applauding.

And suddenly Margaret, my wife, her mother, is there beside us, without a coat in this cold, and I hug them both to me, try to warm her, our daughter between us.

Laurel says, "Mom, I feel the little warms from it on my face!"

"Yes," I say, close my eyes to try again—and fail—to find an even darker dark in this black Christmas Eve night.

"It's wonderful," Margaret says, and says, "I'd never have imagined how lovely."

And this is how I know nothing can separate us, how I can imagine we will be together, me, my wife, our daughter, no matter what the world we live in is or might become.

And we go inside, quickly, to warm ourselves, to eat and drink the treats Margaret has prepared, and to watch our daughter delight in the bounty of her Christmas presents, watch her open them, know them with her hands, laugh her bell of a laugh as she delights in the riches of touch and sound and smell of the gifts we give her.

Acknowledgments

These stories, since revised, appeared originally in the following journals:

"Mannequin," *Agni;* "Ed Stein, Ed Stein, Speak to Me!" *World Wide Writers* (England); "Viewed from Lanta & Wally's," *Dark Horse Literary Review;* "Solidarity Forever!" *Weber Studies;* "Without Spot or Wrinkle," *Southwest Review;* "The Divorced Men's Mall Walkers Club," *High Plains Literary Review;* "On Watch for Big Red," *Tampa Review;* "Long Odds," *Boulevard;* "Gilded Quill: The Story of Jones," *Idaho Review;* "Imagining the Structure of Free Space on Pioneer Road," *Crab Orchard Review.*

About the Author

Author of four novels and eight previous short-story collections, including *Four Decades* and *The Way We Know in Dreams* (both available from the University of Missouri Press), Gordon Weaver is Adjunct Professor of English at the University of Wisconsin–Milwaukee. Recognition of his work includes two National Endowment for the Arts Fellowships, the O. Henry First Prize, the St. Lawrence Award for Fiction, and numerous other prizes and citations. *Cadence*, the 1991 movie starring Martin and Charlie Sheen, is based on Weaver's novella *Count a Lonely Cadence.*